DYNAMITE DOC
OR
CHRISTMAS DAD?

BY
MARION LENNOX

MILLS & BOON

Dedication:

With thanks to the fabulous Meredith Webber,
whose passion for slithering things reaffirmed my commitment
to this story, and to Trish Morey, whose laughter is magic.

First published in Great Britain 2011
by Mills & Boon, an imprint of Harlequin (UK) Limited.
Harlequin (UK) Limited, Eton House,
18-24 Paradise Road, Richmond, Surrey TW9 1SR

© Marion Lennox 2011

ISBN: 978 0 263 88615 3

Harlequin (UK) policy is to use papers that are natural, renewable and recyclable products and made from wood grown in sustainable forests. The logging and manufacturing process conform to the legal environmental regulations of the country of origin.

Printed and bound in Spain
by Blackprint CPI, Barcelona

Marion Lennox is a country girl, born on an Australian dairy farm. She moved on—mostly because the cows just weren't interested in her stories! Married to a 'very special doctor', Marion writes Medical™ Romances, as well as Mills & Boon® Cherish. (She used a different name for each category for a while—if you're looking for her past Mills & Boon Romances, search for author Trisha David as well.) She's now had 90 romance novels accepted for publication.

In her non-writing life Marion cares for kids, cats, dogs, chooks and goldfish. She travels, she fights her rampant garden (she's losing) and her house dust (she's lost). Having spun in circles for the first part of her life, she's now stepped back from her 'other' career, which was teaching statistics at her local university. Finally she's reprioritised her life, figured out what's important, and discovered the joys of deep baths, romance and chocolate. Preferably all at the same time!

Recent titles by the same author:

THE DOCTOR AND THE RUNAWAY HEIRESS*
DATING THE MILLIONAIRE DOCTOR*
CITY SURGEON, SMALL TOWN MIRACLE*
A BRIDE AND CHILD WORTH WAITING FOR**
ABBY AND THE BACHELOR COP***

*Mills & Boon® Medical™ Romance
**_Crocodile Creek_
*** Mills & Boon® Cherish

These books are also available in eBook format from www.millsandboon.co.uk

Dear Reader

Why do my Christmases always end in chaos? Every year I plan a beautiful Christmas, my detailed lists outlining tasteful table settings, inventive menus, glorious weather and great gifts. But every year…chaos. Glorious, wonderful chaos, with my family chuckling at my lists as they mix sausage rolls with salmon roulade, as they double the amount of brandy in the brandy sauce, as they rock with laughter when my mum gives me an 'abdomeniser'—don't ask, but apparently it's because she knows I can use it…

My Christmas always turns to muddle, and in exactly the same way my hero and heroine, Jess and Ben, are stunned as Christmas brings love and life-affirming magic. They're a man and woman whose Christmas chaos gives them what they need most of all—each other.

If you're reading this before Christmas, then good luck with those lists. If you're reading afterwards… Hooray—that was another muddle, and wasn't it fabulous? Meanwhile, happy reading. Christmas and romance—my very favourite mix.

Marion

CHAPTER ONE

'ALL I want for Christmas is a males-only island. One bearded Santa with all-male reindeer, dropping gifts of boys' own adventure books without a girl in sight. Nothing else. While I waited for the Blythe baby I read of a monastery where they don't even allow hens. Research it for me, Ellen. I'll spend Christmas there.'

Ben Oaklander's secretary was sorting the last of her boss's documents into his briefcase. She didn't blink. After working for Ben for five years, very little made Ellen blink. 'You don't need a monastery,' she retorted. 'Cassowary Island has cassowaries. There won't be a lot else.'

'Except a conference load of obstetricians. I'll bet at least one's female.'

'If you don't like women, why be an obstetrician?'

'I like my mothers. I like my colleagues.' Ben eyed his secretary and finally decided compromise was a good idea. 'Thus I like you. I also like babies, whatever the sex. But that's the end of my attachment.'

'Yet you choose to date,' she said, unruffled. She searched the desk for his USB stick and placed it in his briefcase. Back-up. Not that it'd be needed. Ben Oaklander was nothing if not meticulous. His keynote speech would be backed up four different ways, and he wouldn't refer to notes once.

'That's it. Dating. Nothing more.' Ben raked his long fingers through his dark, wavy hair, leaving it rumpled. Rumpled was Ben's constant state. Sleepless nights delivering babies, plus a hectic research and teaching load meant crazy schedules, a constant five-o'clock shadow, shirts crushed from catnaps during long deliveries...

But his rumpled state made not one whit of difference to his innate sexiness, Ellen thought. It was no wonder he had woman trouble. Her boss was thirty-five years old, tall, dark and drop-dead gorgeous. As an obstetrician known for non-interference, Ben spent a lot of time waiting. While he waited in the small hours he used the hospital gym and it showed. His body...well, a sixty-year-old secretary shouldn't think what Ellen was thinking about his body.

And then there was his intellect...

Ben Oaklander was fast gaining a reputation as one of Australia's foremost obstetricians. The invitation to be keynote speaker at the international obstetrics symposium—held in Australia this year for the first time—was a signal to the world that he was on top of his game.

But not 'on top' of women.

He'd dated seven women in the years Ellen had worked for him. Each time there'd been a hint of serious he'd walked away.

'So what's happened with Louise?' she asked.

He sighed. And shrugged. 'Louise organised herself a flight to Cassowary Island as a surprise Christmas gift to me. Then somehow last night a casual walk ended up in front of a jewellery shop. She pointed out the rings she liked. She pointed out that it was two weeks until Christmas. I thought...no use not being honest.'

'Uh-oh,' Ellen said. 'Let me guess. She didn't appreciate honesty?'

'She hit me.'

'Ouch.' Ellen peered closer, saw the faint red mark across her boss's strongly boned jaw. Winced. 'That must have hurt.'

'It did,' he said, rueful. But also seemingly bewildered. 'But it was totally undeserved. I spelled it out at the beginning. No strings.'

'It's a bit hard to stop strings forming,' Ellen told him, returning to packing. 'It's nature. They just sneak up on you.'

Louise, the lady in question, was a thirty-four-year-old pathologist. She worked in the same hospital; she popped into the office often. Ellen had seen the normally single-mindedly professional pathologist glancing at Ben's patients, at the mums-in-waiting, at the babies. She'd seen where Louise's dreams were drifting, strings or no strings.

'She'd make a lovely mum,' Ellen said, a trifle wistfully. Her own children weren't showing any signs of making her a grandma. She wouldn't mind if her boss…

'With someone else as dad,' Ben said grimly, and snapped his briefcase closed. 'Not me.'

'What do you have against families?'

'I have nothing for them and nothing against them. I just don't have anything to do with them. Or women who want them. Which is why I'm staying on at Cassowary Island after the conference. The rest of the world can celebrate Christmas, and I'll lie on the beach and wait for Santa to drop by with my *Boys' Own Adventure*. That's not to say I don't wish you a wonderful Christmas,' he said, hauling an exquisitely wrapped box from under the desk. 'Merry Christmas, Ellen. Have a wonderful time.'

'With my family,' she said sadly. 'You know I'd love you—'

'No,' he said. 'And it's time you stopped asking. I love you, Ellen, but even for you…even for anyone, I don't do families.'

'All I want for Christmas is my dad.'

'That's not exactly a practical wish.' Jess was perched on the end of her small son's bed, listening to his Christmas list with dismay. Until now Dusty's Christmas list had been easy. Fire engine. Spider-Man outfits. Computer games.

She'd thought she had a couple of years until the troublesome teens, but lately they'd been showing signs of emerging. For Dusty wasn't smiling with Christmas excitement. He was glowering, his ten-year-old face trying hard to look mature and solemn, not sulky and childlike. He wasn't quite managing to pull it off.

'You know your dad died when you were three,' Jess said, as gently as she could. 'Not even Santa can fix that.'

'I know that,' he said, intelligent kid speaking to slightly thick adult. 'But all we have is three photos, and even they're blurry. That's what I want. A whole bunch of pictures. And other stuff. Pictures of my…my ancestors. And things. Real things. Like a cricket bat he used, so when Mike talks about his dad I can show him…something.'

So that's what this was about, Jess thought. Mike Scott was Dusty's new best friend. Mike's dad had died of cancer last year and Mike's mum, an anaesthetist, had moved to London to be closer to her mother. The two boys had become friends in the hospital's after-school child-care programme, two ten-year-olds, smart as paint, both with dead fathers.

Difference? Mike had a lifetime of memorabilia. Dusty had three grainy photos.

Which was hardly surprising. Mike's parents had been happily married. Jess was a single mum. She'd met Nate in her first year in medical school. She'd been desperately lonely and desperately unlucky, in her choice of boyfriend, in her choice of contraception, in…life.

She was much better at it now. Life. Somehow she'd scraped through medical school. Somehow she'd managed to raise a normally cheerful, healthy ten-year-old who hardly ever asked anything of her.

Who was looking at her now with the expression she knew well.

He seldom asked for anything, but when he did…

'There's nothing I can do about this,' she said, knowing only an adult answer would do. 'You know your father wasn't ready to be a proper father when you were born, and you know he was killed when you were a toddler.'

'When I was three,' Dusty said belligerently. 'There must be photos.'

'There aren't.' She'd never been able to tell him the whole truth, that his father had never come near, had never seen his son, had even disputed fatherhood. 'Dusty, we weren't photo-taking people.'

'Then someone else must have been,' Dusty said, clinging grimly to his need. 'When he was a kid.'

'Your grandpa was a grouch,' Jess said. Here at least she could be honest. Or a little bit honest. 'I asked if he could let us see something of your dad's childhood and he told me he wasn't interested in sharing.'

And that summed up an appalling interview. Memories flooded back, Jess at twenty-one, using all her courage and failing. She'd hoped Nate had told his father about Dusty, or if he hadn't…she'd hoped he'd be pleased he had a grandson. She'd hoped wrong.

She remembered standing in the marble hall of a house that had taken her breath away. Nate had been dead for three months. His child-support payments, tiny and grudgingly given but still desperately important if she was to keep studying, had stopped completely.

She'd known Nate's family was almost obscenely wealthy. She'd known those payments would mean nothing to them, but they'd meant everything to her.

So she'd faced the old man-and watched him turn choleric with rage and disdain.

'How dare you come near me with your lies and your schemes? My son would never have a child with the likes of you. Get out of my house; you'll not get a penny out of me. Nothing.'

It had taken her two years to calm down, to find the cour-age to write. This time she'd enclosed a picture of Dusty, who looked just like his father, saying that even if he didn't wish to help support Dusty, she'd like some kind of recognition that Dusty had had a dad.

She'd received a lawyer's letter in response, threatening her with a defamation suit.

She could prove it in a minute, she thought. Nate had known it; that's why he'd grudgingly paid child support. DNA testing would be conclusive, either from the old man or from Nate's brother.

But what was the point? Prove paternity she already knew? Pay a fortune she didn't have in lawyer's fees?

Dusty needed to forget it, as she almost had. 'There's nothing we can do,' she told Dusty now. 'I know this is hard, but you need to accept that your dad's dead. So's your grandpa. There's nothing left to show you of your dad's family.'

'You said Dad had a brother.'

'He hardly talked of him. I don't think they liked each other.' She didn't think the whole family liked each other.

'So let's find him.'

'Dusty, he won't want to see us. He's probably grouchy like your grandpa.'

'No, but we could see him,' Dusty said. 'It'd be like an adventure. Just…looking. I might be able to take a picture with my zoom lens. Then when Mike asks I can say he's a secret and we had to sneak a look…'

And it'd be something to talk about, Jess thought. A game…

'I'll look him up on the internet,' she promised. 'I'll see.'

'It's all I want for Christmas,' Dusty said, belligerent. 'To see my dad's brother.'

'What about a skateboard?'

'Not even a new gaming console,' Dusty said grandly. 'And looking at an uncle would be cheap.'

Sneaking a photograph of this uncle wasn't going to be cheap. It was free.

With Dusty in bed, she searched the internet and up he came. Ben Oaklander.

Nate's brother was in Australia, and information about him was everywhere.

Apparently he was a doctor, an obstetrician, just as she was, only this guy was seriously good. He was five years older than she was, but about twenty years older in terms of career.

She remembered the first time she'd met Nate. He'd been studying law, and she'd been in first year medical school. Her friend introducing her as 'my friend, Jess, who's just started medicine.'

'What, a save the world do-gooder like my sainted brother?' Nate had snapped, but then he'd looked at her, focused, apologised for his bad manners and set himself out to be charming. Which had been very charming indeed.

His brother had hardly been mentioned again.

And here he was. Nate's brother.

A do-gooder?

Not so much.

She was at a site advertising a conference being held in December, at somewhere called Cassowary Island off Australia's Queensland coast. Keynote speaker, Benjamin Oaklander.

A biography.

One of Australia's most eminent obstetricians. Youngest professor… Contributor to three texts, author of thirty journal articles. Top of his field. Highly regarded researcher.

A picture. He was dark where Nate had been blond. He was about the same height, though, standing tall among a group of colleagues at an award ceremony, and he had the same lovely eyes, a deep, azure blue. He was smiling straight at the camera, and that smile…

She remembered that smile. Dangerous.

But this would do, she thought. There was no need for sneaky zoom lenses when she could show Dusty this.

She closed the computer with a snap.

But then she thought—it wouldn't do. She knew Dusty. He didn't see the internet as real. He wanted real contact.

Maybe when he was older she'd try and contact this man.

She opened her laptop again.

That smile…

She was so over that smile. Just looking at it…the arrogance, the lies, the deceit. *'I'll take care of you for ever…'*

Well, she'd looked after herself, she told that smile. There was no way any insidious smile could breach her defences. Once was enough.

'Mum…'

Ouch. She flicked the backward arrow on the internet. It wouldn't do to show Dusty a blank screen. He came up behind her, rubbing sleepy eyes. 'What are you doing?'

'Don't ask questions,' she managed, trying to sound Santa-Claus mysterious.

But he was already behind her, looking. 'Oh, yum,' he breathed. 'Is that an island?'

She looked then—really looked. Cassowary Island, close to Australia's Great Barrier Reef. A small research centre dedicated to cassowaries, with a privately run, wildlife rehabilitation sanctuary attached.

Nothing else, apart from an international-standard conference centre with eco-resort accommodation. Miles of glorious beaches, turquoise waters, rainbow coral, multicoloured fish, turtles, dolphins… Resort mantra: 'Take only Photographs, Leave only Footprints.' Oh…

'Oh, Mum,' Dusty breathed. 'Are you thinking about holidays?'

'Just dreaming,' she said.

And suddenly she was. How long since she'd had a proper holiday?

She'd gone over her head into debt to finish her medical training. Then her mother's health, always precarious, had failed even further. She'd died two months ago. This would be their first Christmas without her.

Christmas without her mother didn't bear thinking of.

'We might go somewhere,' she said, glancing wistfully at turtles.

'Why not there?'

'It's the other side of the world.'

'It'd be warm.'

'I guess.' She could even afford it now, she thought. She'd been earning for a while now and with the sale of her mother's small house… Maybe she could.

'It says there's an obstetric conference happening.' Dusty's face was alight with excitement. 'Is that why you're looking? The nineteeth to the twenty second of December. Mum, that's cool. School finishes on the fifteenth.'

'You don't want to go to a conference with me.'

'I bet we can't afford to go unless it's for work,' Dusty said wisely. 'You never do anything not for work. Or for Gran. Or for me.'

'Maybe I can make an exception. We could find lots of places that are warm. Maybe you could ask for that for Christmas instead of finding out about your dad.'

And her son's face closed. 'I want to find out.'

'Dusty, we can't.'

'You said we'd have two weeks' holiday for Christmas. I bet we could find something out in two weeks.'

'I'd rather go somewhere warm.'

'Then let's do sleuthing and then go somewhere warm,' Dusty said, sliding his hand into hers. 'We can sleuth really fast.'

'Dusty…'

'You have to help,' Dusty said, smiling his gorgeous ten-year-old smile; the smile she'd disconcertingly just seen on the screen before her. 'I bet you'd like photos, too. It can't be nice not having any pictures of Dad. I'm sure you want some.'

She didn't.

But then…she knew where Dusty was coming from. Her own father had died when she was twelve. The albums filled with pictures of her father holding her, playing with her, had assumed almost supernatural importance.

She tucked her son back into bed. Threatened him with no Santa if he didn't stay. Went back downstairs and stared at a stranger's smile; a smile that she knew like it was part of her.

Kill two birds with one stone? It looked a great conference.

She could 'just happen' upon Ben there, tell Dusty who he was, then they could have a week on the island when everyone left.

She glanced through the window into the night. Sleet was slashing the frozen streets.

Tropics. Turtles. Sun.

A wildlife sanctuary… She read a little about it. Apparently it was independently run by three women, fiercely passionate about their cause. The care and rehabilitation of injured wildlife.

Her father had been a park ranger. She'd been brought up with animals; with passion for their care.

Cassowary Island had been decimated by a cyclone fifteen years ago. Efforts were being made to re-establish the cassowary population; to restore the native flora and fauna.

Echoes of her childhood. Echoes of her father's passion.

She'd love to go to this island.

And Dusty? He'd been silent and clinging since his grandmother had died. The need to find out about this uncle might be part of his grief, she thought. Insecurity. A need for a wider sense of family than just she could give him.

There was little chance that any Oaklander would give him any sense of family, she thought, but still… It might help if she showed him she was doing her best to help. The holiday itself would be wonderful for them both, and if they went to this conference he could see his uncle without it being a big deal.

Good idea, or an unmitigated disaster?

Or an unmitigated disaster?

How could it be a disaster? Ben Oaklander had no hold on her. He was nothing to do with her. She didn't need him as she'd needed his brother.

So go take a look, show Dusty where he got his smile and then walk away. Even if Ben reacted coldly—which she'd expect—they'd have an awesome holiday afterwards to make up for it.

They might even have fun. Heaven knew, they deserved it.

It was only…

She glanced back to the computer, to the conference blurb. To Ben Oaklander's image.

The Oaklander smile.

It was no longer dangerous—surely?

It couldn't be.

CHAPTER TWO

SATURDAY morning a month later, they were halfway between the north coast of Australia and Cassowary Island.

Ben Oaklander was sitting not ten yards away from her.

She was feeling…weird. Confrontation wasn't supposed to happen this fast.

The conference wasn't due to start until Monday. A hovercraft had been organized to bring delegates to the island on Sunday night, so the daily ferry was almost empty. It held a skipper, a deckhand, two elderly women who looked to be wildlife carers—the 'Cassowary Island Habitat' emblem on their jackets gave them away—and one solitary male who sat in the bow and read.

Who happened to be Ben Oaklander.

She'd known who he was the minute she and Dusty had climbed aboard. Dusty hadn't noticed. He was blown away by the ferry, the sea, the prospect of what was before them, and the guy on the foredeck in casual clothes was a long way from the formal, suited headshot she'd shown him on the net.

But Ben's profile was unmistakable. Jeans, T-shirt, faded trainers. A body to die for.

A true Oaklander.

Gorgeous.

Also aloof and arrogant.

He'd thanked the crewman who'd helped lift his impressive computer gear aboard, he'd assisted one of the elderly ladies who seemed to be limping, but he'd shrugged off her thanks, cut off her attempts to chat, settled in the bow and read.

His body language said, Leave me alone, I'm not interested.

Well, she wasn't. He was Nate's brother and apart from a tiny amount of idle curiosity, she'd pass him in the street and move on.

Except that he was stunning. Silhouetted against the morning sun his profile was one of pure strength. He was a darker, stronger, harsher version of his brother. Don't mess with me, his profile said, and she remembered his appalling father and she thought she wouldn't.

She should tell Dusty—and she would; this conference was all about letting Dusty see this guy—but not yet. Not in the close confines of the boat. She'd told Dusty his uncle would be there as one of the conference attendees but how to introduce them took some thinking about.

She didn't feel exactly ready. She wasn't actually sure that she would be ready.

Dusty had enough to think about right now, she told herself. He was practically bursting with excitement as they approached the island.

They'd timed their arrival early, to settle, to find things for Dusty to do while she attended the conference; to simply enjoy themselves.

It seemed Ben Oaklander had the same idea.

But by the look of the textbook in his hands… Enjoyment? Heavy didn't begin to describe it.

Jess thought of the medical journals on her bedside table, gathering dust. She hadn't brought a single one.

This was why this guy was a leader in his field, while she was simply a doctor who delivered babies the best way she knew how.

She glanced again at the forbidding profile. Then she glanced at Dusty, who was watching dolphins. The similarity was almost frightening.

Keep it simple. Would the best plan be to introduce herself right now, explain what Dusty needed and go from there?

She didn't quite have the courage. The sight of this guy... She hadn't expected to feel like this.

An Oaklander...

Dusty had been photographing the dolphins. Now he turned and started photographing the ferry. Everything in the ferry.

'Not the guy in the bow,' she told him. 'He looks like he wants to be left alone.'

'I'm not being a pest,' Dusty said virtuously. 'I'm only taking pictures. Of everything.'

Everything. She couldn't argue with that.

Maybe he was being paranoid but he didn't think so. He was being watched and the sensation was unnerving.

A woman was glancing at him covertly—a woman who almost took his breath away. Maybe it was the morning, the sunlight glinting off the sea, but the sight of her glossy, chestnut-coloured curls, rippling a little in the soft sea breeze, her laughter at something the child said, the simplicity of her clothes, the maturity on her face that belied the fact that she looked little more than thirty—the total effect was breathtaking.

And beside her...a small boy who looked like Nate.

He was imagining things. Yes, the little boy was blond and blue eyed, just as Nate had been. He had the same wavy hair, the same cheeky grin. But he wasn't Nate. He was ten or eleven years old and he belonged very firmly to the woman beside him.

The child had the woman's build, slim, fine featured, almost elfin. She was wearing jeans, a plain white T-shirt and plain white sandals. The only note of colour was a simple, sea-green scarf knotted casually around her throat. It was the same colour as her eyes.

Alone she'd have had him riveted.

But still his attention went back to the child.

Memories of Nate... Unwanted memories.

Once upon a time he and Nate had been friends, two years

apart, ganging up against their bully of a father and their icy, aloof mother. But then Nate had figured what would please his father, following in his footsteps, and Ben had left.

Yeah, well, that had been a long time ago. There were lots of blond-headed kids in the world. He turned back to his text.

He could sense the little boy's camera raising, aiming.

He looked up as the camera clicked. The child let the camera drop to his knee. Gazes locked.

The child gave a tentative smile.

Nate!

The woman…

She intercepted his look, flushed, took the child's camera. 'Sorry,' she said smoothly, liltingly, and she smiled, a smile which wasn't the least like the child's. 'We bought Dusty a new camera for the holiday and he's practising. He doesn't have the legal ramifications of point and shoot covered. We'll delete that shot if you like.'

Her smile might not be like her son's but it was a good one. Her smile said smile back.

He couldn't make himself smile. The child's face.

Nate.

Suddenly he was eleven years old again. His mother's words: 'Forget your brother. Your father doesn't want you—he and your father are one family, we're another.'

Only he and his mother weren't a family. He'd been used as a possession to be claimed in a messy divorce. Nothing more.

'I'm Dusty,' the child said, happy to chat. 'Who are you?'

The child wasn't Nate. He needed to pull himself together.

'I need to read,' he said, almost reluctantly. Even without the unsettling resemblance to his brother, there was something about the pair of them that made him want to know more.

No! This woman looks like a single mother, his antenna was saying. What about his resolution? No women for Christmas.

But his antenna was still working overtime.

Nate…

There were a million children in the world who'd look like his brother, he told himself. Get over it.

'Sorry we bothered you,' the woman said, and smiled again, and her smile was almost magnetic.

That smile…

Back off. Now.

He was being dumb. 'It's fine,' he said, gruffly. Why not tell the child his name? 'And I'm…'

'Leave the gentleman alone,' the woman said. 'He wants to read.'

His thoughts exactly. Only they weren't…exactly.

Uh-oh. Jess was feeling disconcerted, to say the least. She'd had no idea the presence of this man could have such an effect on her.

He was an Oaklander. What was it with this family?

Danger.

But then, thankfully, one of the elderly ladies, the one with the limp, produced a baby wombat from inside her jacket, and started to feed it.

This event was so extraordinary Dusty's interest switched in an instant. Yes! The last thing Jess wanted was introductions all round.

Had Nate told his brother about Dusty's existence? She suspected not, but his father might have relayed his dealings with her. Her name might mean something.

As did the fact that Dusty looked like Nate.

But the brothers hadn't been close. In fact, Nate had shown nothing but disdain for his big brother.

She should relax. It was unfortunate that they were on the same boat, but the trip would soon be over. She could figure out how to introduce them when she had herself more together. And meanwhile…

A baby wombat…

Fascinated herself, she moved closer.

The woman had been wearing a sleeveless fleece jacket, which had seemed a bit unnecessary on such a fabulous day.

Now she realised why. The wombat had been tucked into a pouch, taking warmth from the woman's body. It was still snuggled in the jacket which was now being used as a blanket.

The creature was tiny, the size of a man's fist. It was pink-bald, with fur just starting to develop across its back. It lay cradled in the fleece, while its carer patiently encouraged it to attach to the teat of what looked like a miniature baby bottle.

'It's a wombat,' Dusty breathed, edging closer to the woman, fascinated. 'A baby. Where's his mum?'

'His mother was hit by a car,' the younger of the women told them. 'Horrid things, cars.'

'You're taking him to Cassowary Island to look after him?'

'It's a wildlife shelter,' the woman said, talking to Dusty as if he were an adult. 'There are no predators for wombats over there. He'll be safe.'

'What are predators?'

'Things that want to kill wombats.'

Dusty inched closer still, and so did Jess. The other woman also had a bulge under her jacket. As she tried not to look, it… moved.

'You both have passengers,' she breathed.

'Don't tell the skipper or we'll have to pay,' the wombat lady said, chuckling. The name tags on their uniform said they were Marge and Sally. Marge, the wombat lady, looked to be in her late seventies. She looked drawn, Jess thought suddenly, the professional side of her kicking in. In pain? But all the woman's attention was on the wombat she was feeding. 'We smuggle our babies all the time,' she told Dusty.

'The skipper knows,' the lady called Sally retorted. 'We're not doing anything illegal. But they do need to be carried under our jackets.'

'Why?' Dusty was riveted.

'Body warmth,' Marge said. 'Pop your hand under your T-shirt and tell me that's not a warm, soft place to keep a baby.' She cast him a shrewd look. 'If you like, after he's fed, I'll let you wear the pouch until we reach the island. If you promise to be careful.'

'Oh, yes…'

'How old is he?' Jess asked.

'About two months,' Marge told her. 'He was born about the size of a jelly bean. He had no hair, and his skin was thinner than paper. But like all baby wombats, after he was born he'll have managed to wriggle into his mum's pouch. Normally he'd stay in his nice, safe pouch for about eight months but this little guy has a horror story. His mum was hit by a car and killed. It was only because a passerby knew to check her pouch that he came to us.'

'You're using a special formula?' Jess was crouched on the deck, watching the tiny creature feed, as riveted as her son.

'In an emergency we can give normal powdered milk, half-strength,' Marge said. 'But now he's with us, we give him special wombat formula. Sally has a half-grown echidna under her vest. They're both mammals. They drink milk but they need their own milk. Cow's milk is for baby cows.'

'And for us,' Dusty said.

'Not when you were tiny,' Marge retorted. 'I bet you had your mum's milk.'

'Did I?' Dusty demanded.

'I… Yes,' Jess said—and for some dumb reason she blushed. Which was stupid. As natural a thing as breastfeeding. What was there to blush over in that?

But…an Oaklander was listening.

He'd abandoned his reading and strolled along the deck to see.

Ben Oaklander…

'Every species has its own particular milk,' he growled, but his voice was softer now, no longer repelling. 'Designed exactly for that baby.'

'So my mum's milk was designed for me?' Dusty demanded of him, and Jess saw Ben start a little, as if he hadn't expected to be drawn into a conversation with a child.

She watched him turn professional as a way to deal with it. Maybe he hadn't wanted to talk but the sight of the little creature had drawn him in. He squatted and touched the tiny wombat, stroking him lightly with one long finger, all his attention on the baby. 'Yes,' he said, softly, looking at the little wombat and not at Dusty. 'When you were born, your mother had immunity from the germs she meets every day. By drinking her milk as a baby, you'll have been safe from those germs, too.'

'Are you one of those obstetricians?' Sally asked him. 'One that's coming to the conference?'

'I am.' He stood, retreated a little, starting to look as if he was regretting coming over, but the women weren't letting him off the hook.

'We might need you,' Sally said, casting a questioning glance at Marge. 'We're so pleased you're all coming. We were sort of hoping to meet one of you.'

'I doubt I'm much good at delivering wombats,' he said, and the thought had him relaxing a little. The sunlight glinted on his dark hair. His eyes were narrowed against the sun, and he looked suddenly at ease.

Why had he been defensive at first? What had he thought, Jessie wondered—that she and Dusty were somehow intending on intruding on his private space? Or... She glanced at Dusty and then at Ben. The similarities were really marked. Maybe he'd seen.

'We have a dog,' Marge said, a bit shamefaced. 'A pug. She's sort of...pregnant.'

'She's very pregnant,' Sally retorted. Sally was a wiry little woman with a mop of grey curls, considerably younger than her friend. Late sixties? 'Dogs aren't allowed on the island, but Pokey is fat and quiet and no threat to anything. She belongs to Marge's sister, but Hilda had to go into a nursing home last month. Having her put down would have broken her heart. And because we run the shelter...'

'We sort of sneaked her in,' Marge admitted. 'There's three of us there, Sally and Dianne and me. The rules about animals on the island are strict—and good—but in this case we thought it wouldn't hurt to hide her. But then she started to get fat.' She sighed. 'Or fatter. And now…'

'She's definitely pregnant,' Sally said. 'So we're sort of in trouble. And if *she* gets into trouble we have no vet.'

'You have no vet on the island—and you're a wildlife refuge?' Ben said, clearly confounded.

'We've done specialist wildlife training,' Marge said, with a touch of reproof. 'Sally and Dianne and I, we pooled our money to set this place up. We plan to stay here until we die; it's our dream retirement. We have a vet come over once a week, and we can do most things. But we can't afford for him to come every day. And we sort of haven't told him about Pokey.'

'He might say she shouldn't stay,' Sally added, and Jess intercepted a worried glance at her friend. There were problems, Jess thought. Undercurrents. The words *We plan to stay here until we die* had been said almost with defiance. But then Sally caught herself and gave a rueful smile and the moment was past. 'Okay, he *would* say she shouldn't stay,' she conceded. 'Marge's daughter's coming home from New York after Christmas and we hope she'll take her, but meanwhile we need to care for her. We're worried,' she conceded. 'Native animals don't have trouble giving birth. Joeys, baby kangaroos, wombats, possums are born tiny. If Pokey gets into trouble we don't know what to do.'

'But then we found out about the obstetrician conference,' Marge said. 'So we thought we'd find a nice-looking doctor and confess. And you…you look kind.'

Silence. Did he look kind? Jess wondered. An Oaklander? Kind? Hardly.

'My mum's an obstetrician, too,' Dusty said into the silence, and then there was even more silence.

Jess and Ben… Two obstetricians and one pregnant pug.

Two elderly ladies looked defiant but hopeful. Jess started feeling exposed.

'You're here for the conference, too?' Ben asked Jess at last, and the wariness was back in his voice.

'Yes,' she said. 'But I'm not stealing your patient.' She managed a smile. 'Pokey is all yours.'

He didn't laugh.

He was wary, Jess thought, and maybe not just of being pulled into an illegal dog-birth situation. She saw him glance at Dusty.

Definitely wary.

'It's okay,' Jess said. 'We're not about to intrude on your privacy.'

Why had she said that?

It was just that…his body language was all about protecting himself. He was acting as if she and Dusty and maybe also these ladies and their weird animals were a threat.

Familiar anger started surging. Kind? Ha. He was an Oaklander.

She was reminded suddenly of the night she'd told Nate she was pregnant. He'd closed down. Backed off. Disclaimed responsibility.

The Oaklander specialty.

'If your mother's going to the conference, what will you do?' Sally asked Dusty, seemingly unaware of the undercurrents running between Jess and Ben. Between Ben and everyone. The assumption was that the question of Pokey had been solved. The belief was that Ben would help.

Would he?

'I'll play on my computer,' Dusty said, switching instantly to martyr mode. His specialty. 'I have to do that when Mum has to work and I can't go out. Mum says there'll be a hotel person to sit with me. Whoever that is. It's okay. I'm used to it.'

Uh-oh. All eyes—including Dusty-the-Martyr's—gazed at her with reproach. She could feel herself flushing. Neglectful mother, abandoning child to uncaring hotel person and mindless computer games.

Guilt…

She'd checked there was a child minding service before she'd come. She and Dusty had talked about it. They'd go to the beach early and she'd skip less important conference sessions. Dusty wouldn't suffer.

'Try being a single mother yourself,' she muttered under her breath, and practically glowered.

But Dusty was soaking it up. Pathetic-R-Us. 'It's okay,' he said again, manfully. 'I don't really mind.'

'Would you like to help us in the wildlife centre?' Sally asked Dusty. Taking pity on The Orphan.

'We can use some help,' Marge agreed, smiling at The Orphan as well. 'That is, if you like animals. Your mum could walk you over to the refuge in the mornings before the conference and pick you up afterwards. It's not too far. If you think you'd enjoy it...'

'We look after lots of things,' Sally told him. 'Possums, echidnas, kangaroos, goannas, birds, turtles; there's always work to do. You look like the sort of boy who'd enjoy helping.'

So they'd seen his hunger.

Dusty's fascination with animals had started early. Even as a toddler, he'd been fascinated with the photographs of his mother's childhood. His grandma's cat who'd died just before she did was the extent of Dusty's hands-on animal contact, but he'd read it all, and now, even while he was playing the neglected orphan, he hadn't taken his eyes from the baby wombat. He'd known instantly what it was. He knew his animals.

'If it's okay with your mother,' Marge said, and it was still there, that faint accusation. Abandoning your child...

'It must be hard to be a doctor and a mum as well,' Ben said suddenly, and she glanced up at him in surprise. She'd been carefully not looking at him, expecting the same accusation. But instead what she got was almost...empathy?

'Patients don't understand that doctors have families,' he said gently. 'Emergencies don't always happen in school hours. And if Dusty's mother wants to keep up with the latest developments in obstetrics so she can give her mothers the best of care, then she needs to undertake professional development. Like coming to this conference. I'd imagine coming with his mum would be much more fun for Dusty than leaving him behind.'

'Yes,' Dusty said, finally abandoning the pathetic. 'Mum went to a course last school holidays and I had to stay with Mum's Aunty Rhonda for three whole days. *And* she made me eat roast beef and soggy vegetables for three days in a row. Coming here's better than that.'

There was a general chuckle. The tension eased and Jessie's anger faded. Or not so much anger. Defensiveness.

She hated leaving Dusty alone. She loved her work.

Push, pull. The minute she'd turned into a mother the guilt had kicked in. No matter what she did, she couldn't get it right.

'Well, Dusty, what about helping in the wildlife shelter instead of computer games?' Marge asked, and her tone had changed. Ben's interjection had helped.

'I don't know…' Dusty looked dubiously at Jess.

'Come over tomorrow and check us out,' Marge said warmly. 'You could all come.' She beamed at Ben, including him in her invitation. 'You're here early for the conference. You can't come to Cassowary Island and not see what we really do. Come at ten and we'll give you a guided tour.' She hesitated and Jess saw her wince. Once again, that impression of pain, and this time she conceded it. 'My leg's a bit sore at the moment,' she admitted. 'Maybe you could even give Sally and Dianne a hand with the cleaning. Would that be okay?'

'I'll be busy,' Ben said.

'Too busy to take an hour or so out to see how our shelter runs?' Marge sounded incredulous. 'And you'll want to meet Pokey.'

'I don't need to meet Pokey.'

'Well, we need you to meet Pokey,' Marge said, with asperity. 'And if we're looking after your little boy during the conference then it's the least you can do.'

'He's not my little boy,' Ben snapped.

'He's not?' The wildlife worker visibly reran the immediate

conversation through her head. She looked from Ben to Dusty and back again. 'You mean you don't know each other?'

'No.'

'But he looks like you.'

There was a moment's silence. Dusty stared at Ben. Turned to his mother. Opened his mouth.

'We don't know each other,' Jess said, cutting Dusty off before he could say a word. She wasn't ready. Panic.

Panic was stupid, but there it was. Not now. Please.

'But you're both obstetricians,' Sally said, sounding thrilled. 'How wonderful. That's exactly what Pokey needs. So ten tomorrow? Marge will pick you up in her beach buggy. Be ready. And whatever you charge is fine by us.'

'I don't…' Ben started.

'Accept payment?' Sally said blithely. 'We thought you might say that. A donation to your favourite charity is okay with us. And we understand all care, and no responsibility. So if there are no other objections we'll see you tomorrow.'

'I need to read,' Ben said, retreating.

'Of course you do,' Sally said. 'Work now so you'll have time for us tomorrow. Now…' She looked at Jess. 'Would your little boy like to hold a wombat?'

CHAPTER THREE

THE convention centre and associated resort was as good as the internet had promised, maybe better. Quite simply, Jess couldn't believe her luck.

The rooms weren't built as a standard hotel, but as a series of bungalows, each with a mini-veranda overlooking the beach. With the windows swung wide, it was as if the beach was in the room. You could run from the bungalow into the sea in a minute.

The staff were lovely, casually dressed, seemingly casually behaved, but nothing was too much trouble.

A very pregnant receptionist—Kathy—accompanied them to their bungalow and made sure they had everything they needed, chatting to them about how wonderful the island was. There was no doubting her sincerity—this wasn't a pre-prepared spiel. She organised beach equipment and told them how to organise surfing lessons for Dusty. A cassowary strutted past within two minutes of their arrival.

Dusty was too hornswoggled to think any more about his flash of insight as to Ben's identity, and Jess had let it slide. Thankfully. Ben Oaklander could be forgotten. For now. They headed for the sea and she blocked him out. Almost.

Not wanting to face one of the resort restaurants—and not only because Ben might be there; jet lag was taking its toll—they had room-service dinner brought to them by the lovely Kathy. They fell into bed, exhausted. When they woke, the sun was streaming into their little house, sandpipers were darting back and forth on the sand right under their window, the sea was turquoise and sparkling and Jess thought she'd died and gone to heaven.

Ben Oaklander or not, this was the right thing to do. To bring Dusty here, away from the grief of his first Christmas without his beloved gran, without London's sleet and bitter cold…

Happiness was right now.

Dusty was waking, his hand automatically groping beside his bed for his spade. Kathy had organised Dusty a man-sized bucket and a businesslike bushman's spade and Dusty had glowed. Last night they'd built a sandcastle to top all sandcastles. He'd washed his shovel with care, it rested on the floor beside him and sometimes during the night she'd heard him stir, remember it and reach down to touch it. As if to reassure himself this place was real.

She needed the reassurance, too.

Beach and breakfast. But then…

At ten she was getting into a beach buggy with Ben Oaklander and heading to the wildlife shelter.

Even Ben Oaklander was hardly a blip on her happiness radar. Should she talk to Dusty about him now? Maybe not. They'd talked about it back in England. She'd told him she thought his uncle would be here. The plan was that when Ben figured who they were, it'd be treated as a coincidence, so the less she said about it now the better. They certainly hadn't come all this way to find him.

It was an aside, she told herself. A tiny part of a huge adventure. She wouldn't worry about it.

She glanced out at the shimmering sea and felt at peace.

This holiday marked the end of a very long struggle. Years of financial hardship. Years of worrying about her son and her mother.

And they lived happily ever after…

That's what this was, she thought. Happy ever after. No matter that their time here was short, they'd take memories of this place home in their hearts.

And when Dusty confirmed who Ben was, then Dusty would have memories of him and could tell his friends.

'My uncle lives in Australia. He's a doctor like my mum. He delivers babies but sometimes he delivers puppies.'

She grinned at that, thinking of Ben's horror at the thought of being a pug-doctor.

How would he react when he found out their relationship?

If he was mean to Dusty...

She wouldn't let it happen. She was a stronger person now. She'd quailed before Nate's father. She had no intention of re-acting the same way again.

If it came out—*when* it came out—she could deal with it. She could protect her son.

But now Dusty was waking, gazing out at the beach with awe. A swim before breakfast? Why not?

Who cared about Ben Oaklander? They had ten days of para-dise before them, starting now.

Ben woke to the sound of Jess and Dusty playing in the shal-lows. He gazed down to the water and saw them. They were shouting, laughing, falling into the waves, spluttering, hugging. Mother and son.

He watched them, an outsider looking. He lay quite still, as if movement might make them aware, might mar their happi-ness.

For happiness there certainly was.

She was wearing a crimson bikini. Slim and graceful, she dived through the shallow waves, encouraging her son to join her. Every time she emerged, she swept her mass of curls back from her face, streaming water. She laughed and teased her son and the little boy laughed back at her.

Gloriously content.

Family.

Maybe he could have it, he thought. If he was prepared to take a chance.

He wasn't.

Louise's reaction during their last dinner had shocked him. She'd declared herself a consummate professional, determined not to have children.

They'd had a great relationship, as colleagues, as friends, as lovers at need, when it hadn't interfered with either of their lives.

She'd shocked him by her turn-around.

He'd gone to see her before he'd left. Apologised. 'I'm sorry. I know made things clear at the beginning of our relationship but I should have kept checking.'

'And I should have talked about my change of heart,' she'd admitted. 'I know I said I never wanted family; babies. I can't think why I do now, but I do.'

They'd parted friends. She was already eyeing off the new paediatric consultant, a young widower. A guy with a child already.

A ready-made family…

Once more his gaze drifted to the water. Jess and Dusty.

Dr Jessica McPherson. He'd looked her up last night. English qualifications. Based in London. Accompanied by her son, Dustin.

Obviously here to combine work and holiday.

If she didn't have a child he could spend some time with her, he thought. She fitted his date description. Smart, attractive, funny. Returning to the other side of the world in ten days.

Smart, attractive, funny…

He watched her a while longer. Add gorgeous to that description, he decided. The way she laughed… The way she rolled in the sand with her son, totally unselfconscious. Her peal of delicious chuckles.

She had a child, he told himself harshly. He didn't do children.

And suddenly Nate was there, front and centre.

Nate.

He was in the most beautiful place in the world, in the most comfortable bed with the best view and suddenly the tension inside him was almost to breaking point.

His family was dysfunctional to say the least, but Nate had been his one true thing. Nate, eight years old to his eleven. His adoring little brother. During childhood they'd hardly seen their parents, they'd been raised by nannies, but they'd had each other.

And then something had finally cracked in the social façade that had been his parents' marriage. They'd woken one morning and it had been over.

'Ben, darling, you're coming with me. There's a lovely school in Australia—I believe it's even been used by royalty. And Arthur, the nice man I introduced you to last week, is based in Melbourne. We'll be able to explore together. Your father's decided he wishes to hold onto Nathaniel. Your bags are being packed now. Say goodbye to your brother. Your father's gone out for the day—I don't think he intends to say goodbye to anyone.'

After that... He hadn't seen Nate for years, and when he had Nate had turned into his father. Blamed him. Vibrated vitriol.

To feel like that again...

No. He didn't do family.

Outside Jess and Dusty were whooping up the beach, rolling in the soft sand, then lurching about like sand-covered monsters trying to scare each other.

How would she feel if anything happened to her son? How would her little boy feel if he lost his mother?

Don't go there.

He always did. He always had. Families instilled an automatic dread.

So...

So there was two hours to go before he'd promised to go to the wildlife shelter. He still wasn't sure how he'd been coerced into the visit but he'd get it over with fast. Meanwhile he could have breakfast and head to the beach. A swim would be great.

That's what he would have done if they weren't there.

They were there. A family.

He had work to do. A quick breakfast, a few laps of the hotel pool, then an hour or so on the computer.

He'd meant this time to be a rest. Beach time.

Not if it meant getting involved. No way.

Dusty swam, splashed, dug, then reluctantly returned to their bungalow for breakfast, and when Sally and a rough-looking beach buggy arrived to collect them he was so wide-eyed he was practically speechless. For a child brought up in the heart of London, this was heaven.

He'd almost forgotten that flash of intuition he'd had about Ben on the boat, so when Sally stopped the buggy in front of Ben's bungalow and Ben emerged, Jess saw her son react with something akin to confusion. He had warring priorities. Beach and wildlife—or a guy who might or might not be his uncle.

Should she have said something? Admitted that she thought she'd recognised him? It was too late now. Jess could only hold her breath and hope.

'Hi, people,' Sally said cheerfully. 'You'll have to put up with me driving this morning. Marge is our usual driver. I only got my licence when my husband died and that was when I was sixty so I'm not exactly skilled. But Marge isn't well this morning so it's me, me or me. Don't talk to me. I need to concentrate. Hold onto your hats.'

There wasn't a lot else to hold onto. There were two bench seats facing each other in the back of the buggy.

Jess and Dusty sat on one. Ben on the other. Facing each other.

'Did they give you a spade?' Dusty demanded of Ben.

'No.' Ben was looking…bemused. He was wearing light chinos, a short-sleeved linen shirt, open at the throat, canvas boat shoes. His hair was already rumpled by the soft sea breeze.

He looked far too much like his brother, Jess thought grimly. And like her son.

'They gave me one,' Dusty was saying. 'It's humungous. I

built the best ever sandcastle and moat. We built it just past the high-tide mark and when the tide comes in the water will reach the moat and fill it. Do you want to look when we get back?'

'The doctor will have work to do when we get back,' Jess said, with gentle reproof, and Ben flashed her an appreciative glance.

'I do. I'm presenting first thing tomorrow.'

'I don't know how you find the courage to take on public speaking,' she ventured, trying to think of what a real colleague would say. 'It'd scare me witless.'

'Having a son would scare me witless,' he said.

'You don't have children?' That's also what a normal colleague would ask, she thought. That's also what Dusty would like to know. If he had cousins.

'No family,' Ben said, and it was almost a snap.

'What, no one at all?'

'The wildlife lodge's just over this hill,' Sally yelled cheerfully from the front. 'I think…uh-oh… Hold on!'

A hump. The buggy lurched sideways. Jess grabbed Dusty, Ben grabbed her, Sally hit the brakes and suddenly they were sliding onto the floor.

Sally pulled to a stop. Looked back at her passengers, appalled. 'Oh, my… Marge said not to hit that crest too hard. I forgot. Are you okay?'

'I…' Ben was still holding Jess. She could hardly breathe. 'I think so.'

Dusty was underneath her. Ben was holding him, too.

Dusty giggled.

There wasn't much alternative. She should giggle.

It was just that…she was underneath an Oaklander.

Ben.

She was starting to separate him from Nate in her head, but she still remembered how Nate had made her feel.

Separate or not, he was an Oaklander. But she couldn't pull away.

'I think we're better staying down,' Ben said. 'We can't fall any further.' There was a rubber mat on the floor of the tray. Ben's advice made sense.

He tugged her sideways so she was free to breathe and she tugged Dusty close so they were spooned into each other.

Dusty giggled some more.

And suddenly Jess was chuckling as well—because there was nothing else to do. She was so disconcerted.

Ben's arms were around her waist. An Oaklander, holding her. Ben… Different.

'Okay, Sally, let her roll,' Ben said, and Sally grinned and grated the gears and tried again. With her passengers on the floor. And three minutes later they were there. The buggy pulled to a stop and Jess was almost sorry. And what sort of stupid reaction was that?

Dianne was busting out of the house to meet them, down the veranda steps, exclaiming in dismay as she saw their seating arrangements—or lack. 'Sally! Marge said to go slow.'

'I did,' Sally said cheerfully. 'Or mostly I did. I need to practise.'

'That was…fun,' Jess managed, hauling herself upright. Ben climbed down from the buggy, swung Dusty down, then held out his hands to help her.

She looked at his hands, considered, and then thought maybe not. Climbed down herself. Staggered.

His hand caught hers and steadied her.

Strength…

An Oaklander.

'Well,' Dianne said, glowering at Sally. 'Maybe walking would have been more comfortable. I'm sorry. But now you're here… Our babies are doing fine. The wombat's doing beautifully. I reckon it was that cuddle you gave him yesterday, Dusty. Cuddles cure everything.' Her face clouded a little. 'Most things. Anyway, come and see.'

Yesterday Jess had assumed the place would be a tiny affair, a shelter run by three retired do-gooders with the best of intentions but not much else.

She was wrong. On their home turf Sally and Dianne turned into professionals who knew what they were doing and cared deeply. This was a professional operation, running smoothly and efficiently. It was used in part by the mainland university as a research station. It was used as a centre for breeding and releasing of endangered species. It was used also as a care facility for tending and re-introducing injured creatures to the wild.

The ward they were shown into was amazing. 'Our children's ward,' Sally said proudly, and showed them into a softly lit bungalow with rows of pouches hanging from hooks just above floor level. 'Each pouch has its own electric blanket, set to the individual animal's body needs,' she said. 'Some of our babies can't sweat so it's important we get it right. We have nine babies here right now.'

'Survival rate?' Ben asked.

'Depends,' Sally said, and all trace of the fluffy do-gooder Jess had thought her disappeared. She was calmly competent, a woman who knew exactly what she was facing. And she wasn't trying to dress it up for Dusty. She was treating them as three professional adults.

'Some of these babies are deeply traumatised,' she said. 'If the mother dies without the joey being injured and someone finds it straight away and cares for it properly, then it stands a good chance. But sometimes a baby's thrown from the mother's pouch and not found for a while.' She grimaced. 'Or sometimes there's something genetically wrong with the babies that are sent to us. A weak baby may not be able to cling to the mother. It falls and is left. That's a hard call. We never harden to it; we give it our best shot but we know we can't save them all. Would you like to see our kitchens? We have the best scientific baby formula production area in the known world. Dusty, maybe you could help feed… And we're always looking for help sluicing out cages.'

She grinned at the look on their collective faces. 'Well, what did you expect?' she said, and chuckled. 'We're not open to sightseers but we are open to people who genuinely want to help. We're always short-staffed. And…' Her face clouded again. 'We're even more short-staffed this morning with Marge not well. Your help would be a godsend.'

'Is there anything we can do for Marge?' Jess asked, seeing the worry. But…

'No. It's just a sore leg—she was kicked by a wallaby last week. Kicks go with the job. She had a massage yesterday—that was why two of us went to the mainland rather than just one to collect the animals—but it seems to have stirred it up rather than settled it. She's sounds like she's getting a cold as well. But at least she's accepted she needs to rest.'

'We are doctors. You wouldn't like me…?' Jess ventured, still seeing worry.

'She'd be furious if I asked you to,' Sally said. 'She hates fuss. You know, she's almost eighty. She shouldn't be here, but she says, well, she says she wants to die doing the work she loves and Dianne and I respect that. It'll be what we want for ourselves.' She gave herself a little shake, visibly pushing fears aside. 'But today we've persuaded her to rest and that's huge in itself. She's snuggled into bed with Pokey, but she's feeling guilty and if we push her any more she'll get up just to prove she can. Right. Work. Let's go.'

Work.

They fed babies. They sluiced.

It was kind of fun.

The animals were in separate runs according to age, sex and species. Each run had a patch of natural ground, designed to be as close to the natural habitat as could be obtained, but there were sections in each run where feeding took place, or treating. These section were concrete slabs that had to be meticulously cleaned.

Jess scrubbed out the run of four short-nosed wombats. She worked alone. Dusty and Ben were in the turtle/tortoise run, cleaning the area around the pool. Scrubbing. Chatting.

Jess couldn't hear what they were chatting about.

'Do you want to work together or apart?' Sally had asked.

'Apart,' Jess had said, fast.

But Dusty had said 'Together' at exactly the same time. Ben hadn't responded.

'That's easy, then. Jess, you do the wombats, and Dusty and Ben do the tortoises,' Sally had said, and before she knew it that's exactly what was happening.

She could see them from where she was, fifty yards away, two heads, one small and blond, one adult and dark.

Dusty, asking questions.

Ben, seemingly at ease. Answering. Chatting back. Scrubbing as if he was accustomed to hard manual work.

Dusty manfully trying to keep up with him.

Even from here Jess was sensing the beginning of hero-worship.

'I think this might be Dr Oaklander,' Dusty had whispered to her during the tour, and she'd nodded, as grave as he'd been. They'd introduced themselves briefly as Dusty, Tess, Ben, and she'd seen Dusty react to the name. Ben.

'Check him out, then,' she'd said. 'Maybe don't say anything until you're sure.'

Dusty was obviously taking her at her word, or maybe he'd simply forgotten again and was just enjoying the moment. There was too much else to think about.

He didn't have enough males in his life, Jess thought ruefully as she watched them. No grandparents. No uncles. His teacher was a woman. Even his karate instructor was female.

What were they saying?

This was driving her crazy.

Ben's reaction to Dusty had Ben disconcerted. He didn't react to kids like this. In truth, he hardly reacted to kids at all. Once they'd lost newborn status he had little to do with them.

He was aware of them, of course. He'd even done a stint of paediatrics during training. But now…it was as if his decision about avoiding families had made him tune out from doing more than be nice to the siblings of his newborns.

But Dusty seemed…different.

The kid had him intrigued. He wasn't a noisy kid. He'd sensed the need for initial quiet in the enclosure they were cleaning, not wanting to scare the tortoises. For the first few minutes he'd simply scrubbed and not said anything.

Then, as the creatures got used to them, deciding they were no threat, Dusty started talking. A little.

'There are three different species of turtle here,' he told Ben. 'Look at the markings. And two species of tortoise. I really like tortoises.'

'Have you ever had one as a pet?'

He looked appalled. 'We live in London. These guys would hate it there.'

'I guess.'

Dusty scrubbed on, then peeped him a smile. 'What did the snail say when he was having a ride on the tortoise's back?'

'I don't know.' Ben sat back and enjoyed Dusty's grin. Once more, he was hit by that blast of recognition. Surely this was…

'Wheeeeeeee,' Dusty told him, and Ben found himself chuckling out loud.

The creatures around them didn't even back away.

'Do *you* know any tortoise jokes?' Dusty demanded, and Ben thought about it. He and Nate used to buy books of jokes. Jokes had been their very favourite thing and Ben was blessed with an excellent memory.

'As a matter of fact, I do,' he said, and Dusty chuckled in anticipation.

Just like Nate.

This was excellent, Jess thought. Wonderful. Dusty was getting to know his uncle without the tensions that revealing their relationship might cause. She'd deal with those tensions when they happened, she decided. Meanwhile the wombats were watching her balefully from inside their hollow log. Waiting for their clean house.

She scrubbed.

She kind of liked scrubbing. There were massive eucalypts overhead, taking away the sting of the sun. The wombats were a benign presence, and she thought, Am I doing it to your satisfaction, guys?

This was great for her head. It was taking her away from the grief of losing her mother, from the normal stress of work, the worry she always felt about Dusty…

And that was the biggie. Dusty had been desperately miserable since his gran had died. Now…

He had an uncle.

Any minute Ben might find out.

But when it came out…if Ben reacted well…

She glanced across at their stroke-for-stroke scrubbing. If Ben decided he did want to be an uncle… If he decided to share…

There were too many ifs. And she didn't want to share with an Oaklander.

'I'm befuddled,' she told the wombats, and they eyed her as if they already knew it.

Befuddled but happy?

Yeah, okay, she was happy. She was in one of the most glorious places in the world. Come what may, Dusty had met his uncle. 'I helped my uncle look after tortoises,' she imagined him telling his friends back home. 'He made me laugh.'

For Ben's rich chuckle rang out, over and over, and a couple of research workers in one of the far enclosures swivelled to see. As they would. They were female and that chuckle… Whew.

Had Nate's chuckle been as…gorgeous?

She couldn't remember. Nate was a fuzzy memory, an overwhelming, romantic encounter and then nothing.

Ben was here, now.

He was still an Oaklander. Nate must have had that chuckle. For her to lose her senses as she had…

'Well, I'm not losing my senses now,' she told the wombats, returning to scrubbing with ferocity. 'No way. I'm cleaning your yard and then I'm moving on.'

To the wallaby run. Not to Ben Oaklander. Not even close.

And then she paused. Sally had come flying out of the back door of the house. She looked around wildly. Saw her. Gasped.

'I… I…'

And that look…

Jess was already rising. Switching mind sets. She'd done stints in emergency rooms. She knew that expression. 'Sally, what is it?'

'It's Marge.' Sally's voice was scarcely above a whisper but the words carried regardless. 'It's serious.'

One minute Jess was a tourist, happily scrubbing for wombats. The next…

'Ben,' she yelled, no doubt scaring the wombats, but the look on Sally's face said scaring was the least of their problems. 'I need you.'

CHAPTER FOUR

A SORE leg and a head cold?

Much more.

Marge was lying on crumpled bedclothes, gasping for breath. Even from the doorway Jess could see signs of cyanosis, the blue tinge from lack of oxygen.

Ben was right behind her, and he saw the signs as she had.

Marge's nightgown was buttoned tight to her throat. He strode forward and ripped the buttons open, easing constriction in an instant. He put his hands under her arms and lifted.

Jess dived to shove pillows behind her. They were getting pressure off her chest any way they knew how.

A pug growled from the end of the bed and Sally gasped and grabbed her and hauled her away.

The little dog whined in fright.

Sally sobbed.

Dianne was crowding into the room as well, with Dusty and the research workers behind her.

Marge was still conscious. Her breath was coming in short, harsh gasps, as if every breath was agony.

As Jess pushed the pillows more solidly behind her she coughed, and a splash of crimson stained the bedclothes in front of her.

'Her leg,' Jess said urgently to Ben. 'A kick from the wallaby last week. Massage yesterday to alleviate the pain.'

And with that thought they both knew what they were dealing with. This had to be a pulmonary embolism. A blood clot in the leg, breaking up, moving to the lung. All the symptoms were there—the pain on breathing, the shortness of breath, the lack of oxygen marked by the bluish tinge. A bruise on the leg, a massage yesterday stirring it up…it made horrible sense.

They needed to call for transfer to a major hospital. They needed to clear the room. They needed to move fast. But just for this moment Ben took time for reassurance. Panic would make this much worse. He took Marge's hands in his and he forced her terrified gaze to focus on him.

'Marge, it's okay, we know what's happening and we know what to do about it,' he said, firmly and strongly, and everyone in the room seemed to pause. Marge's harsh breathing was still dreadful, but her eyes fixed on Ben's, a terrified, wounded thing searching desperately for help.

'Sally said you hurt your leg last week,' Ben said, almost conversationally. 'A fragment of clotted blood will have broken away and made its way to your lung. That's what I think is happening. It's causing problems with your breathing; it's stopping your lungs inflating fully. That's what's hurting, your deflated lung. What we need is to get the pain under control so it doesn't hurt so much to breathe, and to give you oxygen so you won't have to breathe so often or so deeply. If I can find those things we'll do it here to make you comfortable. Meanwhile, we'll call for a transfer and get you to the mainland hospital, because that's where they can give you blood thinners that'll stop any more clots forming and causing more trouble. But it's okay. We'll take care of you.'

The doorway was crowded. Everyone was listening. Ben's voice was deep and calm, dispersing panic.

Marge's breathing was still short and sharp and dreadful but some of the terror faded. If Ben could persuade her to relax…

If anyone could, he could. His calm, deep voice was almost mesmeric and his eyes didn't leave hers. If ever there was a man she'd want in a crisis…

This was a crisis and he was here.

An Oaklander. Promising to take care.

That was what Nate had promised, she thought, somewhat hysterically. She'd met Nate as a student in London. It had been a desperately hard time for her. Her mother had been ill in hospital and no one knew what the outcome would be. When her mother had finally been released, her great-aunt had taken her back to Yorkshire. 'You get on with your studies,' she'd told Jess roughly. 'Leave your mother to me; what happens happens.'

She'd been eighteen, alone, terrified. She'd thrown herself into her new university life, she'd let her friends take her where they'd willed—and she'd met Nate. He'd gathered her up and told her he'd take care of her. He'd made her forget.

Stupid, stupid, stupid.

This was different. She knew that. It was also no time to reflect on the past.

She was already moving to help.

She wheeled to the onlookers, thinking fast. 'Sally, you said you had a vet clinic here?'

'Jeff comes once a week to do our small stuff,' Sally managed, her voice faltering. 'Dressings and stuff. He's not here today.'

'But his equipment is?'

'He has a locked store cupboard,' one of the research girls ventured. 'Only Jeff has the key.'

'Take me to it,' she said, meeting Ben's gaze for an instant, an urgent, silent message passing between them. Regardless of Ben's reassurance, the bright blood on the bedclothes meant there was internal bleeding and the cyanosis of her lips, the blue tinge to her skin meant there was real danger of instant death.

'I'm not sure if Jeff would...' the girl ventured.

'Jeff doesn't have any say in what we're doing now,' she told her. 'We'll think about consequences later. Dusty, you can see Marge is sick. She's having trouble breathing and we need to help her.' She glanced at the research girls, their name tags, Sarah and Naomi. 'You guys are working on cassowary breeding programme, right? Would you explain it to Dusty? Naomi, is it okay if Dusty stays with you? Dusty, I'll be with you as soon as we make Marge feel better.'

And that was a promise, too. *As soon as we make Marge feel better...* They all heard it and Ben even managed to give her an appreciative nod. But they needed to move fast.

Dusty was looking terrified. They were all looking terrified.

She needed to focus on medicine.

'In your own time, Doctor,' Ben said, almost as a joke, but she knew what he was saying. *You know what we need and we need it now.*

'Sally, you stay here and give Marge a bit of courage,' she said. She managed a teasing smile. 'Ben might be tempted to give Marge an injection and that's deeply scary. Dianne, you take Pokey outside and give him a cuddle and while you're doing it call the nearest ambulance service. Say we have a lady with a pulmonary embolism.'

'They'll send a chopper,' Dianne said, her voice trembling. 'If it's urgent.'

'Tell them it's urgent,' Ben said, still in that calm voice that said urgent wasn't necessarily scary. 'Marge'll be more comfortable in hospital. She needs full pain relief so make it sound as urgent as you like. Tell them you have a lady in pain from a pulmonary embolism, you have two doctors here and they both say helicopter transfer with all speed.'

Jess opened Jeff's cupboard by attacking it with an axe.

Sarah had offered to try and unscrew the hinges. Jess, who'd seen the axe by the woodshed, went for what was fastest. While Sarah gasped in horror about what Jeff would say, Jess aimed for the hinges and smashed them to pieces.

The door fell forward, very satisfactorily.

Naomi and Dusty had paused to watch. 'Wow,' said Dusty, sounding a bit wobbly. 'I didn't know you could chop cupboards.'

'I didn't, either,' Jess said, but she was already in the store, flicking on the lights, searching.

Yes!

An Aladdin's cave couldn't offer her any more that these shelves offered. The unknown Jeff was a meticulous, careful vet, and his store reflected it. This was a pharmacy and medical store combined. Each shelf was carefully labelled. Each container was clearly marked.

The storeroom was big enough to hold a small refrigerator. She tugged it open. Drugs.

Morphine. Yes!

Syringes. All sizes.

A variety of stethoscopes.

Oxygen concentrator. An oxygen saturation meter. Tubing. Not the tubing she was used to, set up so she could put in a nasal tube in an instant—in this setting every nasal cavity would be different—but the fittings were there, scissors on the side, tape, everything right where she wanted it. Ready to grab.

Back to Ben.

Please…

'Mum…'

Dusty. She paused.

'It's like Gran,' Dusty said tremulously, and she stopped to hug him.

'I hope not,' she said, knowing honesty was the only way.

'Fix her,' Dusty whispered. 'You and my Uncle Ben.'

The urgent things were done fast, oxygen started, morphine administered, Marge reassured as much as they could. Then there was time to pause.

'The chopper will be here in fifteen minutes,' Sally told them tremulously. 'Can I make…tea?'

'Would you like one, Marge?' Ben asked, and the offer settled Marge further. That Ben could focus on anything so mundane as tea…

Marge didn't want one—every ounce of energy she had was focused on breathing—but the offer was reassuring and she relaxed enough not to react with fear when Ben suggested an examination.

The results were frightening. Marge's oxygen saturation was down to ninety per cent, and that was after they'd had oxygen flowing for almost five minutes. And when Ben took the stethoscope and listened, his face remained impassive, but Jess knew...

'Do you mind if Jess listens?' he asked.

The morphine was starting to take hold. Marge was relaxing more and more. 'Go right ahead,' she said, and managed a faint smile as she waved expansively to her chest.

Jess listened—and there it was, the faint but unmistakable sound of lung rasping against ribs. What they suspected was confirmed. The lung was collapsing as the blockage worsened.

Jess handed the stethoscope back to Ben, feeling ill.

The morphine was taking hold now, and the panic had eased from Marge's face, but she was still fighting to get sufficient oxygen into her damaged lung.

Ben had the nasal tube attached, the flow set to maximum.

'I'm almost sure it's a clot,' Ben told her, setting the stethoscope aside. 'I'm afraid you do need to go to hospital. They'll give you a pulmonary angiogram—a type of X-ray—to find out exactly where the clot is. Then they'll start you on heparin to thin your blood and get you better.'

'This is the third time...' Marge whispered.

'Marge's had two heart attacks before this,' Sally told them, her voice unsteady. 'Each time... We're so lucky to still have her.'

Jessie's own heart sank further. Two major infarcts and now this.

What was Marge doing, living in such a remote place? With this medical history she should be living next door to a major hospital.

It was her life. She was living the life she loved.

Sally started fussing round the room, packing. It'd be better if she stayed still, Jess thought. Marge needed comfort rather than fuss.

As for Jess herself, there was little more she could do here. She should go and find Dusty. Reassure him and tell everyone outside what was happening. But as she made to leave, Marge's hand came out and clutched hers. 'Please…stay.'

'You don't need two doctors,' she teased. 'Dr Oaklander's here.' She wasn't pretending she didn't know who Ben was. It was no longer important.

'If I had fifty doctors here I'd want them all,' Marge gasped. 'And you're both baby doctors.'

'Hey, we're all grown up,' Ben retorted.

'I meant obstetricians,' Marge whispered, and managed another smile.

'So we're no use at all,' Jess agreed, smiling, too. 'Unless these are labour pains and there's a baby on the way.'

'No baby,' Marge gasped. 'I've had three. Like you, they're all grown up. And…and you? How many?'

'Just Dusty.'

'He's a nice little boy.'

'He is.' Jess glanced at Ben's face. Ben was holding Marge's wrist. Not good news?

'And you?' Marge asked Ben.

'No kids.'

'What a shame.' She managed a trace of a cheeky grin. 'Maybe you could share. Dusty looks more like your son than Jess's…'

And then she stopped. The remaining colour blanched from her face and her gaze moved inward.

'Oh…' Her hand faltered to her chest, then dropped to the bedclothes, as if it was simply too heavy to hold up.

'Marge!' Sally dropped the overnight case she was packing; was back at the bed in an instant.

'I'm cold,' Marge whispered. 'So cold…'

And then suddenly…nothing.

They might both be obstetricians but their general training was solid and they knew exactly what to do. They moved swiftly, smoothly into cardio pulmonary resuscitation. They had no defibrillator but they had everything else.

Sometimes everything wasn't enough.

CPR was supposed to be the miracle cure-all. Jess remembered her distress as a first-year intern when CPR had failed.

'When the blockage is complete, there's nothing anyone can do,' her registrar had told her gently. 'Don't beat yourself up. We're only doctors. Miracles aren't stored in our doctors' bags.'

There was no miracle here.

The helicopter arrived with paramedics. They took over with practised expertise, with all the right equipment, but they produced no miracle either.

No trace of a heartbeat. Nothing.

She was seventy-eight years old, Sally whispered in answer to one of the paramedic's questions, and Jess thought of Marge yesterday, as they closed her eyes, as they removed equipment, as they let death take its peaceful course. She thought of Marge on the ferry, sitting in the sun, feeding her baby wombat, surrounded by her friends, doing the work she loved. The grief around them was real and dreadful, but it'd be something, she thought, to be grieved for as Marge was grieved for. To die as Marge had died.

Sally was telling them all, desperate to talk. Marge had three children. Seven grandchildren. She had colleagues, friends, a host of animals whose care would be less because this gentle lady was no more.

Dianne came in and sobbed. The paramedics took over, quietly competent.

Sally and Dianne hugged each other.

Dusty was in the corridor, trembling with shock. Jess went out and hugged him, and as she held him she glanced back into the room and saw Ben hugging Sally and Dianne.

A tiny part of her thought, An Oaklander…hugging?

But that was it. The paramedics were in control.

There was nothing left for Ben and Jess to do but to take a white-faced, silent Dusty and leave.

* * *

'Why couldn't you make her better?'

It was the first time Dusty had spoken. Shock seemed to have held him rigid.

Jess and Ben and Dusty were walking back to the resort. It was only a half-hour walk. Sally was in no state to drive, and by mutual silent consent they'd decided a walk was fine.

They'd all stayed silent. The shock. Did you ever get used to it?

Not in ten years' medicine, Jess thought. Maybe never.

Why couldn't they make her better? Oh, she wished...

'We did all we could,' Jess told him. 'We were lucky we had equipment. Ben made the pain stop, he helped her breathe, but sometimes everything we do isn't enough. She had a blood clot that stopped her heart beating. It's sad but that's the way it is.'

'Like Gran,' Dusty whispered, choking back tears, and Jess thought her mother's death was too close; too raw. Dusty missed her so much, and for this to happen...

'You could die, too,' Dusty whispered, and his hand clutched hers convulsively.

Uh-oh. This was the terror of an intelligent only child of a single mother. The terror of a child realising life was fraught.

'I'm young,' Jess said, but thought she didn't feel young. She stooped and hugged him. 'It's okay, Dusty, I'm not going anywhere.'

'My dad died.'

'I don't take risks.'

'But...anything could happen,' Dusty said wildly. 'Like in the buggy this morning. Crashing. Anything. And then there'd be nothing. Nothing and nothing.' He was verging on hysterical. 'And then...then there'd only be Dr Oaklander, and he doesn't even know who we are.'

'Dusty...'

'And you aren't going to tell him. And I don't even know if he likes me. And it's really scary and I don't want anyone else to die and I want to go home...'

The last was a terrified wail. Jess plonked down on the sand and tugged him close, cradled him hard against her, knowing she could only wait until the paroxysm of grief and fear and shock wore off. Dusty had hardly cried when her mother had died. He was making up for it now.

She held him close. Simply held.

Ben squatted down on the sand beside her.

Said nothing.

He had patience. Ben seemed to know Dusty needed this, needed to sob, needed simply to be held. He waited, as she did, for the paroxysms to pass.

And when they did, when Dusty lay limp and exhausted in her arms, when Jess thought she should struggle to her feet, somehow get him back to the resort, Ben touched Dusty lightly on the hand. A feather touch, ready to withdraw at need.

'Dusty?' His voice was calm but compelling, and Dusty took a ragged breath and swivelled in Jess's arms to look at him.

'Dusty, your gran and Marge were both old,' he said, softly yet surely. 'Marge's children are all a lot older than your mum and me. They have children of their own. So I'm guessing that'll be what happens with you and your mum. You'll grow up and when you're as old as I am or older you might get married. You might have a whole lot of kids who'll grow up and be teenagers. Then you'll grow bald and start playing golf and having little naps after dinner. And your mum will get white hair like Marge and she'll be a grandma. And she'll say how can a son of mine be bald? And she'll boss your kids. Then one day in the far, far distant future, when you're almost old yourself and so bald you have to shine your head with furniture polish, it might be your mum's turn to die. But right now she looks very, very healthy. I suspect she'll be bossing you around for a very long time to come.'

There was enough in that to give Dusty pause. Bald… The concept drew him from the thought of death, just a little. Old. Bald. Involuntarily his hand crept to his hair. Just checking.

Ben smiled.

But Dusty had coped with the idea of another death besides Marge and his gran.

'But my dad…'

'He died young,' Ben conceded. 'Accidents happen. Not very often, not if we're careful.' He hesitated, looked at Jess, looked at Dusty.

'But am I right in thinking your dad wasn't careful?' he said, slowly, as if thinking it through as he spoke. 'Am I right in thinking your dad went too fast on a Jet Ski, and crashed? Am I right in thinking your father was my brother? That you're Nate Oaklander's son?'

Dusty stared at him, unable to speak.

Jess couldn't speak either. Too much had happened. Too much was happening.

But there was nothing to do but answer.

'Yes,' she said simply, finally. 'I'm sorry. We should have told you. But, yes, Dusty is your brother's son.'

CHAPTER FIVE

To say he was flabbergasted was an understatement. Ben knelt in the warm morning sunshine and let her words sink in.

He was looking at Nate's son.

His nephew.

It was Nate who was looking back at him. Nate at eight years old. His brother.

His guess had seemed a wild hunch, crazy, but now... Now...

'What kind of a stunt is this?' It was almost an explosion, impossible to repress.

'It's not a stunt.' Jessie's face closed in swift anger. 'I wish it was.'

'We were keeping it secret until we were sure it was you,' Dusty said, looking miserable—or even more miserable than he already was. 'Mum said you'd be crabby.' His pale face contorted in pain. The shock of another death like his grandmother's... His lovely morning ended... It was all too much. 'Mum thought you'd be angry and now you are.'

'I don't understand,' Ben said blankly.

'Dusty wanted to see you,' Jess said, carefully, as if each word was loaded. 'We found you on the internet, as guest speaker at this conference. The conference looked interesting, we needed a holiday so it seemed a good chance.'

'To see me?'

'Yes.'

'Why didn't you tell me?' He sounded furious. Echoes of his father.

'Cos we thought you'd be like my grandpa,' Dusty whispered, his voice muffled as Jess held him close. 'Mum says Grandpa was cross. And now… Mum's right, you do sound cross and I don't know why. I don't know…' His voice broke and he dissolved again.

She had to focus on him.

Life had been hard for Dusty since her mum had died, Jess thought, hugging him close. Dusty had faced grief, moving house, babysitters, child care. He'd been stoic.

He wasn't stoic now. He was shattered and all she could do was hold him. There was no room for her to worry about the reaction of the man beside her.

Explanations were needed—she knew that—but for now all Dusty needed was to be held. He didn't need the distraction of an uncle. 'I'm sorry you had to find out like this,' she managed. 'We're not here to ask anything of you. We don't want anything. And now I think we need to be by ourselves.'

He was staring at her like she was an alien from outer space. Maybe she was. She was his brother's lover.

His brother had been dead for years.

'Go,' she pleaded. 'Dusty only needs me.'

'I can help.'

'You can help most by leaving.'

The sun was blazing down on the sandy track. They should move into the shade.

In a moment she'd get Dusty to move. In a minute. When Ben left.

He knew it. She could see his hesitation, his impulse to do the right thing, carry Dusty into the shade, push help she didn't want. For some reason she could read his expression.

'Please,' she said.

'I'll be back.'

'There's no need,' she told him, as another shudder racked

Dusty's body. 'We're not here to make nuisances of ourselves. Dusty's seen you. That's all he wants. Please…just go.'

His head was spinning. He strode down the track toward the resort and then broke into a run.

Yes, it was hot, but they were out there in the sun. Regardless of Dusty's need to be alone with his mother, he had to do something.

His brother's child.

That meant Jess and Nate…

He couldn't go there. He felt ill.

Why? Nate had had a string of lovers; he'd known that from the time he'd re-established contact. The combination of money, good looks and sheer, unashamed arrogance seemed to have been a powerful aphrodisiac. But as for permanent attachments… His brother had slept with Jess and he'd left her with a son?

As far as he knew, his immediate family had ended with his father's death.

He had a nephew.

He was doing mental arithmetic as he ran. Dusty was about ten. That'd mean Nate would have been in university. He'd 'studied' for years, on and off—mostly off—before he'd thrown it in as not his scene.

That's where he must have met Jess. London. University. Jess going on to be a doctor. Nate going on to do what Nate did best, which was nothing.

Nate dead, because of a stupid, drunken crash.

Leaving a child. Dusty. What sort of a name was that?

A great name for the battered ten-year-old. A little boy with stoicism written all over him.

Intelligence. Humour. Bravery.

Qualities he saw in Jess.

His fingers were clenched into fists as he ran. The old anger. Nate who'd wound his stupidly indulgent father around his indolent finger. Nate who'd hated him.

Now this. Nate's son.

Had he looked after them? Certainly not when he'd died. There'd been no hint of a grandchild in the legal quagmire his father had left behind. Had Nate even told their father?

A tight knot of anger coiled in his gut. He didn't want anything to do with Nate's disasters.

But these weren't disasters. The memory of Jess crouched on the track, hugging the sobbing little boy, was imprinted on his mind. These were Jess and Dusty.

He was approaching the resort, and the concierge was bustling out to meet him. 'We've just heard,' he said before Ben could say what he needed. 'Such dreadful news. Mind, they should expect it when the place is run by such elderly women but it's made your morning dreadful. Can I help?'

'Can you send a buggy back for Dr McPherson and her son?' he said brusquely. 'They're on the track halfway home. They need a ride back here.'

'Certainly, sir,' the concierge said. 'I'll send Doug at once. Would you like to go with him?'

'I… No.' Ben paused. Regrouped. Knew what Jess had asked. *Please…*

She was as distressed as Dusty was, he thought, and he wasn't doing anything to distress her. Nate's woman.

No. Jess. Simply Jess.

'No,' he said again. 'The little boy's very upset but my presence won't help anything.'

Dusty was distraught. All the emotion of the last three months seemed to have been stored and had burst out today, released by the shock of Marge's death, the proximity of Ben, sheer emotional overload. He sobbed until the resort buggy arrived to drive them home. He stayed limp during the ride, he sobbed again as they reached the privacy of their bungalow, and finally he slipped into an uneasy sleep.

He slept most of the afternoon while Jess thought of Marge and thought of her mother and thought grief could strike anywhere. How could she alleviate Dusty's distress? She knew she couldn't.

You never 'get over' grief, she thought drearily, but you finally build scar tissue. Dusty was learning the hard way.

When he woke she rang room service and asked for sandwiches.

Ben arrived, the waiter behind him.

He had his computer slung over his shoulder. He was carrying...Pokey?

The little dog was huddled in Ben's arms like she wanted to be somewhere else but she didn't know where. Heavily pregnant. As miserable as all of them.

'Can we come in?' Ben said gently.

Bemused, she stood aside. What else was a woman to do?

Ben came in and so did the waiter. The man put the tray on the table, smiled at Ben, smiled at Pokey and left.

Um...she had a dog in her room.

There were signs all over the resort. No pets. No non-native animals on the island,

Pokey didn't qualify?

Dusty was still a huddle of misery under his bedclothes. She thought he was awake, but he wasn't reacting at all.

'Can Pokey and I join you?' Ben asked.

What if she said no?

She couldn't. This man was Dusty's uncle. It behoved her to be civil. Even though he was an Oaklander, he'd done nothing to deserve incivility, even though the thought of his presence was disconcerting. Frightening even.

'You said you didn't want anything of me,' he said, still in that gentle voice that did something weird to her insides. 'I don't want anything of you either. If you want Pokey and I to leave then we will. But if you can, I'd like to talk.'

She stared at him helplessly for a moment and then motioned to the chairs at the table.

He sat. Pokey whined. He fondled the little pug behind her ears and she settled on his knee.

'Why do you have Pokey?' she managed. It seemed as good a place to start as any.

'She's Marge's dog. I've been back over there; it's full of distress and people not sure what they're doing. Pokey's presence is bound to be found out. Consensus is that Pokey might be better staying here for a few days.'

'But can she stay here?'

'I can be persuasive.' He smiled at her, and she thought this wasn't Nate's smile. Nate's smile had never been this gentle. 'I'm keynote speaker to an international conference. I've explained I'm using Pokey as a prop.'

'A prop...'

His smile widened. Coaxing her to smile back. 'How's this for fast thinking? My talk's on care for pregnant women in remote areas. I can hardly use a pregnant woman as my show-and-tell, so instead I'm using a pregnant dog. So I fronted at Reception and said she'd arrived on this afternoon's ferry as arranged. I requested dog food, I acted as if there could be no objection in the world, and when they made a tentative protest. I said it had been a condition of my attendance, hadn't they received my advance notice? I sounded haughty—like my attendance is predicated on Pokey being on stage with me. So they were faced with Losing Keynote Speaker. They were so dumbstruck they agreed. I figure when the conference is over she can be quietly slipped back to Sally and Dianne, who'll quietly slip her to Marge's daughter as soon as she returns from overseas. Job's done.'

He was looking like a child who'd just got away with stealing sweets. Mischief and triumph combined. Almost irresistible.

It had to be irresistible. Back away from that smile...

'So you're going to look after her?' she managed.

'I'll be busy at the conference,' he said. 'I do have plans to incorporate her into my presentation—I need to justify this. The rest of the time she can stay in my room. But I did wonder...'

He looked through into Dusty's bedroom then, his smile fading. Addressed the small nose poking above the bedclothes.

'I did wonder, Dusty, if you might look after her for me. Just during the sessions when I can't be with her. What do you think?'

Silence. More silence. Then…

'Me?' Dusty quavered, and the bedsheet was lowered by an inch.

'There's no one else,' Ben said, apologetically. 'She's scared and lonely and she's about to have pups. She needs gentle walks and lots of cuddles.' He hesitated, like a man about to admit a failing. 'I'm not all that good at cuddles,' he conceded.

Dusty's sheet slipped so his face was in full view. The awful blankness had disappeared. 'Why not?' he demanded.

Ben frowned. 'Why not what?'

'Why aren't you good at cuddles? Didn't your mum—?'

'Dusty!' Jess sent her son a warning glance. Shock and distress not withstanding, Dusty was one smart little boy. *He was using the occasion for probing?*

But she wasn't about to stop Ben replying.

'My mum wasn't good at cuddles either,' Ben said, seemingly not fazed by the interruption. 'She died of a pulmonary embolism eight years ago, just before your dad was killed. Her name was Fiona Smythe-Harris. She would have been your grandmother. Your other grandmother.'

And just like that Ben was admitting to Dusty that they were related. She felt…winded.

'Just like Marge,' Dusty said.

'She wasn't a bit like Marge,' Ben said. 'She wore silk dresses and smart jackets and high-heeled shoes. She didn't like dogs.'

'So you never had a dog?'

'No. I need help with this one.'

It was the right appeal. Dusty pushed his bedclothes back with decision. 'Are you cross that you're my uncle?' he asked.

'No. I'm cross that I didn't know about you but that's not the same.'

'You sounded cross with Mum.' He was approaching Pokey with caution. Not, though, with the caution of a child who thought he might be bitten. It was the caution of a child who thought something wonderful might be snatched away.

'I'm not cross with your mother either, even if I sounded like it,' Ben said, and his voice was suddenly harsh again. 'I'm cross with your dad for not telling me I had a nephew. I'm cross that for all these years I've had a nephew and I didn't know. A nephew called Dusty.'

'I'm really called Dustin,' Dusty said, and he slid into the seat beside Ben and started stroking Pokey's ears. Pokey dropped her head sideways to deepen the rub and Dusty obliged. 'After my other grandpa. The nice one. He liked animals, a lot. I have his train set. It's ace.'

Ben's eyes lit. 'I had a train set when I was your age. Would you like to see it?'

'How can I see it?'

'My computer,' he said, and he carefully slid Pokey into Dusty's arms. Dusty looked at the little dog in awe. Pokey wriggled in his small-boy arms, and sighed.

Dusty was used to handling his gran's cat. He held Pokey with care and with firmness, and the little dog sighed again but then snuggled against him. Leaving Dusty free to gaze at Ben's truly awesome laptop.

'Wow,' he said. 'That's about ten times better'n Mum's. Do you have photos on it?'

'Now I do,' Ben said, and he smiled across the table at Jess—who was feeling gobsmacked. 'My secretary back in London is used to some pretty strange requests. I waited until dawn her time to wake her up. She emailed them through. It's taken them a while to download but I thought you might like them.'

Photographs.

Family photographs. He didn't wait for permission; just flicked his laptop open and started a slide show.

At some stage he must have scanned a lot of old photographs onto disk, because these pictures spanned a century.

'That's Oaklands when it was first built,' he told Dusty, and Jess saw the house that had scared her witless seven years ago.

'It was built by your great-grandfather. It's a bit over the top. All those columns.'

'Wow.' Dusty stared at the house in wonder. 'Was your family rich?'

'*Your* family was rich,' Ben said firmly. 'These people are your family, Dustin.'

And it was as if it was a legal decree. *These people are your family...*

With these few words Dusty had been granted a right to his father's life.

A name.

Her son was part Oaklander.

Jess glanced at Ben's impassive face. For the last ten years such a thought had made her shudder. Now...there was another side?

Ben's side.

Once upon a time the Oaklander charm had made her lose her senses. Beware.

She was bewaring as hard as she could beware.

'So do you still own it?' she managed.

'Yes.' He sounded strained, though, as if he didn't like admitting it.

'Do you live in it?' Dusty asked.

'No.'

'Why not?'

'It has twenty bedrooms. How could a man choose which one to use? I loan it out to an overseas aid organisation. Meanwhile this one's your grandfather and grandmother on their wedding day. I think you have your grandpa's nose.'

'Can you make it bigger?' Dusty asked, entranced, so Ben did, magnifying it and magnifying it again so all they could see was pixilated nose.

'See,' Ben said. 'Exactly the same.'

Dusty felt his nose, looked at the pixilation—and giggled.

It was a great sound.

The day was being turned around.

'Maybe we can do better than that. All sorts of displays are being set up, right here. Technology companies are spruiking their equipment, and some are already testing, wanting to make sure nothing goes wrong. I noticed one team this afternoon—they produce tiny portable scanners, state-of-the-art stuff. The team leader was telling me they're getting close to as good a result as they are from much bigger units. If we were to head over there now...' He looked at her, considering. Almost teasing. 'Professor Oaklander, keynote speaker, and Dr. McPherson, senior obstetric physician at London Central...'

'I'm not senior.'

'If you take off your flip-flops,' he said, grinning, 'you might look senior.'

'How did you know I worked at London Central?'

'Professors have their ways. You want to try?'

Dusty was looking worried. 'You want to do an operation on Pokey?'

'That's exactly what I don't want,' Ben said. 'That's what ultrasounds are for. It's a method of photography, of seeing exactly what's inside our Pokey. We can look at the puppies, measure their heads and make sure they're all pointing in the right direction. Then we can all relax and wait for the puppies to come. Shall we try?'

'Now?' Jess demanded, startled.

'Why not? Is that okay with you, Dusty?'

'Yes,' Dusty said, the last of the morning's trauma set aside. He smiled shyly at this wonderful new uncle. 'Yes, it is.'

CHAPTER SIX

THEY walked over to the convention centre, Pokey in Dusty's arms. Ben suggested she walk but Dusty wanted to carry her and the little dog seemed to like it.

'You really think these guys will let us use their state-of-the-art ultrasound on Pokey?' Jess demanded.

'Watch,' Ben said.

The convention centre was another world; almost incongruous in this beautiful island setting. It was a vast glass rotunda, looking out in all directions at the beauty of the island. It was decorated for Christmas but there were no garish decorations here. The Christmas tree was a live Australian bottlebrush, twenty feet high, each 'brush' its natural crimson with sparkling golden tips. It was stunning.

So was Ben.

The woman in charge of the scanner was in her fifties, cool, clinical, reminding Jess of the consultant in charge of her first-ever training placement. Almost scary. Jess could see her assessing the foursome as they approached. Jess had tugged on a neat skirt and blouse to do her best to look professional, but there was no way she could stop Dusty looking tearstained, and Pokey, fat and frumpy, was hardly a fashion accessory.

'Dogs aren't permitted in the resort,' the woman began, but Ben held out his hand and gripped hers before she could say any further.

'I'm Professor Oaklander and this is Dr McPherson from the UK. You must be Elizabeth Morey—I've heard great things about your team and your product. I'd like to mention your work in my keynote address tomorrow—it fits magnificently into my theme of remote medicine—but I thought I'd arrange the ultimate test first. I've persuaded Dusty here to lend us his dog. Pokey's here by special arrangement with management. Her pregnancy's almost full term. If your machine can show us her pups in minute detail, it must be capable of detecting abnormalities in human presentation. Would you be happy to agree?'

'Ultrasound…a dog?' Elizabeth was clearly taken aback.

'We have obstetricians coming from all over the world,' Ben reminded her. 'Many of them care for women in remote areas, or teach those who do. That's one of my pet projects—improving on-site care so women don't have to be transferred to cities without need. Now, I know you can't do a human ultrasound—any presentation would need to be video only—but what I propose is one step better. I propose we record Pokey's ultrasound, and show it, at the same time producing Pokey as show-and-tell. If she's amenable we might even be able to repeat the ultrasound on stage. Our audience can see how small she is, how small the pups are and what your machine's capable of. I suspect it'll make my job easier—persuading doctors that these machines can be useful—and it'll certainly make your sales pitch a whole lot simpler.'

And she was sold, just like that.

It was as much as Jess could do not to giggle.

She didn't. Ben was being professional. So must she.

She squeezed Dusty's hand, but Dusty was looking up at Ben and she could see…awe? The beginning of belief. This new uncle was…wonderful?

He wasn't bad, Jess conceded, but she wasn't about to think wonderful. She couldn't afford to let herself forget he was an Oaklander.

She'd been stunned by an Oaklander before.

Elizabeth led them into an anteroom where her team was

setting up their display. Briefly the woman outlined what Ben intended—and immediately she had three technicians onside, desperate to prove the efficacy of their new toy.

And Pokey proved herself a worthy subject. A dummy of a pregnant woman was put aside. Dusty set Pokey on the examination table in her place. With only the slightest encouragement Pokey rolled over. When stroked, she obliged by sticking her legs straight up, dead-dog position, exposing her swollen belly for inspection.

The technicians loved her. Even the rigidly proper Elizabeth came close to smiling.

Jess had thought they might need to shave her, but she had very little hair on her underside. They anointed her with gel, the wand slid easily over her swollen bulge and images started appearing.

'Can you people explain this?' Ben said. 'I'm good at big babies but puppies... Is it even possible to get detail?'

The technicians practically purred. Doctor admitting he knew less than they did. This was their baby, and they were out to prove their mettle.

'Head circumferences...' Ben murmured.

'What, for all of them?' the junior-most technician said, and Elizabeth quelled him with a glare.

'Of course,' she snapped. 'We can do that, can't we, Tony?'

'I'm guessing yes.' The senior technician was intrigued and challenged. 'But let's count heads first.'

'Quads,' Ben said in satisfaction as they stared at the fuzzy images on the screen. Four. 'We've been worried about octuplets. Head sizes for eight might be a problem.'

'With eight we'd have a puppy knot,' Tony agreed. 'This will be hard enough. But doable. Let's focus on this guy first in line to come out.' He grinned. 'You don't want sex, too?'

'Why not?' Ben asked, and everyone chuckled—including Elizabeth.

'It'd be something if we could get it,' she murmured, and Jess saw sales in her eyes and satisfaction in Ben's.

And in twenty minutes they had it. A perfect picture of exactly what was going on inside Pokey. The little dog had been patience personified. Dusty had stroked her, spoken gently to her as the technicians argued about what belonged to what, how best to get head circumference, how to try and sex them. They even thought they knew.

'I'm betting three boys and a girl,' Tony said. 'There's no head circumference that'll cause problems with a pelvis that size. That first little guy looks perfectly presented. Whoever Pokey's obstetrician is can relax. Dad can pop out and stock up on cigars; this is as good as in the bag.'

General chuckle. General satisfaction. Pokey's tummy was wiped, she almost reluctantly ceased her dead-dog roll and they were done.

'Four puppies,' Dusty said, awed. 'Can we keep one?'

Uh-oh. She should have seen that coming. Hospital apartment on the other side of the world...

'Never count your chickens before they're hatched,' Ben said, scooping Pokey out of Dusty's arms, tucking the confused little dog into the crook of his own arm and then taking Dusty's small hand into his large one. 'And that goes for puppies. You might take one look and think, yikes, they're pink.'

'Pink!'

'You never know with babies,' Ben said solemnly. 'Do we know for sure who the daddy is? Was he pink?'

'No, I—'

'Then we just have to wait until they're hatched,' he said. 'Meanwhile, did you say you had a spade?'

'Yes.' Dusty was thoroughly bemused.

'Then I want one, too. It's ageism to give you a spade and not me. I'm off to complain to the manager right now. And once I have my spade, what I propose is beach.'

'Beach.' Dusty was having trouble keeping up.

'Beach,' Ben said definitely. 'I've checked out your castle from this morning and I'm sorry to tell you that the moat hasn't protected the foundations. I have a suspicion your castle now has water in the basement. So I suggest you guys go put on your swimmers. I'll complain to the management about my lack of spade, demand one for myself, and while I'm at it I'll ask for a picnic rug, a picnic basket and a sleeping basket for Pokey. My plan is for fast castle repairs, then supper on the beach, then a swim and then bed. We all have a big day tomorrow. I'm talking at the conference. You're Pokey-minding. Your mother has to listen to me talking. That'll be the hardest task of all. So do we have a plan?'

She was more bemused than Dusty was. Swept away…

Keep your feet firmly on the ground, she told herself. This guy is an Oaklander.

No. This man was Ben and right now he was wonderful. He was making her son happy. She had no intention of being swept up in his smile, but she could relax for a little. She could even agree to his plan.

She could even smile back.

She was lying on the sand, a small fat dog curled up beside her, watching her son play in the shallows with his uncle.

How easy was this?

She could have approached this man years ago. He would have accepted the relationship, she thought. He seemed to be… kind.

Pokey wriggled beside her, trying to find a comfy spot for her very pregnant body. She stroked her and thought what an amazing act of kindness, to take this dog. She was under no illusion as to how hard it must have been. He'd have had to spin a very tall story. He might even have had to play a bit dumb. 'Dogs not permitted? How was I expected to know?'

There was no way anyone of less standing—and less critical importance to the event's success—could get away with it.

He'd even manoeuvred Pokey an ultrasound.

'He's impressive,' she murmured to Pokey, and Pokey rolled over and did her dead-dog thing again so she'd get another tummy rub.

'That's enough of pleasure for you in this pregnancy,' she said, trying to sound severe—and failing. 'The rest is hard work.'

Pokey looked at her with doubt.

'I wouldn't worry. You have one of the world's best obstetricians to help you,' she told her, and tickled her tummy some more.

And glanced at the water.

Ben had Dusty on his shoulders. He was chest deep in the surf, holding Dusty's hands, and Dusty was falling forward in a practice dive. His first ever diving lesson.

He was going right under, something he'd always been afraid of. Spluttering and laughing. Being swept up and put on Ben's shoulders to try again.

Like father and son.

Not quite.

Nephew and uncle.

It was more than she'd expected. More than she'd hoped for.

It was…just a little bit scary.

That's why she was here, lying on the sand, watching. The temptation to join them was almost irresistible but she'd been chuckling with the two of them, being splashed, splashing in turn, when suddenly she'd stopped enjoying herself. She'd felt fear.

Had Ben guessed? She'd told them she was getting cold but in truth it had been no such thing. Ben's gaze had met hers, and there was a flash of something between them.

He was being kind to Dusty. That was all.

They were staggering out of the water now, waving to her. No, not waving to her but to someone behind her. She turned and one of the resort staff was walking down the track toward them. Kathy. Carrying a basket.

Supper.

Supper and then bed. Tomorrow the conference started. Ben would be surrounded by professional colleagues, their separate worlds would take over, this time would be over.

He and Dusty could keep in touch, she thought, hopefully.

Email was great. Maybe even Skype so they could see each other.

For Dusty to have an uncle on the other side of the world was a gift.

And maybe it was just as well he would be on the other side of the world, she told herself, feeling breathless as she watched her son and his uncle walk hand in hand up the beach toward them. Ben was wearing boxer-swimmers, nothing else.

Had Nate's body been so…ripped?

She couldn't remember.

She would have remembered if it had looked like this, she thought, and by the time they reached her she was struggling to subdue a blush that seemed to be enveloping her from the toes up.

Luckily they were preoccupied. 'Excellent,' Dusty said, in tones of someone who hadn't seen food for days. 'I'm starving.'

'You had a really late lunch.'

'That was hours ago.' Kathy reached them and set down the basket. 'Hi,' Dusty said, abandoning his habitual shyness. He'd met this girl twice now, he was growing accustomed to the relaxed tone of the staff, so obviously it was time to move to familiarity. 'Are you pregnant?'

Kids… She had to talk to him about this, she thought. If Kathy had just been overweight…

She wasn't. She was wearing a hotel uniform resewn as a maternity smock, with a tiny white apron, tied high. Very high, Jess thought suddenly. She'd been preoccupied and tired the first couple of times she'd met her. Now she thought…it was tied very high indeed.

'Good guess,' Kathy said, smiling and stooping to put the picnic basket on the sand, but Ben was before her, taking it from her.

There was that smile again. Jess watched as the girl responded and she thought no wonder the man was such a successful obstetrician. Who could panic in the face of this smile?

'You shouldn't be carrying picnic baskets,' Ben said. 'Not this heavy.'

'I'm fine,' Kathy said.

But she didn't look fine, Jess thought. She looked...strained. It really had been too heavy for her. Suddenly she was professional again, homing in on the woman's body, the woman's needs.

She looked young. Nineteen? Twenty? Not much older than when she herself had had her baby.

Kathy. She sounded Irish.

'I can't believe you persuaded management to let you keep the dog here,' she said.

'I'm very persuasive,' Ben said. 'Now, about this basket. Isn't there something in your pregnancy handbook that says you shouldn't be carrying anything heavy this close to delivery?' He frowned. 'Come to think of it...this place is classified as remote. Should you even be here?'

'Of course I should.' Kathy's face shuttered, and there was suddenly a trace of panic in her voice. 'I can work until early January, four weeks before I'm due. Can you sign the chit, please? I need to get back.'

'You're closer than thirty-six weeks,' Ben said.

'I'm not,' she said, flatly and definitely. 'I'm thirty-four weeks. I'm fine. Please, please, don't make trouble for me.'

'Would it be trouble,' Ben asked softly, 'if your baby was due earlier?' He assessed her for a long moment, and so did Jess. The baby was lying low. Maybe it was the end of a long shift. The girl looked exhausted.

'It's not,' she said.

'If it was...'

'I want to stay. I have friends here. I help out at the sanctuary on my days off. I just... Please...sign.' She thrust the voucher at Ben as if it was hot coals.

He signed it, looking troubled. His eyes didn't leave hers.

'I'm not making trouble for you,' he said.

'You've no cause.'

'You know the resort's full of obstetricians who might guess…'

'There's nothing to guess. It won't come for weeks. Months even.' She tried to smile, but it didn't quite come off. 'Anyway,' she said, 'I have a lovely day tomorrow. I'm rostered on to kids' club, which means my job's to be companion to Dusty.' She turned to Dusty. 'I'm not very good at knowing what guys like, so I hope you'll tell me. And my boss now seems to think dog care is in there as well, so I figure…you take care of the dog and I'll sit round and make sure you don't fall in the pool. Is that okay?'

Jess watched Dusty respond to the girl's nervous smile, and thought the girl had skill. She'd approached Dusty just the right way.

But her pregnancy…

'Just tell me you've having regular antenatal checks,' Ben growled, and the girl nodded.

'I'm having regular antenatal checks.' She was a bad liar.

But there was nothing they could do. Jess watched Ben hesitate, she almost saw the mental shrug, the decision that help wasn't being asked for, wasn't wanted, wasn't welcome.

Ben backed off.

'See you tomorrow,' Dusty said happily, and plonked down on the picnic rug and set to important business.

Supper.

More important than babies any day.

CHAPTER SEVEN

WITH supper over, Dusty drooped. The day had been too much. Jet lag was still catching up with them. Jess was feeling exhausted herself and when Dusty leaned against her and fell fast asleep she wasn't surprised. She was only surprised she was still awake herself.

The light was fading. The night was still and warm. The surf was a soft hush-hush on the golden sand, and Ben was overseeing all like a beneficent genie.

He'd spent time taking photographs of Pokey—'for tomorrow's presentation,' he'd said, but wouldn't elaborate. Then he'd fallen silent, watching sandpipers scavenge in the shallows. He was…restful, she thought, though maybe restful was the wrong word. Every nerve ending was aware of him, but in a weird kind of way, like he'd somehow infiltrated her normal tense self and set her fears aside.

'I guess we take our babies to bed,' he said at last, and it was all part of the dream. Take our babies to bed… Like they were a family.

I'll take care of you for ever… Nate's promise was suddenly there, front and centre, and she was wide awake.

There was no for ever.

This guy was Nate's brother.

She shifted Dusty so he lay curled on the rug while she started shoving stuff together.

'Leave them,' Ben growled. 'No one's going to steal the

spades. I'll come back down for them later. You carry Pokey, I'll carry Dusty.'

'I can carry—'

'Pokey,' he said.

'It's not me who's pregnant.'

'No, but you were,' he said softly. 'And Nate left you. I know enough about my brother to realise you'll have done this alone. You're still doing it alone. There's no way I can help that, but for tonight at least I can be family.'

'I don't need—'

'Neither do I,' he said. 'We've both learned that the hard way. But it seems Dusty wants me as his uncle. I figure I can play family for a few days if that's what he wants. Let me carry him to bed. Please.'

There was nothing to say to that. She stood back, and let him be family.

Dusty didn't stir as Ben carried him back, set him on his bed and left. Jess sponged the worst of the sand away and tucked him in. She'd set Pokey's basket at his bedside and Pokey didn't stir either. She kissed Dusty goodnight, gave Pokey a pat and went to the living area.

Ben was standing outside, leaning on the veranda rail, watching over the moonlit sea.

Could she just sidle into her bedroom and leave him to it?

He'd been kind.

She owed it to Dusty to create some sort of relationship with this man. Family…

He didn't feel like family.

He was, though. She had no brothers or sisters. Apart from her, Ben was Dusty's closest relative.

Dusty wasn't the only one who'd thought, if anything happened to her…

It was a thought every parent faced; didn't want to face but did all the same.

After her mother died it had been a black hole. There had been nothing there, no back-up.

If this man…

Um, no. Let's not go there.

It was selfish not to. If you took insurance you didn't need it. Take insurance. Open the door and talk to him.

'Coffee?' she asked, and he turned. His expression in the moonlight was troubled.

'No. Thank you. You need to be in bed as well.'

'So you're planning on sentry duty all night?'

'In case of bunyips.'

'Bunyips?'

'Scary Australian wotchamacallits.' He drew an imaginary line across the top of the veranda steps with his toe and pointed to the far side. Lowered his voice and growled. 'Here be bunyips.'

'Okay, you're on sentry duty.'

He grinned but it didn't last. His expression went back to troubled. 'How did I never hear about you?'

'I guess your brother and your father weren't communicative.'

'My father knew?'

'Yes.'

His expression grew even more grim. 'There was no provision…'

'For Dusty? No.'

'My aunt left Nate a fortune,' he said. 'Nate died wealthy even without my father's money. That money should have been used to support his son.'

And what a difference that would have made. If her mother hadn't been almost hysterically insistent that she keep studying she would have opted out. As it was, those early years had been a nightmare. Study and a night job. Debt…

He read it in her face. He was good, this man. Intuitive as well as kind. How had that happened? In such a family…

'I'll make it good now,' he said. 'My father's fortune came

to me—he didn't want it to but he hardly had a choice. Nate's money's in that mix. It's sitting unused. I'll sign it into a trust for Dusty. You'll be able to use the interest for his care. I suspect it'll make things easier for you both.'

'I don't want your money.' It was an intuitive snap. Cold. Uncalled for.

'I'm not offering you money,' he said, suddenly formal. 'I'm signing Nate's legacy over to his son.'

Silence.

A really long silence.

There was so much happening in her head. She felt... bewildered.

'I'm sorry,' she said at last. 'I shouldn't have snapped. I know you're not your brother.'

'I'm not.' Grave agreement, nothing more.

'You don't deserve my anger.'

'My family deserves your anger. Fortunately I'm the last of the line. My family was singularly unworkable. It deserves to die out.'

'It can't,' she said. 'There's Dusty.'

'So there is.'

'And...and you? I mean...you're not married? Children?'

'Heaven forbid.'

'So you're the same as Nate.'

'I am not the same as Nate.' It wasn't just a snap; it was an explosion, and Jess took a startled step back.

'I...I'm sorry.'

'I'm sorry, too,' he said, suddenly rueful. He raked his hair. 'I assume you loved my brother. I imagine something's still there. Every time you look at Dusty...'

'I see Dusty,' she said evenly. 'I don't see Nate. I never have.'

'Wise. You're better off on your own.'

'As you are?' she said, curiosity getting the better of her. 'You're not married. You said your father left you his fortune against his inclination. Nate never talked of you. How young were you when you cut yourself off?'

'Young,' he said. 'As I said, my family didn't work. Much better to be without one.'

And there was that in his face…

Maybe it was because she knew Dusty so well, and this man had her son's features. This man had her son's eyes. She could read Dusty.

She could read Ben.

She saw emptiness lying beneath an exterior that had been schooled to face the outside world.

She thought then of something she'd read. When Nate had died. When she'd been trying to locate his father.

It was a brief entry in a business who's-who, a fraction of personal biography above his business interests.

Joseph Oaklander. Married Fiona Smythe-Harris, divorced, disputed property split, elder son Benjamin, now resides with mother, who's based in Australia; younger son Nathanial remains with Joseph.

She'd figured it out. The divorce date would have been when the boys were eleven and eight?

It was one of the reasons she hadn't tried to get in touch with Ben. He'd been divorced from Nate as well.

And for the first time she thought about it. Brothers, torn apart with their parents' marriage.

'How hard was it?' she asked gently, knowing it was none of her business. 'That your mother took you away from Nate when you were so young? That your family just…ended?'

'It wasn't much of a family anyway,' he said grimly. 'I don't do families.' He hesitated, his face growing even more grim. 'No matter what I'm saying to Dusty.'

She came right out onto the veranda then, carefully closing the door behind her, as if somehow, in doing so, she could protect her son.

'What do you mean?'

'Just what I said. Dusty obviously needs a link to a guy he thinks of as his dad. You've both been given a rough deal. I'm happy to fill in the gaps, let him think he has a connection. But in a few days you'll be back in the UK and I'll be here. Half a world apart. I'm happy to answer questions, send copies of photographs, move Nate's money into trust for him. Even spend this Christmas with him if I must. But anything further… I don't need the connection.'

'Because he reminds you of Nate when you were a family?'

It was a shot in the dark, an impertinence, none of her business. But she saw him flinch and she knew she'd hit home.

Had she wanted to hit home? Did she want to pierce this guy's armour?

No.

He was right. In a few days they'd move back to their separate worlds. Dusty could keep his illusion of family as he needed it. But it would be an illusion. *Spend Christmas with you if I must*… Ben Oaklander didn't do family.

That was fine by her. What he was offering was more than Dusty had ever expected.

A few days with Ben. Dusty was old enough to remember it, to carry it with him. As he grew into his teens, made his own life, the connection would be less important. There was no need to press further than she already had.

There was no need to ask questions…

But she had already asked questions. One question. *Because he reminds you of Nate when you were a family?* She wasn't even sure why she'd said it, but it hung, unanswered, and for some reason it felt like the dark was closing in. *'Because he reminds you of Nate?'*

'Maybe,' he said at last, his face rigid. 'But it was an illusion. Nate turned out to be someone I didn't like very much. I reacted to our separation with grief. Nate responded with anger. It must have been gut wrenching, to lose us both, to be left with my father, and it changed him. The Nate I knew…the Nate I thought I knew would never have abandoned you.' He hesitated. Shook his head. 'Enough. It's history.'

'Except…' she said quietly, and she couldn't help herself, there was something about this night, this man…

Unresolved grief. She could feel it. She could almost touch it. Without knowing why, without even realising what she intended until it was done, she reached out and touched his hand. It was a feather touch, nothing more.

'Except it's not the end,' she said softly. 'I wish Nate was alive so you could talk about it. About how that loss must have felt to him as well as to you. Maybe how he was… Maybe that was the grief thing as well.'

'Or maybe he just learned earlier to build armour, and it got too hard,' he said roughly, but he didn't move his hand from the veranda rail. From under hers. 'I need to go,' he said, even more roughly. 'I have work to do. I'm presenting first thing in the morning.'

'With Pokey?'

'Pokey's scheduled for ten.'

'How do you know she'll behave?'

'I've figured it. Anything for a scratch on the tummy, our Pokey. No pride at all.' He was searching to get his voice under control, she thought. Somehow she'd touched him.

But maybe that was a conceit. It wasn't her. It would have been the events of the whole day. The unexpected death this morning. The revelation that he had a nephew. The effort of making Dusty happy.

Only it hadn't seemed an effort. It had seemed as natural as breathing, taking a small boy's world and turning it around. Giving Dusty such a gift. The gift wasn't in caring for Pokey, or laughter, or the beach, or sharing of photographs. It was in giving himself. It was in knowing what Dusty needed; what would make him happy.

Maybe Dusty was more like the child-Nate, the little-brother Nate, than Ben would admit. There was an instinctive knowledge. They were family, even if Ben didn't admit it.

'I won't hold you any longer,' she said. 'You've done so much already. Just…thank you for today. Thank you for sharing.'

'I'm not sharing, at least, not after we've left here. I'll even spend Christmas with you if that's what you want but that's all.'

'If it's all that's on offer, it'll do,' she said. 'Dad for a week.'

'I'm not Dusty's dad.' It was said with such force that she took a step back.

'No. I… Of course not.'

'I'm just a relation. For a week.'

'And then back to being on your own.'

'This is about you and Dusty, not me.'

She hesitated. Tried to tell herself to stay silent. Failed. 'Ben, I met your father,' she said. 'I can guess what sort of damage he'll have done to Nate. To you. For you to be so alone… I can't…'

'Leave it.'

She'd already gone too far. She was in no-man's land and she wasn't sure why she'd gone there, or how she could extricate herself.

She had to extricate herself. This man was nothing to do with her. He had a connection to her son, nothing more.

It was just… It was just…

The night. The warmth. The emotion of the day. The way he looked at her with her son's eyes. The kindness he'd shown, to Pokey and to Dusty.

The need.

And there it was. She wasn't sure how she knew, she only knew that she did. The emptiness.

I'll even spend Christmas with you if that's what you want…

It was a barren statement and it made her feel cold all through. She couldn't bear it.

He went to turn away but before he could she reached out and she took his hands in hers. Strongly. As if she knew what she was doing. In some way she did, but it was like she was split in two, one section of her moving with instinct, the other part of her screaming, *What on earth are you doing, are you nuts?*

But right now the instinctive side of her was winning, and she had no choice but to let that part of her hold sway.

'Ben, I don't believe you're really an Oaklander,' she said softly and surely. 'You say you'll spend time with Dusty, and for that I thank you. He'll believe it's like spending time with his dad. But it's not. You're nothing like your father or his. But maybe Nate as a kid…the Nate you loved… Maybe that's what I was attracted to all those years ago. Maybe that's the connection I want for my son. The connection that can love.'

'I don't—'

'You have loved in the past,' she said, more firmly still. 'And you will again if you let yourself. I want that for Dusty.'

'I don't intend…'

'No,' she said. 'But you might. Dusty's a great kid, and he is your family, like it or not.' She smiled up at him, feeling his trouble, feeling the need in him. He had such a reputation. Professional brilliance. Power. Fortune.

And all she saw was the part she knew. The part of him that was Dusty. And maybe it was true, it was the tiny part of Nate that she'd loved, the part that had been supplanted by character faults too big to ignore, but the part that, in this man, she recognised again.

A good man, struggling against conditioning so great it threatened to overwhelm him.

She looked at his face, she saw the trouble behind his eyes, she saw the pain. And here it was again, instinct, whether she willed it or not.

And before she knew what she intended doing it was done.

She tugged his hands, using the motion to push herself up on her toes—and she kissed him.

It was a feather-light kiss, a mere brush of her lips on his, and why it burned…

It did burn.

Her feet touched ground again and she looked up at him and saw…recognition?

Need?

What was she doing? Was she insane?

Get this on a logical level. Fast. Get this on a level you can handle.

'That…that was a thank-you kiss,' she managed. 'From… from someone who could have been your sister-in-law if things had been different. Goodnight, Ben. Thank you for this afternoon. Thank you for rescuing Pokey and thank you for caring for Dusty. I'll see you in the morning.'

And finally the sane and sensible Jess got it right. Finally the sane and sensible Jess managed to turn around and walk inside.

Closing the door behind her.

What had just happened?

He'd been kissed by his brother's ex-girlfriend.

Jess.

The feel of her hands was still in his. He could still taste her. He could still smell the salt of the sea on her body, and more, a citrus-clean perfume, hardly there but still drifting in the night. The scent that was all Jess.

He did not want involvement.

When he'd started dating Louise, he'd said no strings. It had placed been solidly out there. Louise had changed her mind. She'd been angry when he'd proved immovable, but she'd conceded that he'd played fair.

With Jess…

There were strings already. Dusty. His brother's child.

The fact that his family had ignored Jess, had made her live in poverty where an infinitesimal amount of the family fortune would have made, he suspected, a vast difference made him feel indebted and involved.

But there was more than indebtedness behind what he was feeling.

Jess.

And her child. The way Dusty looked at him. Dusty's giggle. Dusty's shy smile.

It wasn't working. He was trying to drag his attention back to her son. He couldn't.

Jess.

Jess was nothing to do with him. She was merely Dusty's mother, someone his family had treated with injustice. He'd right the injustice and move on.

His mind wouldn't move on.

Jess.

His fingers were balled into fists.

What was he thinking? Why was he reacting like a terrified kid?

He wasn't. He was simply a man who'd made a decision not to get involved. The pain when his mother had torn him from Nate had been indescribable. He couldn't survive that kind of hurt again. The trick was not to get close in the first place. It was a rule of life and he was sticking to it.

Jess was giving Dusty all the love he needed. He'd provide the kid with memorabilia, with the concept of an uncle, with financial security. Jess could do the rest. It was what she wanted.

But Jess herself…

There was the enigma. There was something about her that tugged him as he'd never been tugged. That twisted something inside until it hurt.

'Get over it, Oaklander,' he told himself, suddenly savage. 'You have work to do. You need to rewrite your presentation to include the dog.'

He forced his thoughts away from Jess; thought instead of Pokey. He thought of the ultrasound, 'dead dog' with four legs in the air, delirious with pleasure from the gentle strokes of the scanning wand.

What would happen to her after the conference? Did anyone want her?

It wasn't his problem.

Nothing was his problem. He was here to give a keynote speech, spend time with his colleagues and get back to Sydney. He didn't get involved. Ever.

So there was nothing in what had happened today to make him stand with his hands deep in his pants pockets and stare sightlessly out to sea.

Marge's death.

Pokey.

Dusty.

Jess.

Nothing to do with him. Not.

Go and change your keynote speech and go to bed.

She'd kissed him.

Yes, she was insane. Stupid. Totally, absolutely nuts.

'He's an Oaklander and I kissed him.' She shoved her head under her pillow and practically moaned. Then froze as she heard footsteps on the veranda.

He was still out there.

She lay motionless, hardly daring to breathe. Finally she heard more footsteps, leading down the steps. Silence, apart from the gentle sound of the surf.

He was gone.

Go to sleep.

Pigs might fly. She flung out of bed, headed to the front drapes and peeked.

He hadn't gone completely. He'd walked down the beach. He was staring out to sea, tall, rigid, unmoving.

A man with demons.

They weren't her demons, she told herself. He was nothing to do with her.

So why had she kissed him?

She was out of her mind, that's why.

There was a thump from the direction of Dusty's bedroom. A small shadow waddled across the living-room floor, stopped at the water bowl and drank. Pokey. The little dog gazed at the water bowl for a moment, considering, then put her two front paws right in. She stood, soaking it up, like the man on the beach was soaking up the night.

It was a hot night.

Pokey had lost Marge.

Ben had lost so much more.

At least she could do something about Pokey.

She stooped and clicked her fingers. Pokey swivelled in the

water dish, made her decision and clicked across the tiled floor to Jess, leaving wet splodge marks behind her.

Jess sat down on the tiles. Pokey scrambled into her lap and snuggled in.

She sighed deeply.

Her tummy moved.

A belly full of pups…

As an obstetrician, the most Jess had ever had to contend with was triplets but she still remembered the young mother, moaning late in pregnancy, 'All I want to do is put them down…'

That's what Pokey's sigh was. She was hot and tired and in an unfamiliar environment.

She wouldn't know where she was ending up tomorrow.

'You'll be on stage with Ben,' Jess whispered, gently hugging her. 'Unless you don't want to. It's an invasion of privacy.'

But then she thought… Ben will have the ultrasound wand, the gel.

'You'd sell your soul for that wand,' she whispered, and smiled, and then she thought of Ben's strong hands scratching Pokey's tummy, his long fingers, his smile…

'Obviously he's a fine obstetrician,' she told Pokey. 'You can put your trust in him.'

Put your trust in an Oaklander?

Put your trust in Ben. It was a very different concept.

Um, maybe she'd best go take a cold shower. A long one. Maybe there was something in her wiring that made her respond to Oaklanders. She'd reacted like a lovesick fool when she'd met Nate. She'd held onto her practicality, her sense, her instinct for self-preservation ever since.

Until tonight…

Tonight she'd kissed him.

An Oaklander.

Ben.

'Bed,' she said, more sharply than she intended, and Pokey jerked a little and then sighed an even deeper sigh. She hugged her, instantly repentant. 'Sorry. I mean…it's just that we're all a bit tired. A bit overwrought. Tomorrow things will be back to normal.'

Pokey sighed again.

'Hey, you might have puppies. That'd be great.' Pokey looked up at her as if she'd lost her mind.

'The only way through it is through it,' she told the little dog. 'There's no choice. Just take one moment after the other until it's done. Like me being here with Ben.'

The little dog's eyes widened, seemingly filled with reproach.

'Okay, I know,' she admitted, hugging her again. 'Keeping my hormones under control in the face of a gorgeous Oaklander is nothing in comparison with giving birth to four babies. But I have had had one baby. It was a long birth. In the end I needed forceps. But I'm telling you now, right this minute keeping my hormones in control seems almost impossible in comparison.'

CHAPTER EIGHT

MONDAY morning. First day of the Cassowary Island International Obstetric Symposium.

Back to professional.

Dusty and Pokey were with Kathy, on the beach. Jess, on the other hand, was in a pencil smooth black skirt, white blouse, sheer panty hose and black court shoes with kitten heels. Her hair was dressed in the neat chignon that had taken her years to perfect. Her make-up was flawless.

Around her neck she wore her conference lanyard displaying the conference insignia and her name card. She was a professional obstetrician, in the midst of a bevy of professional obstetricians. She even knew some of them; a few of these people had trained at her hospital; a couple of her old bosses were here. She could mingle and chat.

She could stay away from Ben.

She could hardly be unaware of him. He was on the far side of the reception area. Surrounded.

Moths to flame, she thought. The man's professional reputation made students listen, colleagues raise issues they thought he could help with, drug companies propose research ventures.

She was trying to listen to an elderly obstetrician from the States complain about the lack of dress code of the hotel staff.

She was watching Ben.

He looked up and their eyes met. Whoops, that was so not meant to happen.

He smiled.

'Excuse me, I need to find a seat,' she said hurriedly to the dress-code stickler, and practically bolted into the auditorium.

Where to sit? Three-quarters of the way back, to the side, so she wouldn't look like she was avoiding him, but also so she wouldn't look like she wanted to be close.

There were only a dozen or so people seated before her. She was a wee bit early.

'Why not front and centre?' Ben said from the doorway.

She was stowing her conference satchel under the seat. She didn't look up. More delegates were filing in. It was possible he wasn't talking to her.

'Hey, Jess,' he said.

No help for it. She looked.

'Dr McPherson's helping me care for Exhibit A,' Ben said to the conference organiser beside him. 'Jess, how about coming on stage to help, hands on?'

'I'm here to listen,' she managed, and thought she sounded petty.

'You won't help?'

'I'd rather not.'

'British,' Ben said to the guy beside him, and the corners of his mouth twitched. 'Once upon a time they were useful to us colonials. Now, just because we're winning the cricket…'

'You'd both be more useful if you played baseball,' a US doctor retorted.

Tension dissipated amid general laughter. Ben gave her a slightly sardonic look and gave up on asking her to help.

He wouldn't need help anyway, Jess thought. He looked in control.

Except…wasn't he using Pokey? She should have figured how that was going to work.

'Do you want me to fetch Pokey?' she asked. It was the least she could do, volunteer to help in a tiny way.

'Sit yourself down, Dr McPherson. I've organised things with Kathy,' he said. 'As you said, you're here to listen. I'd hate to intrude on your listening.'

She listened—and was stunned.

What had she expected?

Ben Oaklander was a leading researcher, his field of expertise being births taking place outside the safe environs of major hospitals. He was here to teach the teachers.

These delegates would be the ones teaching family doctors, midwives, even those without medical training but finding themselves in remote areas with no choice but to deliver.

She'd expected statistics, technical data, discussions of complications.

What he gave was Pokey.

He must have changed the entire presentation, she thought as he spoke, because Pokey was front and centre.

He'd taken photographs from all angles. The first shot was of Pokey just before dinner last night. Pokey had watched the unpacking of the picnic basket with hope, and then the first sausage roll had gone into Dusty's mouth.

The little dog was all anxiety, quivering with terror that a poor starving dog would get none.

Ben was using her as an analogy for a pregnant woman, needing help.

'You never know how your mum will present,' Ben said. 'Your mum might be in a car out the back of the tablelands, her only help a retired bricklayer who stopped to help. Or she might be a fifteen-year-old who hasn't told a soul about her pregnancy, ending up in your clinic via an appointment for a sore knee. Or there's the forty-year-old mum who has a team of birth-partners, a spa-bath full of hot water and incense sticks. For whatever reason, the biggest obstacle you need to overcome is fear. So meet Pokey, the Pregant Pug. I met her yesterday and my priority was to make her think all was right in her world.'

The screen changed to a sausage roll, offered and gratefully accepted. Pokey was shown Dusty's impressive hole in the sand, and was encouraged to share digging duty.

Interspersed with slides of Pokey were slides of very pregnant women being offered tea. Women in the outback, drinking tea from tin mugs. Women in ornate waiting rooms—but the mugs weren't much fancier. 'I like mugs like you'd find at your nanna's,' Ben said. 'Get rid of those white cups that say "Central Coast Medical Service". What you want is a good big mug, a bit worn, the kind your nanna would use when she's giving you cocoa after school. Or similar. If your mum's hungry, don't offer her sandwiches in plastic, take them out and put 'em on a saucer. Better still, offer her an egg on toast. Make it yourself if you need to.'

Then there was Pokey being cuddled. More analogies.

A hand touching a hand. A hand on a shoulder. A finger brushing a cheek.

'No one's going to sue you for giving reassurance,' Ben told his audience. 'Touch can be better pain relief than drugs. Human contact. Reassurance that you'll be there for her until she's holding her baby. If she's at the end of the phone, same thing. I know most of you can't hold a phone for hours; but if she's frightened then introduce someone who can. Or talk about the old guy who'll end up being support person. Say, "Mac'll be with you every step of the way. Mac likes being yelled at. Tell him what you really think about this force taking over your body."'

General laughter.

Then Pokey and her hole in the sand. Analogy three.

'Unless your mum's in second stage there's no need for her to stare at the ceiling and wait for the next pain. Distraction, distraction, distraction. Most human mums can't think of anything but their baby, so work with that.'

He had his audience riveted, Jess thought. She was riveted. Professional, competent…extraordinary.

He flipped the screen to what looked like a jigsaw but in fact was a montage of suggestions. Pictures. Words.

'Ask about names,' he said. 'More. Where's the baby's bed?

How many nappies do you have? How big's your washing machine? If your mum doesn't want to answer she doesn't need to; don't push, but have the questions there so if she needs a break from thinking about the next contraction it's a gift she can latch onto.'

This was so simple, Jess thought with astonishment. A professor of obstetrics talking kindness… As simple and as difficult as that.

He talked of trials where volunteers were assigned to be with anyone who'd like them. Their role? Comfort, diversion, reassurance.

Result? Caesareans down. Forceps deliveries down. And most amazingly, postnatal depression down.

'In our high-tech world, sometimes we forget the important things, and these things can be as important as the high-tech stuff,' he said. 'But the high-tech stuff's great, too.'

Then he moved seamlessly into introducing gear that could be bought and used by clinicians in remote areas. Hooked up to video links so obstetricians could read results remotely. And finally he made the introduction to the ultrasound team of the night before.

And Pokey.

Right on cue she arrived, carried to the stage by…Dusty.

Jess gasped, half rising. *I've organised things with Kathy…*' That had sounded like it had nothing to do with Dusty.

Kathy was standing back, still acting as official child carer, but Dusty needed no carer. He was carrying Pokey onto the stage, beaming.

Ben beamed right back at him.

Identical beams. Beams to make her heart twist.

Jessie's body seemed like one huge gasp.

'And now it's time to meet our mum,' Ben told the audience. 'This is Pokey and her birth partner, Dusty. So let's get these steps right. First step—reassurance that this place isn't threatening.'

Pokey didn't look threatened. She did look a bit wary.

Ben produced doggy treats and she forgot wary.

'A mug of tea might do the same,' Ben told the audience. 'Or a chocolate biscuit or an offer of a back rub, or a shower. Keep scary equipment out of sight until you absolutely need it. If your mum enters a room and sees stirrups, you're asking for panic.'

There wasn't a lot of panic on the stage, Jess thought.

Ben stroked Pokey behind the ear, then down her back, rolling her over, finding the exact spot on her tummy that made her back leg go crazy. Around Jess, the world's eminent obstetricians were starting to enjoy themselves.

This session was being videotaped. What an amazing lesson for young doctors, Jess thought, and then she thought what an amazing lesson for old doctors.

Ben had them in the palm of his hand.

'We can't ask Pokey to go into labour just for this presentation,' Ben said. 'But we can use distractions for essential medical checks as well. Like an ultrasound. Most of you know of these new little machines that let us see what's going on without the need to transport our mums to central hospitals. Let's see how good they are, while we see if we can distract our mum.' This was a risk, Jess thought. What if Pokey objected? But then she thought…maybe it wasn't a risk.

The examination couch was padded and comfortable. Pokey had spent a busy morning on the beach. She had Dusty right by her, plus the guy who knew her magic spot.

Dusty rubbed her behind the ears—proud birth-partner growing more proud by the moment.

Pokey looked up at the ultrasound wand. Her tail waggled in delighted recognition.

She moved straight into dead-dog position.

'Dusty, can you use the wand like you saw it being used last night?' Ben asked.

Dusty was in control?

The woman in charge of the ultrasound team looked like she was about to protest—but then she pulled back, realising what Ben was doing.

If Dusty could handle this machine, how much more easily could a nurse do it, maybe flying into a remote station five hundred miles from the nearest radiologist? These machines could be used by anyone.

'These images can be beamed via the internet straight to someone who can interpret them,' Ben said. 'But Dusty can interpret them now. What are we seeing, Dusty?'

Dusty moved the wand methodically back and forth, instinctively copying the movements he'd seen last night. Puppies. He focused the wand on each small head in turn. He paused while the technician beside him clicked to take a still image.

'Okay, Dusty, tell us what we have,' Ben said. He was asking Dusty to explain?

Dusty looked out at the audience, then at Ben. Ben smiled.

Dusty nodded. Firmed. Started to speak.

Four puppies. Legs, tails, heads. He faltered at first as he spoke, but after the first couple of moments he started enjoying himself.

'This is the biggest puppy. We're pretty sure she's a she but we're not really certain. But you can measure the head. We did last night. My Uncle Ben says there's room for this puppy to get out, and she's in a great position. She'll come out first and the rest should come out easily after.'

This could make a real difference, Jess thought, stunned. Ben had the undivided attention of every person in the room. This recorded video would be used over and over. It could be taken to a local service club. This ultrasound demonstration would hold an audience—any audience—riveted. A small community could conceivably purchase one of these.

Its use? Measuring head size, presentation. Checking for abnormalities. Let a woman continue in labour, or organise emergency evacuation.

This was a magnificent tool for decision-making. And, meanwhile, no panic.

Anyone less like panic than Pokey she had yet to see. The

little dog had gel on her tummy and was loving the wand. Her legs were still sticking straight up. Doggy heaven.

She glanced at Ben and she saw his expression had stilled. And instinctively she knew what had caused it.

My Uncle Ben...

Could he possibly be proud of Dusty? She was so proud she was ready to burst.

'I rest my case,' Ben said, sounding a bit...different. But it didn't matter because the presentation was done. Delegates were laughing and clapping. Dusty gathered the little dog into his arms and Jess saw her son's small chest expand. His beam practically split his face.

She watched Ben's hand rest for a moment on Dusty's head and she felt her heart twist.

It stayed twisted. Something had changed.

My Uncle Ben.

Something cold and hard that had formed around her heart ten years ago was cracking and falling away.

'Magnificent,' the doctor beside her breathed.

'He... It was.'

He was.

Ben Oaklander was.

Oh, she was in such trouble now.

The session was over. Delegates filed out for coffee. Jess filed out, too, but coffee was the last thing on her mind.

She felt very, very exposed.

This was stupid. This wasn't about her. It was all about a successful presentation, turning patients into people. Dispelling fear.

There wasn't a lot of dispelled fear where she was. She felt like she was on the edge of a precipice.

She wasn't needed. Kathy in her hotel uniform was the official carer, beaming with pride at her charges. Dusty was practically bursting with the joy of a plan successfully executed. He was carrying Pokey in his arms like a mother would carry a baby. Pokey looked in seventh heaven. Every person who came near was encouraged to scratch Pokey's tummy and tell Pokey how awesome she was. And congratulate Dusty on his wonderful dog.

His wonderful dog. Uh-oh.

'We need to think a few things through,' Ben said into her ear, and she jumped. Literally. She landed and he was still there, smiling quizzically. 'I think our Dusty's falling in love.'

Our Dusty.

An Oaklander, claiming a right.

It had been an offhand remark, a throwaway line. It meant nothing. Move on.

My Uncle Ben.

'You...you were brilliant,' she said, a trifle breathlessly. 'I'd defy any doctor here to treat a scared new patient now without thinking of your three edicts.'

'That's what this is all about,' he said lightly, but she knew it wasn't light. This was something that he was passionate about; she could hear it in his voice.

'And there's no way hotel management can ask for Pokey to leave.'

'Not while I'm here.' He surveyed Kathy and Pokey and Dusty with avuncular pride. 'I love it when a plan comes together.'

'Dusty's moving straight into hero-worship,' she said, trying to sound brisk. 'You realise he'll still want to stay in touch after Christmas.'

'Emails are fine,' he said.

'Phone calls?'

She saw his face still. Saw thoughts she couldn't read. 'Maybe not,' he said at last. 'I think I made it clear I don't do family.'

She nodded. Relieved? She should be.

Why was she feeling cold?

'Okay,' she said. 'I understand. If you're nice to Dusty until Christmas, that's all I ask. I'll explain the emails-only rule to Dusty. He doesn't need a family. He has me.'

* * *

How cold was that? Why had he instinctively put up a barrier? *I don't do family.*

She'd been…hurt?

Her reaction to his presentation had been one of genuine enjoyment. He'd glanced up at her as Pokey had assumed the dead-dog pose and he'd seen laughter. She'd been enjoying herself.

He'd made Pokey happy. He'd made Dusty smile. Then…

'I don't do family.'

It was what he'd told Louise. He'd made himself clear. He always did at the start of a relationship.

Except, with Jess, he wasn't at the start of a relationship. Single mother. Former lover to his brother. No and no and no.

Regardless, he'd hurt her and he felt a heel.

Someone hailed him from across the hall, an American professor who wanted his name on a dodgy research paper. How to say no without wounding?

He'd never conquered the art.

Jess stayed for the next session, an in-depth presentation on natural childbirth after previous Caesareans. Excellent stuff. At lunch she disappeared to find Dusty. They were back in her little bunglalow and were all fast asleep, Dusty and Pokey on the bed, Kathy curled on the sofa.

Kathy was keeping guard? Despite her hotel uniform, she looked more a kid than Dusty did, Jess thought, and just as vulnerable. She looked exhausted. No matter what sort of dangerous deception Kathy was playing, at least she had these days free from the normal fetch and carry of hotel duties. Dusty was an easy child to mind.

But she wanted them to be awake.

She sort of wanted…grounding. She didn't want to return to the conference lunch and talk medicine and watch Ben work the room.

No. He didn't work the room. The room seemed to revolve around him. His session with Pokey would only increase his already awesome reputation. Some might call it simplistic, but his research had him slotted as a brilliant doctor. He'd reminded them what was important.

What was important?

She gazed at her sleeping son and she thought she should remember it, too. This and only this.

She should go back.

No. The remains of Kathy and Dusty's lunch was still on the table. Much less unsettling than being in the same room as Ben.

She was being neurotic.

She didn't care. She sat on the front step and ate and very carefully didn't think about Ben.

The first of the afternoon's sessions was split into two. One technical, the other a panel. Ben was on the panel.

A no brainer. She needed technical.

The last session of the day was a presentation of the latest anaesthetics for Caesareans. She'd been to a course on that in Glasgow six months ago. She could leave that one.

Okay. Return, do the one technical session without Ben, then leave.

Kathy was being paid to take care of Dusty all day.

All to the good. She could ask her to stay, say she had research papers to read. If roles just happened to reverse, if Kathy slept while she played with Dusty…excellent.

She'd be playing Lady Bountiful by missing conference sessions. She wouldn't be avoiding Ben at all.

He didn't need to learn about anaesthetics in Caesareans. The woman presenting the paper had run it by him for comments. He knew it inside out.

He had teams wanting to run research projects past him. He had three hours to dinner. He could fit them all in and catch up with others after the meal.

Only…

He'd hurt Jess.

No. This had nothing to do with Jess, he told himself. This

was a great opportunity to keep his promise to Dusty—to spend tine with his brother's son.

That was all.

He slipped away from the conference, changed into beach gear and headed for the beach.

Jess would be there.

He was going to find Dusty.

Jess would be there.

He reached the beach just as Jess did.

There were kids on the beach with Kathy and Dusty. He recognised Harriet, the wife of one of the conference organisers.

Harriet, too, was an organiser. Her sons were twelve, ten and eight. Her umbrella was set up beside a truly enormous ice cooler. She'd organised a pair of sun lounges in the shade. Kathy was on the spare sun lounge.

If anything, the baby looked even lower but the tension he'd seen in her the night before was gone. She looked relaxed.

Jess was standing beside her looking a bit nonplussed. Dusty was whooping in the shallows with Harriet's boys, a cork surfboard apiece, the three little Australians instructing Dusty on the art of catching waves.

Pokey was asleep on a rug under Kathy's sun lounge.

He saw Kathy half rise, and he saw Jessie's instinctive recoil.

She'd see as clearly as he did, he thought, that Dusty was totally, gloriously happy without her. And Kathy needed that sun lounge.

'No,' she was saying as Ben approached. 'Kathy, don't get up.'

But he saw her warring needs.

Her own need, to spend time with her son.

Dusty's need—learning to surf with mates.

Kathy's need.

'You don't need me,' Kathy said, rising regardless. 'The hotel charges for my services by the hour. I've been feeling guilty enough being here with Mrs Holland. I'll sign off now.'

'But we weren't planning on collecting Dusty, were we, Dr McPherson?' Ben said, and Jessie's eyes widened.

'I...'

'Dr McPherson and I need to talk about a plan for joint co-operation between our two hospitals,' he said smoothly. 'Jess was so impressed with my research presentation this morning she's proposing joint authorship of a paper—city birth versus country. We thought we'd take a walk across to the wildlife sanctuary, check on Sally and Dianne and discuss the project as we go. Is it's okay with you, Kathy, to work a little longer? And, Harriet...these guys aren't annoying you? Pokey's not snoring?'

They all laughed, Kathy included, her face brightening with pleasure. Two more hours in a sun lounge.

Harriet was a midwife, Ben recalled. Excellent. Maybe she'd winkle the girl's background out of her; make her see sense.

'Have a drink first,' Harriet ordered, fishing lemonade from her cooler. 'Wear your hats and don't forget sunburn cream.'

'No, ma'am,' Ben said meekly, and the thing was decided.

For the first part of the walk they said nothing. Jess appeared... winded.

He'd been a bit autocratic, Ben thought. He might possibly have ridden roughshod over her.

He hadn't actually intended to take her away. On her own. Unwise? Very.

But if she hadn't been Dusty's mother...Nate's girlfriend...

She was. Step away from the edge, he told himself, but the sensation of walking beside her was doing something weird.

She was out of bounds. Forbidden fruit. That was all it was, he thought, lusting after something, someone he couldn't have.

'I'm sorry,' he said at last as the sandy track left the beach and headed inland into scrub. 'I hoped you wanted Kathy to stay with Dusty. I could see your dilemma.'

'It was brilliant,' she said. Sounding strained.

'But not what you wanted?'

'I wanted to play with Ben.'

'So did I.'

Her eyes flew to his in astonishment. And disbelief.

'Really,' he said gently. 'And I also needed to talk to you. I was out of line this morning. I hurt you and I'm sorry. I thought I'd skip this afternoon's session and come down and make it right with you. Give Dusty a good time.' He grinned, rueful. 'It's a bit levelling to realise he's having a much better time without us.'

'You're telling me.'

'Lots of mothers would have pulled him away.'

'Lots of mothers aren't me.'

'You could have sent Kathy back to the hotel. I saw your face. I guessed you didn't want to do that.'

'You guessed right.'

'But still it hurts.'

'Letting go's hard.'

'It must be.' He thought suddenly of Nate as he'd seen him on that last morning, eight years old, ashen with shock and grief, and there it was, that gut wrench that never left him. Letting go...

They walked in silence. Neither was well equipped for walking. Jess was wearing strong enough sandals, but under her sarong he could see the outline of her crimson bikini. It was hardly hiking gear, but the walking was easy. She'd plastered herself with sunscreen and wore oversized sunglasses. Her hair was loose from the formal chignon she'd worn at the conference. Her curls were dancing down from under her oversized sun hat. She looked...free.

Forbidden fruit.

'I've only seen the one cassowary,' she said, stiffly. 'I'd like to see more.'

'The researchers are excited about two nests but no one's saying where they are.'

'I guess that's a good thing—that they're protected.'

'Yes.' Great conversation. Or not. All he could think about was how she looked. All he could think about was…

No.

He looked deliberately away.

Froze.

CHAPTER NINE

ONE minute she was walking along the sandy track, caught up in a million emotions she had no idea what to do with. Totally aware of the man beside her. Thinking, at the conference, in his dark suit and crisp white linen shirt he'd looked handsome. Now, in baggy shorts, a faded, long-sleeved shirt, sleeves rolled up, missing the top three buttons—a baggy hat, and rope sandals—he looked…awesome. This man must spend serious time in the gym. He was…

Grabbing her. Sweeping her off her feet. Lifting her off the ground and giving her no time to so much as squeak before he had her three, four yards back from where she'd been walking.

'What…? What…?' Her voice was hardly a squeak.

He held her hard against him, still high in his arms, holding her tight, but all his attention was below.

'What…what do you think you're…?'

'Snake,' he said, almost absently, glancing back to where she'd been standing. Looking down again. 'I'm making sure there aren't more before I put you down.'

'Snake…'

'You almost stood on it.'

She gazed back to where she'd been walking.

He was right. Definitely there was a snake. Five feet long. Shimmering black, with a brilliant red underbelly, the creature looked almost beautiful against the golden sand.

Snake. Aaagh.

What was she doing, thinking of a million other things while walking along a sun-baked Australian bush track in open sandals?

She knew better than that. Had her father taught her nothing?

There had been grounds for distraction, though, she conceded. There were still grounds for distraction. Even though the snake had most of her attention, she was being held tight against Ben Oaklander. Her body was hard against his chest. His arms were like iron.

She could feel his heartbeat.

How could a snake compare with a heartbeat?

There was, however, a snake. She needed to get a grip.

She needed to stand on her own two feet.

'Can you put me down?'

'Still checking,' he said, rotating three-sixty degrees. 'I'm not putting you down on another snake.'

'I can check, too. We're both in sandals.'

'We're both idiots.'

'A non-planned hike,' she said, a trifle shakily. 'With the best of intentions. It's okay, I'm not scared. Believe it or not, I know snakes. Now I've been reminded to be wary, I'm wary. Please put me down.'

He did. With reluctance? Maybe that was just her. How long since she'd been held by a guy?

By a guy who felt like Ben Oaklander? Never.

'You know snakes?' he asked. He sounded cautious, like she'd just been caught in questionable research. Like he didn't believe her.

'Yes.' The feel of his arms receded into the background. Not forgotten, but put aside for the moment.

Medical need replaced it. She was checking out the snake, and the professional side of her was kicking in. 'It's hurt,' she said.

'What's hurt?'

'The snake,' she said, with patience. 'It's hot. Snakes are cold blooded. They soak up the sun. The hotter they get, the more active they are. We've just given this one a fright…'

'We've given it…'

'And he's hardly moved.' She started edging to the far side of the track so she could see the snake from a different angle. It wasn't in attack mode; in fact, it seemed to cringe away and then stop, as if it couldn't move.

'You're worried about the snake?' Ben sounded stunned. 'You're English.'

'Like you're Australian,' she retorted. 'Not completely.'

'I came to Australia when I was eleven.'

'And I came to England when I was twelve. Before that, Africa. There are snakes in Africa. My dad introduced me.' She was as close to the snake as she dared to go but still she had the feeling all it wanted was to retreat.

'Some snakes are vicious,' she remembered her dad telling her. 'But most of them just want to mind their own business. They're much more afraid of you than you are of them.'

That was the case here; she was sure of it.

'There's a wound running along his belly. Nasty. It's being attacked by ants.' She hesitated, looking around and seeing skid marks in the sand. 'This is the spot where Sally did her hair-raising speed-hump trick yesterday. She might have hit this guy. Either that or he's been attacked by something. I'm not sure what. There aren't supposed to be any predators on the island. But it looks like it's dying.'

'There are signs everywhere saying don't disturb the wildlife under any circumstances,' Ben said, dubiously. He edged round to where Jess was crouched and winced as he saw the jagged, raw wound along its side. 'Does that mean we let nature take its course?'

Jess was squatting on her heels to get a better look. She was about ten feet from the snake, but edging closer. The snake's beady eyes were looking at her, but it didn't seem a threat. To Jess the eyes were looking dull.

How long had it lain wounded? If had been hurt yesterday

maybe it had dragged itself into cover but then been desperate for warmth. Come out into the sun and been attacked by ants.

The wound was ugly, a jagged tear about eight inches long. It looked filthy, and bush ants were all over it.

'Let nature take its course? Not when we can help,' Jess decreed, and hauled off her sarong. Sounding businesslike. 'I need a stick. Long. Stout.'

'You're planning on killing it?' Ben sounded incredulous. 'Why are you taking off your sarong?'

'To make a bag, and no, I'm not killing him. We'll take him to the sanctuary, clean him up, and see if he recovers. But I'll need help.'

'Help…'

'I'm not asking you to help catch him,' she said, patiently. 'I just want you to hold things.'

'You've done this before?'

'Yes.'

'When?' he demanded, astounded.

'When I was twelve,' she conceded. 'I watched a lot but I was only allowed to catch one by myself. Then Dad was killed and…'

'Your father was killed?'

'Yes.'

'By a snake?' He took a step back and looked at her like she'd grown horns.

And, amazingly, she chuckled. 'Nothing so exotic,' she told him. 'He rolled his truck—the roadside gave way after rain. He taught me how to face lions. He didn't warn himself about road-slips.'

'Lions…'

'Okay, lion cubs,' she conceded, and chuckled again at the look on his face. 'I need a stick,' she repeated. 'A strong one.'

'You're wearing a bikini and sandals and you're planning on catching a snake?'

'I do feel a bit bare,' she admitted. She was fashioning knots in the edges of the sarong. 'But I need a bag. A gentleman might lend me his shirt. Your shorts are more decent than my bikini.'

He stared at her like she was something from out of space.

She went on knotting her sarong.

There didn't seem much choice. He handed over his shirt.

She smiled her thanks, and promptly pulled it on over her bikini.

He was stunned. Stunned was all he was feeling right now. He couldn't get past it.

This slip of an English doctor was proposing catching a wounded snake. With her sarong/bag? While wearing his shirt.

The sensible thing to do would be to pick her up and cart her away. She was clearly a lunatic.

'Stick,' she repeated, and, bemused, he backed off and searched for a stick.

'These guys can be strong,' she warned. 'A twig's not going to do it. I need one three fingers thick at least. And I want your hat as well.'

'Not my pants, too?'

'You can keep your pants.'

'Your generosity leaves me speechless.'

She chuckled some more. She was watching the snake the whole time, though, and he suddenly thought this woman would be a magnificent doctor. She was thinking on her feet. She had time for humour. She was intrigued and committed to what she was doing.

It was up to him to match her for professionalism. One stick, three fingers thick.

Finding such a stick was easier said than done, especially as he had to go off the track to find it and he had a mind to keep his eyes on the ground for snakes as well as sticks. Every stick looked like a snake.

Paranoia didn't begin to describe it.

He found a stick. He returned with it to Jess.

'Excellent,' she said, and he felt like an intern being praised by a senior consultant.

'Now what?'

'Now we put your hat there, with my hat next to it. The plan is to get this guy into my makeshift bag. The cloth's a bit thin and I don't fancy getting bitten, so once he's in the sack we'll coil him into my hat. Then we stick your hat on top and we have a snake-proof container.'

'It seems to me,' he said cautiously, 'that your definition of snake proof might differ a little to mine. How long are those fangs?'

'So what's your alternative, Dr Oaklander?' She put her hands on her hips and he thought, wow, that shirt never looked this good on him. It could never look this good on anyone.

An alternative...

'We could fetch help from the refuge?' he managed, struggling to focus. 'Find someone with the right equipment who knows what they're doing?'

'Leaving this guy to suffer for another half-hour? Maybe manage to crawl away to die? Not happening.' She was laying her sarong/bag open on the ground between the two hats. 'If you're nervous, stand back. Come to think of it, stand back anyway, just for a moment. I'll need you, but not for a minute. Here goes.'

She didn't wait for his approval. She simply stepped forward briskly, approaching the snake from behind, allowing no time for hesitation. Before he guessed what she intended, she was pressing the stick down squarely and firmly, just behind the snake's head. And with the head trapped... She was stooping... And holding...

She was gripping a snake in her hand!

It was maybe five feet long. Thick and solid, and suddenly writhing.

'I need your help now,' she said calmly. 'He's too strong for me to lift with safety. If he hangs and writhes he's likely to hurt himself more. Can you support him under his body? If he's not too strong we'll coil him into the bag.'

To say he was thunderstruck was an understatement. She was holding a snake almost the size that she was.

She, however, was in charge. He was deemed medical assistant, assistant snake charmer, assistant idiot.

He stepped forward and took the snake's body, just past midway.

Its strength was astonishing. It writhed and he held and Jess held as if it was totally commonplace that she was standing half-dressed, holding a snake by the head.

How lethal?

He didn't want to know. There was no way he was asking.

'I have him nicely under control,' she said, sounding just that, nicely under control. 'Can you lower him gently into the bag? Use the bag itself to control the coiling. He's terrified. Once he's almost in, then we put the bag into my hat. My hat's the biggest. It'll seem dark in there. He'll want to go deeper. I'll be able to tug the bag closed over his head.'

And, amazingly, it worked. He believed her now, that she'd seen this done before, even that she might have actually done it. Under her direction it was almost easy. He held the snake just below the gash, he lowered the slashing tail into the bag. The bag contained the slashing and gradually he eased the rest of the snake in. Because Jess had the head firmly in her grasp, there was no threat—it just took physical strength.

Quite a bit of physical strength. This guy might be wounded but he was putting up a fight.

She couldn't have coped on her own.

Would she have tried? He wouldn't put it past her.

She had him fascinated. A London obstetrician, a slip of a girl, coping with a snake as if this was just another terrified patient, presenting for birth.

One with fangs.

He had him inside. Her makeshift bag was doing its job. The whole bag was writhing.

Jess still had the head.

'Now we lift him into the hat,' she ordered. 'Thanks be, I wear a big one.'

It was big. He recognised it from the hotel gift shop—a fun sombrero-style straw hat with a red stripe.

The snake was squirming wildly in its bag, but contouring inside.

'Excellent,' Jess said. 'Now, if you stand back, I'll drop him in and tug it closed.'

'No,' he said. 'I'll take the top of the bag up over its head and bring it down behind your hands.'

'You risk—'

'So do you,' he said. 'You have a son. I don't.'

'There'll be anti-venene at the hotel.'

'You know there can be complications. No argument.'

She glanced up at him and read his face. She didn't argue.

She shifted her hands back as far as she could without giving the snake any leeway to swivel.

'One, two, three, go,' Ben said, and with that he hauled the bag up, back over the fangs, back to Jessie's hands. A split-second movement that left no room for error. He hauled the bag tight shut, knotted it at the top and let it fall. He grabbed his hat, used it to scoop the rest of the sarong/bagbag fully into Jessie's hat, shoved his hat on top and held.

They had a parcel. Two hats, a sarong bag and a snake inside.

'Nice,' Jess said. 'It needs a bow.'

She took the sleeve of his shirt and ripped it off. She ripped it again, all the way to the cuff, so she had a long line of linen.

'Gift tie,' she said, and he held the hats while she tied it four ways, around the hats, leaving a loop at the top for carrying.

'I liked that shirt,' he said mildly, and she chuckled.

'I was scared you might say that. That's why I didn't ask.'

She was enchanting.

Nate had walked away from her?

'Let's get this guy to help,' she was saying briskly. 'I know he seems strong, he fought really well, but that'll be adrenalin. The sooner we get that wound cleaned and closed and get him into a warm, dark place where he can recover, the better his chances. Wild animals die of shock and snakes are no exception. Will you carry him, or will I?'

'You organised the gift wrapping,' Ben said faintly. 'I believe the least I can do is carry your package.'

The wildlife shelter was still a wall of grief. Marge had been truly loved, they could see it in the faces of everyone there.

Sally, though, managed to pull herself together enough to help. 'It'll be a red-bellied black snake,' she said when Jess described it. 'They're lovely snakes, not as venomous as most, and quite timid. And endangered. They eat the introduced cane toads, you know, and whole populations are being wiped out with the cane toad's poison. They're so beautiful. And not nearly as venomous as some. But Marge used to look after the snakes.' She sniffed. 'I…I know it's dumb but I'm scared of them. So's Dianne. Our vet's coming over tomorrow. We'll pop him into a shelter and hope he survives.'

'If Marge used to treat them, you'll have equipment,' Jess said.

'Gloves and things?' Sally pulled herself together but it was a visible effort. 'There's a whole cupboard for reptiles. If you want, I can show you.'

'You're proposing treating it?' Ben asked, but he already knew the answer. He was beginning to be in awe of this woman.

'Of course. Didn't you hear Sally? It's not very venomous.'

'Just a little bit venomous,' he said. 'Meaning you have to be bitten quite a lot before you die. Quite cute really, when you put it like that. Almost cuddly.'

She grinned. 'You needn't worry. I'm not proposing cuddles or letting anyone get even a little bit bitten. If Marge has what I hope she has, there'll be a leather hood. We'll put the snake in that. It'll be fang proof. We figure where the head is through the bag, we fasten the hood around its upper body, then we slip the back end out. *Voilà*, we have a treatable body.'

'*Voilà*,' he repeated, dazed.

'Just like a magician,' she agreed.

'I don't think...' Sally seemed dumbstruck. 'I'm not sure... Our insurance...'

'Do you have anti-venene on hand?' Jess asked.

'Of course, but—'

'Then there's no problem. Neither Ben nor I are about to sue, even if we do get a nibble.'

'Oi,' said Ben.

'But we won't,' Jess said. 'We're good, we are. Two highly trained specialists. What a pity our snake isn't pregnant. We could do a package deal.'

Ben just...looked.

The hood worked like a charm. It was Jess who was nominally in charge, but it was Ben who did the hooding, who made sure the snake was secure, who lifted him free from the hat and laid him full length on the table.

'Anaesthetic?'

'I don't actually know how to anaesthetise a snake,' Jess admitted.

'Really? I'm shocked.'

'I know,' she said, looking crestfallen. 'Snakes seems to have been overlooked in Anaesthesia 101.'

'We could phone someone.'

'Set up a video link with a team of city specialists?' She glanced around the austere little treatment room. Apart from general concern, Sally and Dianne had left them to it. They were on their own. 'Maybe not.'

'I'd imagine these guys can feel pain,' Ben said.

'Of course they can, but as for putting in an intravenous drip...'

'Imagine trying to find a vein. So that leaves us with...'

'Working clean and fast and hoping for the best.'

Ben nodded. He was examining the wound. Within the darkness of the leather hood the snake seemed to have relaxed. The big body lay limp, the full length of the table.

It did look like tyre damage, he thought. Skin crushed at the side, torn, the surrounding area grazed.

'Clean, then super-glue,' Jess said. She was foraging in the cabinet. 'Here we are.'

'Super-glue?'

'Fancy name but I bet it's just that. Dad used to use it all the time and it's brilliant. How long do you think stitches would hold? We clean, we haul the sides together, we glue, we tape until it holds. And then we hope.'

'You're nuts,' he said, and grinned at her. He was, after all, a man who liked a challenge.

And she grinned back. Their gaze met, locked, held.

There was work to be done. That smile…it had to be kept until later.

As a challenge?

It took a good half-hour to clear embedded sand and gravel, to debride damaged edges, to make sure the wound was clean enough to prevent infection taking hold. Then, gradually, painstakingly, Ben pulled the jagged edges together and glued them closed.

Ben was better than she was, Jess conceded. She might have rudimentary snake knowledge but Ben had better hands.

Jess loved her small hands when she was confronted by a tricky birth that needed careful manipulation; she could use her hands where most obstetricians had to use forceps. Ben, however, had fingers that worked with such delicacy she would have had to use tweezers and they'd have tugged, torn. He seemed to know how to push the skin together using the snake's whole body, gently squeezing until the edges met, making sure each sliver of skin was in position, holding, waiting until Jess dropped a tiny dollop of glue, waiting with all the patience in the world until it held, then adjusting the tape and then moving along.

The tape was hardly needed. The snake could shear it off in the next couple of hours, but by then the glue would hold fast.

It was a tedious task. Skilled. All to save a snake that might have bitten them if they'd stood on it.

A snake that might yet die.

The snake lay limp and unresponsive. If Ben's gentle handling, careful probing was hurting, it made no sign.

Um… Maybe it was already dead?

'We're going to look pretty silly if we take our patient into Recovery and find he died half an hour ago,' she said.

'So take his vital signs.'

'How do you take the pulse of a snake?'

'And how do you do CPR?' Ben demanded. 'Our medical training is indeed lacking. I believe that's the end. Last piece closed. The glue's worked like a charm.'

'He'll hardly have a scar,' Jess said admiringly.

He grinned, tension easing. Stepped back. 'Yes! The operation is declared a hundred per cent successful.'

'Even if he's dead?'

'Immaterial, my dear Dr McPherson. Our work here is done.'

'Except for putting him into a cage.'

He looked suddenly nervous. 'Uh-oh.'

'Wuss,' she said, and grinned back at him. Feeling…excellent. 'I'll hold his head, you take the body.'

'Nope,' he said. 'Fair's fair. You held the head last time. Fifty-fifty risk.'

'Only this time the head's wearing a leather hood.'

'There is that,' Ben said, and grinned some more. 'I'm not stupid.'

Release, in the end, was easy. Dianne led them to an enclosure she'd cleared for him and explained the procedure Marge used.

'These hoods are designed to be released from a distance. Undo this first knot. Pop him into the pen and leave this long cord trailing. Close the wire and then tug. The whole hood will come free.' She glanced dubiously at the limp snake hanging over Jessie's arm. 'He's not dead, is he?'

'If he is, I'm volunteering Dr Oaklander for CPR,' Jess said firmly. 'He's the brave one. Okay, let's release and see what we have.'

The reptile pens were at the side of the house. In the main pen, lizards and goannas snoozed peacefully in the sun—Jess saw a goanna with a splinted leg!—but she was starting to worry about the snake's limpness. It'd be such a waste to have him die now.

Dianna led the way to a small enclosure at the rear. A rocky base, a patch of weeds, a hollow log. Half in sun, half in shade.

Convalescent heaven.

If he was still alive.

They carried him warily inside. Placed him on a sun-drenched rock. Ben sent her out. Undid the first knot as Dianne had shown him. Retreated with haste.

Closed the pen door and tugged the cord.

The hood slid free.

He was alive. He shifted, just a little. He stared around with his tiny, beady eyes. A ripple ran through his long body as if reassuring himself, too, that he was alive.

The sun shone on his brilliant black scales, on the amazing crimson markings. Dangerous. Venomous. Beautiful.

Worth saving.

Ben tugged the hood out of the enclosure, and with no panic at all the snake slithered around and hauled itself into the shelter of the hollow log.

Coiled himself in. Settled.

Only his tiny eyes showed in the shadows.

'He'll do,' Dianne said in satisfaction. 'Marge always says...' She faltered. 'Always *said* that if they can make their own way into shelter they have a ninety per cent chance of making it.'

'He'll make it,' Jess said, a trifle unsteadily. 'Dr Oaklander makes the best snake surgeon.'

'Snake surgery seems to be my splinter skill,' Ben said modestly. 'But it's nothing to Dr Matheson's catching skills.'

'Yeah, three-quarters-dead snakes that have been run over, I can catch 'em in my sleep.'

'No matter,' Dianne said roundly. 'You make a lovely team. Where's your little boy?'

She still saw them together, Jess thought. No matter that it had been explained, man, woman and child made family.

'My son's back at the resort,' she said. 'I might bring him over to visit Slash if Slash recovers.'

'Slash.' Dianne stared into the shadows at the coiled snake with taped slash. 'That's a great name. I reckon that'll stick.'

'What will you do with him when he's better?' Ben asked.

'Release him, of course,' she said. 'Exactly where you found him. I know they make me nervous but they're the most beautiful creatures. The introduction of cane toads on the mainland has decimated their numbers but here... The more we can build their numbers, the happier we'll be. They're not an aggressive snake and they belong here more than we do. Now, was there anything else you were needing?'

'We came to see how you were coping,' Ben said.

'Kind as well as competent,' Dianne murmured. She gave herself a little shake. 'We're fine,' she said. 'We're...we're managing. The only thing is...'

'What's the only thing?' Ben's voice was gentleness itself and Jess found herself looking at him in astonishment. Gentleness. He had her more and more confounded. That this man could possibly be an Oaklander...

'Marge's daughter was in New York when she heard of her mother's death,' she blurted out. 'She gets back tomorrow. We...we sort of thought it'd be nice to have the funeral here but Rebecca says Brisbane. She thinks it'll be easier for the family. And she's scheduled it for Christmas Eve. At midday. It leaves us stranded. We'd have to fly down on the twenty-third. Then it's too late for us to fly back after the funeral and there's no ferry back to the island on Christmas Day. Sally and I are desperate to go, but the research girls are going home for Christmas. The vet won't be here. So the animals... They have to be cared for. We can't leave them.'

She took a deep breath, trying hard not to cry. 'It's okay,' she said. 'We know we need to stay. But it seems wrong. Marge's been part of our lives for the last twenty years. To not be able to say goodbye…'

She sniffed. A tear ran down one weathered cheek.

Jess swallowed. Uh-oh.

No choice. No choice at all.

'Then there's only one thing to do,' she said, before she could stop herself, before she gave herself time to think because time to think made for complications and what Sally didn't want right now was complications. 'I don't promise miracles,' she said. 'But I'll do what I can. You teach me what to do and Dusty and I will take care of your animals for Christmas.'

'You'll take care…'

'We'll enjoy it.'

'But we have almost forty animals. To feed them all…'

'Dusty will help.'

'Neither of you are experienced,' Sally said. 'It'd take you all day and you'd never get around them.'

'Then I guess you'd best count me in, too,' Ben said dryly. 'I was wondering how I was going to spend Christmas. I think I've just found my answer.'

He'd just agreed to spend Christmas with forty rehabilitating animals, one pregnant pug, one small boy and one woman.

A woman called Jess.

No women. He'd said it to Ellen less than a week ago and he'd meant it.

This was no woman. This was Jess.

They walked silently home along the track—keeping a decent lookout for snakes—and he kept right on thinking… Really convoluted thoughts.

Jess.

She was walking beside him, still in her tiny red bikini, her now slightly battered hat, his shirt, one sleeve missing.

She had blood on her shirt. His shirt. She had dirt on her face.

She looked…happy.

'Wasn't that wonderful?' she said, and suddenly she spun around on the sandy track, her arms outstretched like a grubby, bedraggled angel. 'We've saved a snake.'

'Slash lives to bite another day,' he said dryly, and she chuckled and spun some more.

'Yes, he does. I can't wait to tell Dusty. Hooray for us.'

'Do you get this excited when you deliver a baby?' he asked, and she considered. But not for long.

'Yes,' she said. 'I do.'

He had a sudden vision of her in a birthing suite, wearing drab theatre gear, baby safely delivered, professional needs passed, spinning with the sheer happiness of the moment.

Nate had walked away from this woman?

'Dusty and I will stay over here,' she said, growing serious. 'At the sanctuary, I mean. There's only a couple of babies needing night feeds. I can handle that. If you walk over during the day and help with anything heavy…'

'I'm staying, too,' he growled before he was even aware he was going to say it.

'There's no need,' she said, astonished.

'What if…I don't know…Slash gets a fever.'

'How would you know if a cold-blooded snake has a fever?' She frowned. When she frowned her forehead got this cute little dimple. 'Fevers in snakes. Maybe I need to do some fast research.'

'Maybe *we* need to do some fast research.'

And his hand brushed hers. Just…brushed. Nothing more.

She stopped. Turned to face him. Searched his expression.

'I can do this alone,' she said, and suddenly it was about much more than a snake. 'I don't need help.'

'I'd like to give it.'

His hand was still touching hers. It seemed…important that it was.

She stared down at the link—and then she drew back. 'If you weren't Nate's brother,' she said. 'Maybe…'

And suddenly it was about much more than a snake.

If you weren't Nate's brother.

She was thinking exactly what he was thinking. Like there was some indiscernible bond, some link, something that caught and held.

Something he'd never felt before, and maybe she hadn't either. For there was wariness in her expression.

Fear?

The feather touch of his hand on hers. It was touch only, but it had been much, much more, and both of them knew it.

No involvement. No commitment. It had been his mantra.

His mantra until he'd met Jess.

'I'm not Nate,' he said.

'You're an Oaklander.'

'You're holding that against me?'

'I'm not holding anything against anyone. I'm not in the market for a relationship.'

'Are we talking relationships?'

'No,' she said flatly. 'We're not. So I hope I read this wrong. Please, please accept my apologies for being presumptuous. It's been a long time since...' She broke off. 'No. Sorry. This is a dumb conversation. No one wants to take it further. You're Dusty's uncle and that's great. I'll stay at the sanctuary over Christmas because it'll help Sally and Dianne, and Dusty and I will love it. If you'd like to come over during the day and help, you're very welcome. Dusty will love getting to know his uncle a bit more.'

'And you?'

'I already know you,' she said softly. 'I know you as much as I want to know you. Any more would be just plain scary.'

CHAPTER TEN

HE SHOULDN'T want her.

The more he thought about her…the more he knew he had no choice in whether he wanted her or not. It was just…there.

He didn't want anything to do with any woman who looked like needing a long-term relationship. The appalling example of his parents' marriage, their bitter vitriol, the shock of losing Nate, had all combined to give him a deep-seated knowledge that commitment wasn't for him.

It still wasn't for him. But Jess saying, 'I already know you as much as I want to know you…' It was like a challenge and it wouldn't go away.

Jess wouldn't go away.

The conference was huge, but Jess seemed to be everywhere. At every session he seemed to sense where she was in the room. He'd glance up and she'd be speaking to someone, smiling, laughing, and he wanted to edge whoever it was away and take right over.

He'd go into one of the smaller workshops and she'd be asking questions that showed the depth of her intelligence.

He watched her, intent, in a workshop on the increasing gaps between mothers with money and resources at their disposal and mothers without.

He watched her care.

He watched her give her total attention to what was happening in the conference sessions—and then he saw her assess the programme, decide a session wasn't necessary, escape.

Sometimes he just happened to escape as well. He'd head down the beach and find her transformed. She had two bikinis, the crimson one she'd worn on snake-day and a sea-green one with silver stars.

He couldn't decide which he liked most.

As soon as she was out of the confines of the auditorium her hair escaped as well.

Professional chignon or flowing curls? No choice. He definitely knew which he liked.

But he wasn't permitted close.

Oh, she wasn't stopping him seeing Dusty. As soon as he approached she'd greet him with pleasure, tug him into whatever game she was playing with Dusty—and two minutes later she'd excuse herself.

'I'd like to catch up on a text for the next session. With you and Kathy here, there's no need for me to stay.'

He was brother to someone who'd treated her appallingly. How could she ever get over that?

Did he want her to?

Yes. The response rang clearer and clearer.

Was it just because she was unattainable that he wanted her?

Was it just that she was mother to a child who looked like Nate?

But the more he saw her… The more he listened, watched got to know her from the sidelines… The more he thought no.

And then…the final conference dinner. Black tie.

The last paper had been presented. The conference had been brilliant—it was common consensus. Holding a conference on remote birthing in such a remote place had been inspired. The attendees would go away with so much more than they'd come with. The mood of the delegates was benign, happy, in the mood to celebrate.

And it was two days until Christmas. The hotel was a blaze of Christmas decorations. The staff were all wearing Santa hats

Wear red if you can,' the conference flyer had said, so almost ll the men were in dinner suits with red bow-ties.

And the women...

The woman.

Jess.

She walked into the room and she took his breath away.

Specialist obstetricians were not usually known for their lack f money, and money hadn't been an issue for most of the women n the room tonight. Most of the women's gowns were amazing. But Jess...

Jessie's gown was so simple it stood out in its understated legance. Bright, clear crimson, shot with some sort of silver hread that shimmered as she moved. Tiny shoe-string straps. The dress itself, the bodice cupping her lovely breasts, accentu-ting their soft swell, then curving into her waist like a second kin. Hugging her hips. Falling to mid calf, still clinging, but lit at one side to mid-thigh, revealing bare, sun-kissed legs.

Simple crimson heels, stilettos, making her legs look as if hey went on for ever.

A tiny blush of make-up. Her curls floating free around her houlders.

Two tiny Santa Clauses, one in each ear, blinking through he mass of curls. On someone else they might look twee. On ess they looked perfect.

The guy Ben had been speaking to stopped in mid-sentence nd stared. 'Whoa. Where's this lady been? Four days of con-erence and I only see her now? Excuse me.'

He was gone.

He wasn't without competition. The dinner tables were pre-lanned, with name-tags on each place. Ben saw at least three ame-tag changes take place for the seat beside Jess before it vas time to sit down.

He noted the last.

Ben was expected to be at the top table. Abe Hildenbrand, the rofessor he was due to sit beside, was Professor of Obstetrics t one of the world's most prestigious medical schools. He was also a personal friend. Ben outlined his plan with a few well chosen words. The professor followed Ben's gaze and grinned

'If I was forty years younger and my dear wife wasn't sitting beside me I'd cut you out, but if not me… Go right ahead, my boy, and I wish you all the luck in the world.'

It was time to sit. An up-and-coming young gynaecologist from Auckland slid into the seat beside Jess with a satisfied smirk.

Thirty seconds later Ben tapped him politely on the shoulder. He lifted his name-tag from the seat beside Jess and motioned to the head table.

'Dr Ross, Professor Hildenbrand has specifically asked for your company tonight. Apparently there's a research proposal he's interested in sharing. He's asked if I'll forfeit my place at the top table so he can discuss it with you.'

The young doctor stared up at Ben with suspicion. Well-deserved suspicion. He glanced at Jess, who was looking surprised. He looked towards the head table.

Professor Abe Hildenbrand, world expert, was beaming at him. Crooking one finger. Beckoning.

The man knew when he was beaten.

Ben handed him his name-tag, put his own in its place and slid into the chair beside Jess.

'What do you think you're doing?' Jess muttered.

'Being ruthless. It's what Oaklanders are principally famous for.'

'Go away.'

'There's no more places,' he said, and picked up the menu. 'I hate this. Chicken or beef, alternate placings. If you get beef can we swap?'

'No!'

'You're a hard woman.'

'I do what I must to protect myself.'

'I can see that.' He sighed. 'Okay, I can handle this. If I need to eat chicken to make you happy, so be it.'

She hesitated. Looked confused. Then said, 'Why?'

'Why what?'

'Why do you want to make me happy?'

Time to drop the levity? His smile faded. 'I'm not sure,' he said at last. 'But it seems I do.'

'You don't owe me anything.'

'This isn't about owing, Jess. This is about the way I'm feeling. Do you know how beautiful you are?'

'Nate told me,' she said, blankly, and went back to menu-studying.

This was armour, he thought. He refused to be diverted. Armour must be too heavy to wear for ever.

'Soup or pâté?' he said. 'Chicken or beef? Chocolate mousse or lemon tart? I'll swap any or all.'

'Please don't.'

'You'd hold the sins of my brother against me?'

'I'm not in the market for any kind of relationship,' she said. 'With you or with anyone else. So, no, I'm not holding Nate's sins against you. I'm holding nothing against you and I'm holding nothing for you. I'm simply not interested.'

'Jess…'

'I need to study this menu.'

'It's simple.'

'No, it's not. It's very complicated, and I'm not about to take any course without very careful consideration.'

For all his contrivance, he passed a boring dinner. He and Jess were seated side by side in the middle of a rectangular table of eight. The four at Jessie's end were discussing the latest pain-relief methods for post-Caesarean patients. Jessie was riveted.

The four at Ben's end were discussing the setting up of a maternal welfare online service, so women could use Skype and find someone to talk to about their concerns with their new-borns at any time of the day. It was a topic Ben was passionate about. The two doctors at the end of the table were delighted he was with them as they were as enthusiastic as he was, and the woman opposite him had drug-company clout.

He'd get what he wanted from this dinner—medically speaking.

But he was finding it harder and harder to concentrate on what he wanted. Or maybe what he wanted had changed.

Jess.

She laughed at something, and her chuckle ran through him like a physical tug. He'd known this woman for, what, five days?

He was falling...

'We'd need trained psychologists on call,' the doctor beside him was saying. 'Postnatal depression's a huge problem for isolated women. It's no use setting up maternal and child health services online if we don't cater for psychological problems. That's going to mean getting Psych Services involved. My brother's the Member for Southern Hinterland. His wife's on the board for South Psychiatric Services. If you're prepared to put your name to it...'

He needed to concentrate. He did concentrate.

Soup or pâté. Beef or chicken. Mousse or tart. Jess ate what was put in front of her and didn't refer to him. The way she held her shoulder...

A barrier.

'You didn't like your mousse,' he said reproachfully as the plates were cleared. Half her mousse was cleared with the plates.

'I'm more a lemon person.'

'Yet you didn't swap.'

'I like my independence.'

'Chicken!'

'No, beef.'

He chuckled. She looked at him. Her lips twitched. She tried desperately not to respond. Failed.

'Okay, I'm sorry. That was petty.'

'Then you owe me,' he said gently. 'One dance.'

The staff had cleared the dance floor. A band had started to play, quietly, while the food was being served but more loudly now. Enticing them to dance.

'I need to go back to Dusty,' she muttered. 'Kathy will be tired.'

'If you let Kathy go now, she'll have to come back to Reception and work until her official knock-off time.'

'I...'

'Shouldn't care abut Kathy,' he said softly. 'But you do. It's yet another thing I'm starting to love about you.'

'Ben...'

'Like,' he corrected himself hastily, watching the flare of panic. 'I meant like. And I'd like to dance. Would you?'

She would. He'd watched her as the music had started, watched her body relax, watched her toe move ever so slightly under the table.

She could dance, he guessed. He guessed she didn't often have the chance.

He stood and held out his hand. Met her gaze, surely and steadily.

'What harm a dance with the uncle of your son?' he said. 'We're practically family. One dance with Uncle Ben.'

'If only you felt like Uncle Ben...'

'You'd like it better if I had a pot belly and whisky on my breath? That's been my experience of uncles.'

'At least then I'd know how to handle you.'

'You do know how to handle me,' he said softly. 'I'm guessing you can dance. I'm guessing I'll be like putty in your hands. All you need to do is trust me.'

'That's not exactly a small ask.'

'Not small, but easy. Take my hand, Dr McPherson, and let me take you to the floor.'

She should never have agreed. The moment they reached the centre of the dance floor the music softened into a waltz. A waltz! What sort of stupid, old-fashioned dance band was this? She'd expected dancing as in two people three feet apart gyrating. She could do gyrating. She did jazz ballet in the hospital gym to keep fit.

Once upon a time she'd also done ballroom dancing. Her parents had loved it. She remembered magical nights of her childhood, music under the stars, her parents teaching her, her father dancing with his little girl as if she was the most important woman in the world.

After her father died, back in London, when the dreariness had become too much, her mother had suggested they might try again. Jess had been astonished, but game, so once a week they'd gone to a seedy, run-down dance hall where Gloria Baker had taught Dance and Deportment—and they'd had fun.

The nights had been as cheaps as chips, the dancers a cross section of all incomes, of all abilities, singles and couples, old and young, people there simply to enjoy themselves. Her mother had been damaged by arthritis even then. She'd only danced the slow ones. The rest of the time she'd watched and smiled and loved what she was seeing.

What's not to love about dancing?

What's not to love about dancing right now?

For Ben Oaklander knew how to dance. He took her into a waltz hold, his body making contact, brushing at the hip, holding her as she needed to be held.

The first step and she melted.

The modern waltz. A waltz Gloria had loved, her mother had loved even more, a waltz she thought no one else in the world knew outside ballroom dancing classes.

The first few steps were standard waltz steps. The next.. Ben made a tentative move with room to back off if she didn't know it.

She felt the response in his body as she did know it. As she moved seamlessly in time with him, in tune with him, as he held her, as he moved with her, as he whirled her effortlessly in his arms.

Gloria could dance like this. As a comparison…Gloria didn't cut it.

How to respond?

No choice. To be held like this…to be danced with like this..

Dangerous or not, this was a once-in-a-lifetime experience. A girl simply melted.

She was aware of others on the dance floor, dancing and watching. The centre of the dance floor was left for them, but it wouldn't have mattered if it wasn't. Ben steered her effortlessly. With no other partner could she have simply abandoned herself like this…totally trusted…

Except Gloria, who definitely didn't count.

She forgot Gloria. She forgot the dancers around her. She was subsumed by the feel of Ben's body, the sensation of sinking into him, the feeling of falling…falling…

Of becoming one.

Like sex, only better…

Someone had said it once at one of their classes. Who needed sex when you could dance like this?

Or…not exactly true, because dancing like this, moving closer and closer to this man's body, it was as near to sex as made no difference.

The music came to an end. People were smiling and clapping and she found herself flushing—but it wasn't because of the heat.

There was a moment's pause while the band collected itself—and then the music changed.

Rock and roll. Straight out of the sixties.

It was like the band had tested them out on sweet and slow and was now trying them on fast and hot.

Better. Not so personal.

Fabulous.

He held her just right. He swung her as a girl wanted to be swung, his strong arm clasping her, tugging her, swirling her, playing with her as she wanted to be played with.

Even the indomitable Gloria couldn't dance like this. The room was swirling, a kaleidoscope of colour and movement. Ben was anticipating every move of her body and she was anticipating his.

She'd never had such fun.

She'd never felt so alive.

They were moving as a couple who'd danced together for years. That was how she felt. Like she'd known this man for years; that he was part of her and she was part of him.

Dancing had nothing to do with life. It wasn't real, she told herself, or she tried to tell herself in the fraction of her brain that had any room to think at all.

But it wasn't enough. Maybe it wasn't real, she conceded, but for now she couldn't resist. She simply surrendered to his skill, to his body, to…Ben.

The final dance was Latin, the samba. She danced as she'd never danced before. She was a little bit crazy—or maybe a whole lot crazy. The feel of him. The texture of his deep black dinner jacket against her bare shoulder. The way his gaze caught hers and held, the way his eyes gleamed with laughter, the way his hand was right there, where she wanted it to be. There was no quarter given or taken. They were simply…one.

And when the music finally stopped…

The door beside them was open. The drapes were fluttering in the warm night breeze. The sounds of the ocean were calling and Ben simply danced her out of the room, out onto the balcony, swung her round and round and round…

And kissed her.

It was inevitable as taking the next breath. The culmination of the dance; of sheer sexual excitement. The final awareness that this man's body meshed with hers, that somehow, somewhere a mould had been split, that two pieces had been apart for years but were now wondrously joined.

Foolish. Fanciful. It didn't matter. All she knew was that she was in his arms, her face was tilting up to his, and he was stooping to kiss her.

And the kiss…

A girl could die in this kiss.

She hadn't been kissed since…since… She'd almost forgotten. Since she'd decided that she didn't need it. Didn't want it.

Her kissing skills had lain dormant, buried, put aside with her past.

But not dead.

She'd decided she didn't want to be kissed.

She wanted it now.

How could she not want it now? She'd danced with Ben. She was being held by Ben. She'd forgotten how a man's kiss could feel.

Or maybe it had nothing to do with a man's kiss. Any man.

Maybe it was Ben.

This night.

This man and no other.

Ben.

And with that thought she felt herself surrender. His hands were holding her, centring her face, so his mouth could merge with hers. Taking her to him…

Fire meeting fire.

That's exactly what this was, she thought, dazed. It was a blast of heat so intense that it sent shock waves washing through and through her body, over and over.

She felt her lips open to his demands. She felt his mouth merge with hers.

She was no longer Dr Jessica McPherson. She was someone else.

A woman loved by Ben?

Ben's woman.

Her arms were still holding his, the last link of the dance made now so much stronger. But it wasn't enough. She lifted her hands, raked her fingers through his dark hair, held him closer, closer… How much closer could she be?

This was nothing she'd ever felt. This was nothing she'd ever expected to feel. An out-of-body experience.

Out of one body. Into another.

Ben.

One body. Theirs.

The night seemed to be dissolving. His mouth was possessing hers. His hands were in the small of her back, moulding her against him.

This was delicious, delectable, dangerous.

Ben.

An Oaklander.

No. Ben. The man in her arms. The man whose eyes possessed her, caressed her, whose mouth was playing havoc with her senses, who'd turned her to fire and want and need.

This was no mere kiss, as it had been no mere dance. It was… possession…

But then… A slight stiffening. A withdrawal.

She could have wept as he pulled away, but the elderly professor was right behind him. His hand was on Ben's shoulder and he was drawing Ben around.

'I'm so sorry to interrupt,' he said, and he was grinning like an elderly leprechaun, a man who'd conjured magic. 'I love it when a plan comes together. But Hilda and I are retiring. We're leaving the island at dawn and flying back to the UK so we can be home for Christmas. So I need to say goodnight. Goodbye.' His smile embraced Jess, and the feeling of leprechaun intensified. 'And good luck.'

'I believe we already have it,' Ben said, still holding Jess, and the professor's smile broadened.

'Well, hold onto it,' he said. 'And, yes, I see you do. Goodnight, Dr McPherson, it was a privilege to meet you. And I believe my wife will be contacting you by email. Something to do with wanting one of Pokey's pups. She wanted to talk to you tonight but you seemed…busy.'

He chuckled, he gripped Ben's hands and he left.

Leaving her with…Ben.

So much to say. Or not to say.

Where to start?

For a moment they didn't even try. So much had already been said or not said that they needed time to take it in.

Ben reached for her hands again but she backed away.

Sense was flooding back. And with it…panic.

'I… Where did you learn to dance like that?' Maybe it was as good a thing to say as anything for rebuilding the armour.

'I had a nanny who loved it,' he said. 'After we moved to Australia. My mother wasn't all that interested in mothering. I still believe she brought me here from avarice, not need—half the property was hers and I was half the property. She and her new boyfriend spent very little time in Australia. Out of school hours I was left with Doreen, a widow who came across as efficient and effective in front of my mother but inside was a pussy cat. A dancing pussy cat. She found me one night sobbing my heart out. Missing Nate. She put Buddy Holly on her sound system and taught me rock and roll. She said—and I believe her—that when your head's trying to connect with your feet, you don't have room for anything else. It leaves you so exhausted that you sleep. As medical therapy it's brilliant.'

'She sounds brilliant,' she said, a trifle unsteadily.

'And you?'

'My parents,' she said. 'One of my earliest memories is standing on my dad's feet, between Dad and Mum, the three of us dancing.'

'Yours is nicest.'

'Do you still see Doreen?'

'I'm godfather to her grandson.'

'Nice.'

'She'll like you.'

'Ben…' Alarm slammed back. Warning bells were starting up all over the place.

He was looking at her with such, with such…

'Jess, I never thought I could feel like this,' he said gently into the night, and her world stood still.

'I don't…'

'Don't feel?'

'I don't want to feel.' Deep breath. Really deep breath. 'You're an Oaklander.'

'And you're a woman. A week ago I was swearing to never have anything to do with the species ever again.'

'A week ago…' She stilled. 'You broke off with someone a week ago?'

It was the truth. She could see it in his eyes.

Imperceptibly she backed even further.

Once upon a time she'd fallen truly, madly, deeply in love with an Oaklander. Had she learned nothing?

'Ben… I need to go.' She couldn't stop the note of panic.

'I'm not my brother.' He said it harshly.

He wasn't, but the real world had raised its ugly head. Sense had to prevail.

'I never said you were,' she said. He wasn't. She knew he wasn't. But he still made her feel…out of control. Like all she wanted to do was put her life in his hands.

How dumb was that? She was a grown woman, a professional, the mother of a ten-year-old. She had her life mapped out. No, he wasn't Nate. She saw pain behind the anger, she saw reasons for why he was like he was—and she also saw reasons for Nate now, as well. Nate, left behind by his mother and his big brother.

She could ache for both of them.

She knew both of them were dangerous to her and to hers.

'Dusty and I are moving over to the sanctuary in the morning,' she said, forcing her voice to be as calm as she could make it—which wasn't very calm at all. 'We'll have a busy Christmas. Dusty will love to see you if you can visit.'

'I told you…'

'I don't want to get any closer. Please.'

'Jess.'

'No!' It was a snap.

She felt right out of control. All she felt like doing was sinking into him, taking his hands, melting into his lovely body.

She'd known him less than a week. He'd just confessed he'd been dating another woman until a week ago.

She might be stupid but she wasn't totally stupid. She needed to step away, even if it felt like tearing herself in two.

'Jess, you and I…'

'There is no you and I,' she said steadily. 'You dance like an angel, or at least like my dad. You sew snakes up really well. You make my son laugh. You'll make an excellent uncle for Dusty but that's as far as we're taking it.'

'Even if we both want…'

'Your girlfriend of a week ago,' she said. 'What did she want? Love? Commitment? Family?'

'That's not relevant.'

'Because you've moved on,' she said, sadly now. 'As you do. As I'm doing right now.'

She took her time going back to the bungalow. There was no hurry. She walked down to the beach. There were other conference delegates walking in the moonlight. In the morning they'd leave, return to their normal lives. They were soaking up this pleasure while they could. Right now they were couples in the moonlight.

For a moment she let herself go down that path. A woman with no ties. Four more days on this island. Ben Oaklander.

She let herself…drift.

His hands on her body. His mouth claiming hers. The rock-hard muscles, the gleaming laughter in those mesmerising eyes, the sensation of dancing, of being in his control, of her body moving in rhythm with his.

She could…

She couldn't.

Most of the people on the beach were in pairs. Husbands and wives. Or not. Delegates from different parts of the globe, coming together for brief holiday passion.

She couldn't join them. Too much was at stake, for if she fell into Ben's arms…

She had fallen into Ben's arms, and it had scared her witless. She'd felt like she was falling into a chasm and she couldn't see what was below.

She suspected what was below. Nate. Chaos.

No. Not Nate.

Ben.

She turned and looked across at Ben's bungalow. His light was on. He was standing on his veranda, just standing. Watching.

One signal from her and he'd join her.

Or she could join him. Kathy was with Dusty until midnight if she was needed.

She wasn't needed. Jess had more sense. She turned resolutely away from the direction of Ben's bungalow and made her way to hers. To hers and to Dusty's. Home.

He watched her go and he tried to think what to do.

Something.

He'd never known he could feel like this.

Never had ended.

CHAPTER ELEVEN

IT TOOK a lot to tug Jess from her trance, but it happened the moment she walked into the bungalow. Kathy was crying.

She was seated at the dining table, her blonde curls sprawled in front of her, her face on her arms, sobbing her heart out.

Jess glanced involuntarily into Dusty's bedroom. Dusty and Pokey were asleep. One single bed. One small boy. One dog.

Things were okay in Dusty's world.

Not in Kathy's.

She walked over and put a hand on the girl's shoulder. Kathy flinched. Looked up wildly with a face blotched and swollen with weeping. Took a gulping sob and pushed herself to her feet.

She was so pregnant...

'I'm...I'm sorry. I should never... It's okay, I'll go now. Dusty's been great. He's been asleep for an hour, there've been no problems. I... Goodnight.' She rose and headed for the door—and Ben was in the doorway.

Kathy looked like she intended to bolt. Jess cast a speaking look at Ben and he moved forward so Kathy had nowhere to go.

'How can we help?' he said, and it was so strong, so direct, that it brought both women up in their tracks. Jess might have said, 'What's wrong?' Ben might have said, 'What's going on here?'

Neither. The simple: 'How can we help?' had the fear disappearing from Kathy's face, leaving only bleakness.

'I have to leave,' she said.

To bed? Back to the hotel?

Ben got it before she did. 'You mean, leave the island?'

'I've been sacked.' There was another gulping sob. 'Frazer, the hotel manager, wanted to talk to me before he went off duty tonight. He rang here. He said…he said…'

'What did he say?' Ben's voice was gentle yet firm, taking the hysteria out of the moment. Making it matter-of-fact—doctor to patient.

'The lady on the beach with the kids…' Kathy managed between sobs. 'Mrs Holland. She's…she's a midwife. She told Frazer there was no way I was due in seven weeks. She said two weeks maximum. She meant well—she said she'd seen me lifting someone's suitcase and she said he ought to know that I could do some real damage. So Frazer's now decided there's legal implications and he wants me off the island. Now. But I can't.'

'Why can't you?' Ben said. He hadn't offered her a seat. She was off balance, Jess thought, and he was keeping her there. If he sat her down, soothed her, she might very well recover enough to clam back into herself, as it seemed, she'd clammed up for her entire pregnancy. A girl from Ireland, doing it alone.

'Mike is in Weipa,' she said. 'And I don't want to be alone for Christmas.'

Weipa.

Jess had never heard of it, but obviously Ben had. He was in professional mode, Jess thought, an obstetrician calming an obviously distressed mother.

'So,' he said, and he did propel her down then, back where she'd been sitting. He sat down in front of her and took her hands in his. Forcing her attention on him. 'Is Mike your baby's father?'

The words seemed a shock to Kathy. If Ben had said your boyfriend or your husband, the words might not have got through, but '*your baby's father*' made it about her child.

'Y…yes.'

'Then what's he doing in Weipa when his baby is here?'

It was still about the baby. Kathy drew in a ragged sob. Choked.

'Cup of tea?' Jess said helpfully, and filled the kettle.

First rule: make things as normal as possible.

Kathy didn't answer. It didn't matter. Jess took mugs out of the cupboard, clattered spoons, decided against tea bags in favour of tackling the teapot. Tried to make the scene domestic.

She caught Ben's eye and won a flicker of recognition. He knew what she was doing and she knew what he was doing.

Normal.

'Where's Weipa?' she asked. No histrionics.

'About as far north as you can go without falling off Australia,' Ben said. 'It's a mining town, full of blokes earning money. So he's earning money for the baby, Kathy?'

'I... Yes.'

'You'd buy a fair few bootees with what he's earning up there,' Ben said reflectively. 'So when's he coming down?'

'After Christmas.' She choked on another sob. 'It's all wrong. We were going to be married last time Mike had leave, only we hadn't given enough notice, and there were hassles with my passport. So we've applied now. On the twenty-ninth of December there's a celebrant marrying some famous couple here at the resort. I asked him if he'd do us, too, and he said yes.'

'That's great,' Ben said. 'A wedding. But let's get this baby sorted first.'

Tears were still slipping down the girl's face, but Ben's matter-of-factness was taking effect. Jess handed her a wad of tissues and she blew her nose. More normality.

'So your baby's due when?' Jess prodded.

'On the fifth of January,' she said, a bit shamefaced. 'I sort of...lied. First babies are always late, my mam always said. It's okay. We'll be back on the mainland by then.'

'Does your mam know you're pregnant?'

'No.'

'Does anyone from your family?'

Deep breath. They could almost see her struggling with hysteria. Jess popped a plate of chocolate biscuits in front of her and hysteria was put aside.

'I...I wanted to be married before I tell them,' she managed 'And we will be. Mike...Mike is Australian. He had a holiday in Dublin last Christmas. I thought he was gorgeous. He said I should come here and I did, and he was still gorgeous, and he loves me and wants to marry me. Only he had to go back to Weipa. He said if he can see out his contract then we'll have enough for the deposit for a house. And if I could work, too, we'd be set for life. Only there aren't any jobs I can do in Weipa and he says it's no place for me when I'm pregnant anyway so I got a job here. He gets triple time rates over Christmas so we thought... Christmas apart, this last time, would be worth it. Only now it really is Christmas and I... It's just... I don't want to be by myself.'

Ben spooned sugar into Kathy's mug and pressed it into her hands. 'Does Mike know how close the baby is?' He relaxed back into his chair. Man in dinner suit, crimson bow-tie, body to die for, sipping tea in the middle of the night and casually discussing Kathy's life plans. While Jess watched in something akin to awe. She'd tried to get Kathy to talk. Ben could just do it.

'I sort of didn't... I mean... I wasn't sure myself. I had it figured for February. Only then... I've been getting really tired so the last time I had a few days off I went over to the mainland and saw a doctor.'

'So you have seen a doctor?'

'Once,' she said. Shamefaced. 'She asked me all sorts of questions. She told me she thought the dates I'd figured out for myself were wrong. A month wrong. But she said...early January. That's still okay.'

'Did you have an ultrasound?'

'No,' she said, sounding scared. 'She wanted me to but I had to get back. I was on duty that night. I thought... I thought...'

She didn't tell them what she thought. She was a terrified kid, Jess thought. When she'd had Dusty she'd at least had her mum. Kathy was totally alone.

'I can do this,' she whispered. 'I'm sorry. When Frazer said I had to leave I got upset, but it was just for a moment. I know all the flights from Weipa will be booked out, even if I wanted to tell Mike to come. Which I don't. I'll book into a backpackers' place, stay there until he comes. It was only…' She swallowed. 'Christmas by myself… I've never…'

'You can't spend Christmas alone,' Ben said.

'Frazer says I have to. He says the hotel won't take responsibility for me.'

'He doesn't need to take responsibility,' Ben told her. 'Jess and I aren't staying at the hotel over Christmas either. We'll be at the sanctuary. The researchers will have gone. Sally and Dianne will have gone. There'll be beds to spare. Jess and I are both trained obstetricians. I do need some reassurance, though, about the baby. If you agree, I'll ask the ultrasound team if they'll let either Jess or I give you a thorough examination before they leave with their equipment. If everything's looking good, why don't you spend Christmas with Jessie and Dusty and Pokey and me?'

Jess was almost too stunned to respond. She was too stunned to object.

Kathy headed back to her hotel quarters, almost happy.

Ben made a call to Elizabeth, in charge of the ultrasound team. Who owed him.

'She doesn't leave until eleven tomorrow,' he told Jess when he finished speaking. 'After the free advertising Pokey and I gave them, she's ready to promise the world. One ultrasound at eight in the morning's a doddle.'

'A doddle,' Jess said faintly. 'To have a woman giving birth in a wildlife sanctuary.'

'She's not due until January. You know Mam's right. First babies are more often late than early.'

'She's stressed, she's been doing hard physical work, and that baby's sitting low.'

He grinned. 'You're saying we can't deliver one baby?'

'You're not staying at the sanctuary.'

'I am,' he said gently. 'I always was. It's only you who's been thinking otherwise.'

'I don't want you to.' And it was a wail.

'Because?'

'Because I'm scared.' There, it was said. Out in front of them, the elephant, right in the room.

'I won't hurt you,' he said at last.

She was standing clutching the bench behind her. As if she needed support. The table was between them. They needed something between them.

'I know you won't.' She swiped her curls from her face. 'This is dumb. How I feel…'

'I believe I feel like that, too,' he said. 'Blown away.'

'You were dating another woman until a week ago.'

'Until a week ago I was thinking there was never a woman I wanted to spend the rest of my life with.'

Silence.

It went on and on.

She should move, she thought. He should move. It was like neither of them knew how to.

She had to break this moment.

'I'm not interested,' she managed.

'Liar.'

'Your brother came close to ruining my life.'

'You think I would?'

'No, but…' Were her curls really in the way or was it just everything seemed in the way? 'I can't divorce it,' she said at last. 'How I felt about him. How I feel about you. You even look like him. You look like my son. And here you are, saying…saying…'

'That I'm as confused as you are,' he said. 'I've met you and fallen in love in less than a week. It hardly makes sense to me either.'

'It doesn't make sense because it isn't,' she said. 'It's not possible. It's not even remotely likely. You've met a little boy who reminds you of a brother you've lost. You've met me and I'm your brother's lover…'

'I could never think of you as Nate's lover.'

'It doesn't matter what you think. I just…was.' She was shaking, she discovered. 'Every time you see Dusty… How could that ever be a basis for a relationship? How could I ever think what you feel for me could be divorced from Nate? How could I ever be sure you're not Nate?'

'I'm not…'

'I can't think,' she said. 'Please, Ben, leave it.'

'I can't leave Dusty.'

'I know you can't.'

'And I will stay at the sanctuary over Christmas.'

'Fine, then.' She sounded dreary. She felt dreary. She thought…this man…he was standing before her, wanting her, and it'd be so easy just to step forward.

He'd been dating another woman until a week ago. He was Nate's brother.

Last time she'd let her heart rule her head…

No and no and no.

'Goodnight, Ben,' she said, and clutched her bench tighter. 'I…I'm sorry I danced with you tonight. I'm sorry I kissed you.' She paused. Met his gaze. Forced herself to go on. 'I let myself be a girl again, like I was when I met Nate. Stupid and romantic and careless. That's not who I am.'

'I know you're not.' His smile was a caress all by itself. His smile was almost her undoing. 'Well, not stupid and not careless. I suspect romantic's still in there somewhere.'

'Then it's staying in there,' she said grimly. 'It's never coming out. Not now. Not ever. Goodnight, Ben. It seems we need to spend Christmas together but after that…we live half a world apart and that's the way I want it.'

He wanted, quite simply, to kill his brother.

If Nate wasn't already dead.

There were excuses for what Nate had become. Ben had come

out of their parents' divorce on the lucky side. At eleven he'd already started coming into conflict with his abusive, overbearing father. Once, when his father had struck his mother, he'd hit him. He'd copped a dislocated shoulder for his pains, he'd suffered his father's ongoing taunts as a mummy's boy, but when the divorce had come through he'd left his father's toxic presence. He'd had a couple of lovely 'nannies'.

Nate had been left with his father. When Ben had finally been able to get back in touch, he'd copped a blast of anger that had astounded him. Nate had blamed him, too, for his desertion.

So there were excuses. But... Nate had almost destroyed Jess.

How could he have hurt someone so beautiful?

How could he have poisoned her against the entire family?

Easy. Jess had met Nate first. Then she'd met his father. How on earth could he expect her to trust him?

Why did he want her to?

A week ago he'd been swearing no women, ever. A week ago he'd thought no family.

She already felt like she was family, and it wasn't because of Dusty; he'd swear it wasn't.

So what was it? What made him feel...? How he was feeling?

It had been Jessie's response at Marge's bedside. Her reaction to a five–foot-long snake; her insistence on saving it, not abandoning it to die. Her intelligence, the way she talked to her colleagues, the way her eyes sparkled with interest and enthusiasm.

The sensation of holding her in his arms tonight.

Kissing her.

Watching her care for Kathy.

She didn't want him at the sanctuary over Christmas. The thought terrified her—he could see that it did. But he'd seen her bleak acceptance, her knowledge that she was trapped.

She wouldn't regret it. He wouldn't push. He couldn't.

If only he'd met her before Nate had...

There was no use thinking of that. No use at all. He simply needed to play the hand he'd been dealt.

Kathy's ultrasound the next morning showed everything as excellent. Beautiful presentation. Perfect baby with good, strong heartbeat.

'Would you like to know if you're carrying a little girl or a little boy?' Ben asked, and Kathy gave him a shy smile and shook her head.

'I'd like Mike to be here when we find out.'

Mike had better hurry, Ben thought, assessing the baby's size and the sheer bulk of Kathy's body, the way she winced as she tried to sit up before he reached and helped her. He'd even done a fast cervical examination, just in case. There was no sign of dilatation but even so...

Maybe he *should* send her to the mainland.

But she'd be alone.

He thought it through. Weighed the risks. Another delegate was staying on in the resort over Christmas as well, and her husband was a paediatrician. In a medical emergency a helicopter could get here from the mainland in twenty minutes. Paediatric back-up. Evacuation. It wasn't so much of a risk.

And the alternative...to have Kathy stay alone, waiting...

If anything happened over Christmas...if she was staying alone in a strange city... There was no real choice and as his examination ended, as he opened the door and found Jess there, waiting to gather Kathy into a hug, as Dusty bounced up and down with Pokey in his arms, saying 'Are you okay, Kathy? Sally's here with the buggy to collect us and she's promised to go really slow', as he saw Kathy's shy smile of thanks, he thought, no, this was right.

The only thing that wasn't right was that he wasn't going with them until later in the day. That was the deal. They didn't need him this morning. Sally and Dianne were flying out tonight. He'd go over then.

For this morning he'd scheduled a meeting with health

department officials. They were discussing pain management in birth situations when there was no doctor on site, contents of medical kits for remote area nurses, proposals for these nurses to have the authority and the equipment to do what was needed.

It was an important discussion.

But he wanted to be…with his family?

CHAPTER TWELVE

THIS promised to be a very exciting Christmas. Possibly too exciting, Jess conceded as they bumped over the track to the sanctuary. One pregnant dog. One pregnant woman. Forty dependent animals.

She sat in the buggy and worried—about all of the above, plus Ben.

Given her druthers, she'd have sent their gear in the buggy and walked, but there was no way Kathy could walk the track, or Pokey either. Sally was driving at snail's pace with her pregnant baggage, and all the time Jess was thinking Ben was coming tonight and then there was Christmas.

Ben.

He was filling her thoughts. The feel of him last night... The sensation of melting into him... Was she a fool for backing away?

But she had no choice. The memory of those first months when she'd known she was pregnant came flooding back. The sensation of being out of control, her mother's distress that she might have to give up medicine, Nate's disdain, the awfulness of having to prove he was the father...

Falling for Ben wouldn't be like that.

There was no guarantee.

'Ooh, I hope we have puppies tonight,' Dusty said, hugging Pokey close. 'Puppies for Christmas!'

'No one's allowed to have babies until Dr Oaklander gets here,' Kathy said.

And Jess thought, Kathy trusts him. She trusts Ben to deliver her baby in the middle of nowhere.

Trust…

Kathy was very young.

Jess knew better.

The good thing about arriving early was that Jess could organise the bedrooms.

Inside were two lovely bedrooms, each with a single bed, occupied by Marg and Dianne. There was also another, stripped clean, but consensus was that no one wanted to sleep in it. Not yet. Marge's loss was too raw.

There were also two beds in a sleep-out, where the students doing research usually stayed.

Easy.

'You'll need the most comfortable bed,' she told Kathy. 'You have Sally's room, Ben can have Dianne's, and Dusty and I will sleep out the back.'

So far so good, she thought as she helped Dianne and Sally with last-minute packing. Keep busy. Stay apart from Ben. Christmas Eve tomorrow, then Christmas Day, then leave.

No drama.

Dianna and Sally left, still thinking up instructions. She and Dusty set to work cleaning cages. Kathy sat down with Pokey on an old settee on the veranda 'just for a moment' and promptly went to sleep. Ben arrived, threw his gear into his designated bedroom and started cleaning pens on the opposite side of the sanctuary to Jess.

So far so good.

Jess moved into evening animal feeding.

She worked one side of the shelter, Ben the other. Dusty stuck with Ben.

Ben had sucked him in, too. Oaklander charm. Irresistible.

She was resisting.

Feeding finished, she turned to dinner. They'd brought sandwiches from the hotel for lunch, but now they were on their own.

'There's food in the freezer,' Sally had told her. 'Even a turkey.'

There was. Sausages, sausages and more sausages. A mountain of sliced bread. One gigantic turkey. Nothing else. She stared into the depths of the freezer with dismay, then checked out the refrigerator. Half a dozen limp-looking lettuces and a couple of bags of rock-hard tomatoes.

The pantry was filled with long-life milk.

Here was a gut lurch. Why hadn't she thought this through? Sally and Dianne wouldn't have had time to think about food over the last few days.

She'd take the ferry across to the mainland tomorrow for provisions, she decided. Fight the Christmas Eve crowds.

She thought suddenly, wistfully, of the beautiful decorations back at the hotel.

One turkey did not a Christmas make.

Meanwhile…tonight…

'I guess it's sausages,' she muttered into the bleak refrigerator.

'Actually, it's smoked salmon roulade followed by pasta with a creamy mushroom sauce,' Ben said from behind her. She whirled to face him. He was leaning on the doorjamb, watching her. Then we have a choice of chocolate mousse or lemon tart. I know, the desserts are leftover conference fare, but it was going cheap. Scrooge has nothing on me. I suggest we eat on the veranda looking over the sea. Dinner will be here in four minutes.'

'You've…'

'Ordered dinner. Unless you really want sausages. I asked Dianne what food she had here. I decided the menu needed a little tweaking.'

'I like sausages,' Dusty said, edging into the room around Ben. He was trying to read his mother's expression. Knowing something was wrong.

'Then we'll cook sausages, too,' Ben said agreeably. 'I'm

mighty fond of sausages. They might take a while to defrost though. Maybe we should have preplanned...'

'You did preplan,' Jess said, and couldn't stop herself sounding accusing.

'I need to. I know what I want.'

His gaze locked with hers.

I know what I want. Uh-oh.

How could she spend three nights with this man?

She had no choice.

'You're talking about food, right?' she managed.

'What else could I be talking about?' he asked, all innocence, but his gaze still didn't leave hers.

'There's a buggy coming along the track,' Dusty said, unaware of tensions. 'Yay, dinner. I don't think I like salmon roulade but I like chocolate stuff. Ooh, what's it got in the back?'

What was in the back was Christmas decorations.

Jess watched, hornswoggled, as the hotel staff unpacked buggies—there were two—onto the veranda.

One vast Christmas tree. Piles of lights. Glittering Christmas balls. Table centres.

'These are from last night's farewell dinner,' she breathed.

'You didn't expect me to buy new ones?' Ben demanded, reproachful. 'The convention centre's not in use until the new year, so I simply asked.'

He'd asked. He'd thought.

He took her breath away.

But... 'Dinner, ma'am,' the guy driving the first buggy said, bringing her up short. 'We've brought it over hot. Would you like us to help set the decorations up while you eat?'

Whoa. Ben might have borrowed the decorations cheaply but for him to arrange hotel staff to bring them here, to offer to set them up, to bring over a hot dinner...

She tried to think of how much this must have cost—and failed.

Scrooge?

Not so much.

He was smiling at her, in a distinctly un-Scrooge-like manner.

She wasn't feeling... She wasn't feeling very...

Actually, she didn't know what she was feeling.

'We'll do our own decorating after dinner,' Ben said. 'It'll be fun.'

Fun. Generosity. An Oaklander.

He wasn't an Oaklander. He was Ben.

He was smiling.

No! She did not need him smiling at her, she told herself urgently. She did not need his smile. Be sensible.

Dinner was served.

Dinner was fabulous.

Dusty wasn't enamoured of the salmon roulade but everyone else was, and Pokey licked Dusty's plate clean, and then went straight into dead-dog mode. Her method of begging for more.

'You're not getting more,' Kathy said, and then giggled as Pokey's disreputable tail rotated like a helicopter blade. 'Dusty, you'll be hungry.'

No chance, Jess thought as she watched Dusty demolish his second helping of chocolate mousse and Kathy her third helping of lemon tart. The sunset was sending a flaming glow over the sea. Each one of the sanctuary animals was warm and fed. She was warm and fed. Ben was surveying all as if he were a beneficent genie—as maybe he was.

She thought of where she could have been for Christmas, in their bleak little hospital apartment, without her mother. This was *some* alternative. A sweet, insidious siren song.

It felt like family.

'Washing up,' she managed, pushing herself sharply to her feet, feeling like the ground might open up beneath her any minute.

'The hotel's sending the buggy to collect the dishes,' Ben said. Then, at the look on her face—her jaw must have dropped round her ankles—he grinned. 'They're hotel plates,' he said. 'You think they'd trust us to wash? Health and safety issues. No one washes them except trained, certified staff.'

'That'd be me,' Kathy said sleepily.

'Nope,' Ben said. 'You're on decoration supervision duty. You and Pokey. Come on, team. Step to it, Dr McPherson, there's work to do.'

And there was nothing for a hornswoggled doctor to do but obey.

They set up the tree in the living room, with the wide French windows open to the night beyond. They strung up lights, inside and out. They hung decorations from one end of the house to the other.

Halfway through Kathy's eyes started closing and Ben ordered her to bed. Dusty followed, reluctant but physically unable to stay awake. Pokey went with him.

But… 'No bed for us until we've finished,' Ben told Jess. 'Tomorrow's Christmas Eve and to not have our decorations in place risks the wrath of every Christmas spirit I know.'

'How many do you know?'

'I'm Scrooge, remember. I've met a few.'

There'd been bleak Christmases in this man's past, Jess thought. She could see it, behind the laughter. Behind the solid resolution to make this perfect.

'I need to take the ferry over to fetch provisions,' she said, thinking Christmas pudding and crackers and party hats and presents for Kathy and…and presents for Ben?

'Now why?' He'd found a stepladder and was attempting to set a recalcitrant star on top of the tree. It wobbled. He wobbled.

Startled, Jess grabbed the ladder and hung on.

'I'm not an orthopaedic surgeon,' she said. 'Babies I can handle. Not broken legs. Have some sense.'

'I appear,' he said, adjusting the star to his satisfaction while she held him steady, 'to have lost it.' His tone was almost conversational. 'Sense, I mean. I came here a week ago a sensible man. Not any longer. I just have to look down…'

'Stop it,' she said. Unsteadily. She was holding the stepladder to keep her steady as well as Ben.

She didn't feel the least bit steady.

'I'll stop it,' he said. 'But we don't need provisions. The resort is putting on a degustation Christmas dinner for guests. They'll be delivering here as well. Every meal. Even Christmas breakfast. Eggnog and truffle omelettes.'

'I don't believe it.'

'And doughnuts for Dusty,' he said smugly. 'Plus I've added a few essentials to the hotel shopping list—they'll be delivered tomorrow.'

'How much is this costing you?'

'I'm not paying. I told you, I'm the original Scrooge. This seems a great way to spend my father's money.'

'What, all of it?'

'No,' he said gently. 'But I've touched none of it. For some reason this seems a very good start.'

He stepped down the ladder then and she didn't step back fast enough. He was too near. Too close. Too…Ben.

'I…I need to feed our little wombat again,' she said, but she backed too quickly, catching her heel on the cord of the flashing lights.

She didn't fall. She couldn't. He had her by the shoulders, and this time it was Ben doing the steadying.

She needed steadying. She felt like her legs were no longer under her.

'Ben…'

'I'll never hurt you,' he said, apropos of nothing in particular. Apropos of…something very particular indeed.

'I know that.' Did she? The way she was feeling… Need. Desire.

Love?

But there was also terror, and he could see it.

'Go feed your wombat,' he told her, but he didn't let her go.

'Ben…'

'I understand,' he said gently. 'It's far too fast. It's hit us both like a lightning bolt.'

'Not me.'

'Liar.'

'Ben…'

'Okay, go feed your wombat,' he said. 'Far be it for me to stand in the way of a medical professional in the course of her duties. But, Dr McPherson, when you revert to Jess again, when you stop being professional…' He hesitated, his smile fading, his gaze all on her.

'When you're Jess again, remember that I'm Ben,' he said. 'Just Ben. Not a doctor, not when I'm with you. Not even an Oaklander. I'll change my name if you like. I'll change anything you want.'

He tugged her forward, lightly, hardly any pressure at all. She could have resisted but she didn't. She couldn't.

He kissed her, soft as a feather, on her nose. The kiss of a friend.

A kiss of a man with all the patience in the world.

'I'm Ben and you're Jess,' he said. 'And tomorrow's Christmas Eve. It's time to make our Santa lists. I know what mine was and I know what it is now. Think about yours, Jess. Think if yours could change. Think if yours could possibly mesh with mine.'

Christmas Eve was busy, and also Christmassy. Because of Ben.

Things kept turning up from the resort. More decorations because he decreed the trees around the sanctuary seemed bare. Santa hats. A full Santa and sleigh to go on the roof, complete with flashing lights.

'Don't tell me the hotel just had these lying around spare,' Jess said, unbelieving.

'They had their last delivery from the mainland this afternoon,' he said. 'I told you—I added a few things to the shopping list.'

'This is ridiculous.'

'No, it's not, it's fun,' Dusty said. He was looking admiringly up to the roof. Ben had spent an hour attaching the sleigh to the eaves and placing Santa on top. 'Kathy, come and have a look.'

'Kathy has backache,' Jess said. Kathy had spent the morning sweeping paths, insisting on helping. Now she'd retired exhausted to her veranda settee.

Jess had checked her. No signs of contractions, but…

She glanced at Ben and knew he was thinking the same as she was.

Kathy's cheerfulness had slipped away, as well as her energy. She didn't come to admire the rooftop. When Jess made her tea, she thanked her and then burst into tears.

'I just want Mike,' she sobbed. And then gulped. 'I know. It's stupid. We were stupid, though, taking this last week just so we'd get the extra pay.'

And not telling him the truth of when you were due, Jess thought, but she didn't say it. She hugged her, found her an extra pillow, set Dusty making paper chains out of fancy hotel Christmas napkins beside her and went back to animal feeding.

Most of the animals were hungry.

Not Pokey. She was circling the living room, looking worried.

Jess got more worried.

'There's not a lot we can do,' Ben said. 'Except research. I spent two hours online after you went to bed last night learning dog delivery.'

'You learned it in two hours?'

'There are still some sketchy areas,' he admitted. 'However, the way I figure it, worst-case scenario is a Caesarean. Our vet cupboard has anaesthetic. I'll play surgeon, you get to be anaesthetist.'

'Gee, thanks.'

'No other problems?'

'I… Slash is off his food, too,' she ventured. 'Sally says he hasn't eaten since we found him. I defrosted a mouse as per Sally's instructions, put it in his enclosure with long tongs, wiggled it about, but he's not the least bit interested. Not that I'd exactly be interested in a defrosted mouse but according to Sally he should be. I hope…'

'Maybe that's all we can do with Slash,' Ben said. 'Hope.'

'I'm out of my depth.'

'You and me both.'

She needed gifts.

As night fell Dusty insisted on hanging stockings, only they didn't have stockings so he used pillow cases. He hung them on the veranda rail, demanding, 'What sort of weird country is this when you don't have chimneys?' He made labels and pinned them on each.

Mum

Dusty

Uncle Ben

Kathy

Pokey

Jess surveyed them with dismay. Tricky.

There was no problem with Dusty's stocking. She'd come prepared.

She'd also made a fast visit to the resort gift shop yesterday. Kathy's Santa would be providing cosmetics, two bibs with cassowaries on the front, and a luscious resort bathrobe.

There'd been nothing that would suit Ben. A book on wildlife of Northern Australia? It was hardly a suitable gift for someone who lived here permanently.

A bath robe? No. It was an okay gift for Kathy but it seemed too personal. And the thought of Ben in a big white bathrobe...

No.

Ben's stocking was, therefore, empty.

'I'm stuck for Ben,' she told Dusty, and Dusty considered.

'He can have the books Aunty Rhonda gave me for the aeroplane,' he said. 'I spilled orange juice on one but the other two still look new.'

'I can't remember...'

'They're guys' books,' Dusty said. 'Old-fashioned, with guns and stuff. I'll wrap them up if you want. I've got napkins left.'

'Fine,' she said weakly. 'Um...' She looked again at the stockings. 'Pokey?'

'That's easy, she loves my red jacket,' Dusty said. 'It's fuzzy. You made me bring it but I haven't had it on since I got here. And she threw up on it yesterday, anyway.'

'Really?'

'I didn't want to tell you,' Dusty said. "Cos you seemed bothered last night. Are you bothered now?'

'I don't think so.'

'It's sad we only have two more nights with Uncle Ben.'

'It…it is.'

'But it's Christmas tomorrow,' Dusty said, cheering up. 'You want to know what I asked for?'

'It's a bit late.'

'No, it's not, because he's here already,' Dusty told her. 'I already have what I want. Only I want him for longer.'

Christmas Day. Christmas dawn.

Something had woken her.

She and Dusty were in bed in the sleep-out. Pokey was under Dusty's bed. Whimpering. Loudly.

Uh-oh.

She slipped out of bed and went to see.

Pokey was as far under Dusty's bed as she could get. Backed into the corner. Staring out with eyes that were terrified.

Another whimper.

Dusty woke and sat up. Stared at his mother. Beamed.

'Pokey's woken us up,' he said, deeply satisfied. 'It's Christmas!'

And as if on cue there was a long, drawn-out moan, not from under the bed—not from Pokey—but from inside the house.

Uh-oh, uh-oh, uh-oh.

'Merry Christmas, Dusty,' Jess said, tugging her little boy to her and kissing the top of his head. Quickly, because she had things to do. 'Happy, happy Christmas. And it looks like no matter what was on our Santa list, Santa's organised us babies.'

Kathy was in very early labour. That early moan had been one of fear more than anything; fright as the first contraction hit.

With the house awake, when they reassured her, settled her on the settee on the veranda, talked her through what was happening, she calmed down. She had one of Ben's ubiquitous cups of tea, and decided she'd like breakfast.

It was only six-thirty. Their gourmet hotel breakfast wouldn't be here until eight.

Jess had headed into the house at a run at first moan. Dusty had headed in as well, in his pyjamas. Ben had reached Kathy before them. He was in tartan boxers and a faded T-shirt.

They should get dressed, only while Jess did a fast examination Kathy decreed she was starving. Ben set Dusty to be useful and there was suddenly a pile of hot toast ready to demolish.

It'd be churlish to let it get cold while they got dressed.

She should have brought a robe, Jess thought. She was wearing pink satin pyjamas with slivers of white lace. Short pyjamas. Very short.

Ben had seen her in her bikini. What difference?

'We should think about transferring you to the mainland,' she told Kathy, and Kathy froze.

'No. Why? There's toast here,' Kathy said, looking panicked and Jess met Ben's gaze and thought, okay, they could do this. Normal presentation. Everything looked fine.

And Kathy was right. There was toast.

Ben brought Pokey out in the washing basket lined with towels and settled her in the shadows behind Kathy's settee. She whimpered, refused toast, looked unhappy.

'It's looking to be a long day,' Jess said, sitting on the veranda steps in the early morning sun, munching toast.

'But an interesting one.' Was Ben looking at her pyjamas?

She flushed. He grinned.

She rose, fast.

'While no babies are actually arriving, I should get the animals fed.'

'You fed the babies at four,' Dusty said, urgently. 'And there's stockings.' It was clear where his priorities lay.

'So stockings are even more important than babies?' Ben teased.

'Yes, they are,' Kathy decreed from her birth centre, eyeing her bulging stocking with a fascination that rivalled Dusty's. For this moment it seemed even contractions couldn't compete with the magic of Christmas. 'We'd hate Santa to think he was unappreciated.'

There was no doubting Santa was appreciated.

Dusty's stocking revealed a pair of tiny field glasses, really strong, the kind a kid with an interest in wildlife could use to develop a life-long passion.

A lot of ten-year-olds might have thought the gift was boring but Jess had guessed right. Dusty was gleeful, hugging her with delight.

He was even more gleeful when he opened a box from 'Uncle Ben'.

A skateboard.

How on earth…? How big had Ben's shopping list been yesterday?

'So where can he skateboard here?' Jess demanded, thinking frantically of airline luggage allowances and having to get it home.

'Up and down the veranda,' Kathy said. And then… 'Owwww.'

That meant a small delay. Jess held Kathy through two strong contractions. Ben disappeared and came back with a canister and a mask.

'Gas,' Jess said, awed. 'How…?'

'I told you. Shopping list and delivery yesterday. I know this is a remote birth but I see no reason why we shouldn't have everything we need.'

'You didn't know Kathy would deliver.'

'I didn't,' he agreed, and then looked a bit silly. 'My reasoning was that if we did full preparation then we wouldn't need it. Logic, huh?'

'It sounds all right to me,' she said, and grinned. Feeling suddenly, absurdly happy.

Dusty was wobbling along, holding onto the veranda rail. Kathy tried out the gas, decided she didn't need it, returned to opening her gifts.

'From Uncle Ben?' Kathy queried as she read Ben's card.

'I thought I might as well be Uncle Ben to everyone,' Ben said. 'I've missed out for ten years. I have a bit of making up to do.'

Kathy opened the bathrobe and bibs and cosmetics from Jess and Dusty. And then, from Ben, she received baby things. A full layette. Tiny, practical clothes, nappies, baby blankets, everything a baby could need and more.

Kathy gasped and sobbed and promptly had another contraction. This time she held onto Jess as if she was drowning.

A big one.

'Oh,' she said as she came out of it. 'I thought...me and Mike could buy this stuff. But now... Oh, when my baby comes...'

She put the contraction aside and went back to Ben's package.

Ben had got it right again, Jess thought. Kathy had obviously done no baby planning at all.

Jess should have thought this through. Normally she would have.

Ben had been distracting her.

He still was distracting her. He was sitting on the bottom veranda step, in the sun in his boxers. Looking...stunning. He was opening his gift from Jess and Dusty.

Two books, courtesy of Aunt Rhonda.

Vintage.

Thrilling Adventures for Boys, Volume One.
Thrilling Adventures for Boys, Volume Two.

He checked them out and then looked at Jess with a very strange expression.

'What?' she said, feeling suddenly...breathless.

'You read my Santa list.'

'I did not.'

'You've been talking to my secretary.'

'Right,' she said dryly, and burrowed behind the settee to check on Pokey.

Pokey was looking very intent. Very intent indeed.

Jess went to stroke her and she snapped.

'She's allowed to snap,' Kathy said. 'If she's feeling like I'm feeling. Oh, my…' She gasped. 'Don't mind me,' she said as she launched into another contraction. 'You open your gifts, Jess.'

So Ben helped Kathy hold her gas mask while Jess opened her gifts.

First was a tissue-box cover from Dusty, made in school, carried all the way from London, only a little bit bent.

She knew she'd use it for ever.

There were also soaps from Kathy, with the resort signature cassowary on each tablet.

'It's a bit last minute,' Kathy told her, breathless and apologetic. 'But I love the bathrobe. You didn't pinch it, did you?'

'No! You didn't pinch the soap?'

They grinned at each other. Friends.

Christmas.

There were crimson parrots in the trees above the veranda, squawking their hearts out. The sea was glittering through the trees.

Jess was sitting by Kathy's settee, holding her hand when needed. Ben started helping Dusty wheel along the veranda rail. She felt… She felt…

'There's an envelope in the bottom of your stocking,' Ben said, off-handed, and she caught herself and fumbled in the pillow case for the envelope and ripped it open.

And gasped and dropped it.

Ben grinned, made sure Dusty's hands were steady on the rail, stooped, picked it up and handed it to back to her.

'It's actually from Nate,' he said, still off-handed. 'Via Uncle Ben.'

She lifted it again and stared. Cautiously.

Two cheques for amounts that made her eyes water.

'Don't you dare rip them up,' Ben said, as she hovered over doing exactly that. 'As I said, they're from Nate. His share of my father's fortune came to me. I haven't touched it. So I made a few phone calls, enquiries about average amounts a normal dad would be expected to pay for child maintenance in similar circumstances. Then I multiplied it by ten years and that's the first cheque, personally made out to you. Nate can never repay you in full for giving him a son, but I wish he could. He doesn't know…he'll never know what a gift that is. The other cheque is the remains of Nate's money. That's to go into trust for Dusty.'

And then he went back to helping Dusty as if the conversation was over. Done with.

Jess stared at the cheques. Thought maybe they could move out of their tiny hospital apartment. Thought she shouldn't take them. But the way Ben had said it…

She knew that she would.

'Why are you crying?' Dusty demanded, looking astounded, and finally she managed a smile.

'I'm not. I'm just…happy.'

'That's 'cos it's Christmas and you've got us,' he said wisely. 'And cool presents. Ooh, hooray, here's breakfast. Doughnuts. Can you fit in a doughnut as well as toast, Kathy?'

'Yes,' said Kathy.

Jess looked up to Ben. He was watching her. Just…watching.

She thought of the bleakness of Kathy's Christmas if she'd been alone. Now, here she was, in full labour but surrounded by Christmas, surrounded by people who cared. By Dusty learning to skateboard. By Pokey having puppies. She thought of the bleakness of their last Christmas, her mother in hospital, knowing the outcome, knowing they'd had to move out of her mother's little house to pay the bills.

She remembered snow and sleet and being alone.

Ben was watching her. Smiling. Asking a question with his eyes.

And she knew what the question was.

If she could just take that step… Find the courage to answer. Courage.

It was too soon. Far too soon.

Maybe I'll put Ben on my Santa list for next year, she thought, feeling panicked. Feeling like she was on an edge and the edge was crumbling. A whimper.

'I think Pokey's puppies are coming,' Dusty said. Unnoticed, he'd dived under the settee to take a look. 'Oh, yuk…'

'Oh…' Kathy moaned, and clutched Jessie's hand.

The edge receded. Thank heaven for professional need.

Dr Jessica McPherson, in her pink frilly pyjamas on Christmas morning, was suddenly all professional.

Just as well. Anything else left her feeling dizzy.

Pokey's four puppies were born at twenty-minute intervals with no trouble at all. Pokey allowed Ben to check each little airway. He needed to break one membrane around the nose, but each pup was perfect.

Four puppies, who looked just like their mother. Three boys, one girl, just as predicted. Marge hadn't known who—or what—the father was but by the look of these, they might almost be pure bred.

'So you were discriminating in your choice of lover,' Jess murmured, feeling emotional. She'd been feeling emotional all morning. She was getting more emotional by the minute.

'She's a good girl, our Pokey,' Ben said.

He'd dressed. Jess had also managed to duck away to pull on jeans and T-shirt. She and Ben were more or less taking it in turns to be Kathy's carer, but there was no need to make it formal. Yes, the animals had to be fed. Dusty needed to be picked up every time he fell over. Pokey needed care.

But it was all happening around Kathy's bed.

The birth was getting closer. Ben rigged up sheets from the rafters that could be let down and taken up every time there was a need for privacy, but apart from brief examinations Kathy didn't want privacy. She was as comfortable as they could possibly make her. Her makeshift bed overlooked the rainforest and the sea. She had two obstetricians on hand. The paediatrician back at the resort had been put on standby, but there wasn't the least hint he might be needed.

She was four centimetres dilated. She was using the gas but she was still in control.

But emotion was starting to cut in, too. 'I wish Mike...' she murmured, over and over, and finally, in mid-contraction, her wishes became pleas.

'Mike...' It was a yell. And after that, every contraction ended up as a yell to an absent partner.

And then, at two in the afternoon, just after they'd finished a very odd Christmas dinner, eaten on the veranda, with Kathy eating only a little mango and lemonade but wanting to see everything and demanding stuff be kept for after...

Mike came.

Jess thought it was the hotel buggy come to pick up the dishes.

She'd been under the settee when she heard it arrive, with Pokey, who was now allowing herself to be stroked, who was conceding that she'd like a little Christmas dinner herself.

She emerged and there was a kid standing by the buggy. Kid just turned to man. Long and lanky, weathered, a bit too skinny. Jeans, tough work shirt and work boots. Looking scared.

'Is this...?' he started. 'Kathy...'

'Mike!' Maybe it was another contraction. Maybe it was recognition but either way the word came out as a long and desperate scream.

And Mike forgot everything else. He was up on the veranda gathering his woman into his arms like she was everything that ever mattered in the world and nothing could matter ever again.

The day wore on, with momentum of its own.

They had the screens up now, permanently. Kathy's contractions were less than a minute apart, and what little attention she had left over was all on Mike. They were cocooned behind the sheets. Mike, amazingly, was coaching her in breathing.

'I've been reading books,' he admitted, sounding almost shamefaced. 'And is that the gas mask? Kathy, love, maybe you could...'

Kathy could. With Mike there she seemed ready for anything. Even birth.

'Call us if she wants to push,' Ben told them. 'We'll check on you every ten minutes.'

Dusty was out on the edge of the clearing, lying flat on his back, gazing with his new field glasses at the parrots up in the trees. He'd be sleepy, Jess thought. She was feeling sleepy herself.

Ben took her hand.

They were looking out over the sea. The sun was warm on their faces.

She should pull away.

She didn't.

'Why did you decide to be an obstetrician?' she asked, trying to make it friendly. Trying to act like the link between them wasn't something momentous.

'And not a money-grubbing billionaire like my father? Or playboy like my brother?'

'I didn't say that.'

'No,' he said. 'You didn't.' There was a moment while she thought he wasn't going any further, he was simply holding her hand, staring out to sea. But then... 'It was other people's families,' he said at last. 'I always felt like I was on the outside, looking in. For some reason medicine fascinated me; it was always what I wanted to do. But I remember my first birth. I was a raw intern, working in a public hospital. The obstetric ward was frantic. We had a mum come in at three in the morning. Her husband worked night shift at a metal fabrication company; they'd pulled him off duty. He was filthy. He had no one to care for the rest of the kids so he brought them all in, three littlies under ten, all in cheap pyjamas, half-asleep. Mum didn't make it to the delivery room—halfway there she delivered on the gurney. I was called out to help. No one else made it. I remember handing the babe to Mum, and then watching them. A family. The reaction to that baby... They had so little and this new little baby was all any of them wanted. I just...wanted more.'

'Yet you decided...'

'That I could never take the risk for myself,' he said. 'Coward, that's me. But watching from the outside...' He glanced back at the veranda where it was obvious another contraction was in full swing. 'I never cease to love it.'

Her heart was twisting. Every single sense was telling her here was something wonderful. Someone wonderful.

Someone she could hold.

Ben was just holding.

'So how about you?' he asked, and she had to force herself to think what he was asking, think what he wanted to know.

Why was she an obstetrician?

'I wanted to be a vet,' she said, simply and surely. 'But I knew because of Mum's illness I could never leave London. My patients of choice weren't in London.'

'Snakes?'

She grinned. 'And lions,' she admitted. 'They were a bit thin on the ground around London, and medical school was closer to home than vet school. Anyway, I got the marks, so I became a doctor. But I was still...drifting. Then Dusty was born. For me it was like life started from that moment. I held him in my arms and I thought birth was the most awesome thing in the world. It still is. Will that do for a reason?'

'It'll do for me,' he said, and the grip on her hand tightened.

She should pull away. She should...

She did nothing of the kind.

'So,' she said at last, and she was beginning to really struggle. 'Mike. Weipa. There's another explanation I want.'

'Business-class fares from Weipa,' he told her. 'Courtesy of my dad. Good old Dad. When Kathy said there'd be no seats left she didn't factor in business class. Then a helicopter to the island. There's nothing you can't get with money.'

'I guess...there isn't.'

'Except what I most want in the world. You do know that I love you,' he said, and the world stood still.

'You can't,' she managed. It was really hard to get the words out. 'You've known me for less than a week.'

'It took less time than that to fall in love.'

'It's Dusty, isn't it?' she said frantically. 'You said yourself… you want a family.'

'Not true,' he said evenly. 'Families scare me stupid. I never thought I could try. I'll admit I'm falling for Dusty, but now… if you were standing on a desert island, just you, no links to my life, no links to Dusty, I believe I'd still love you.'

It was enough to give a girl pause. It was enough to make a woman want to sink…

'Owww…' The scream cut through the stillness and Ben grimaced. Kathy's time was getting close.

They needed to return.

'In my next life,' he said, 'I'm planning on being an accountant. No interruptions. But this lifetime… If you marry me you'll have to put up with babies all the time.'

'I'm not marrying you,' she said, breathless. Panicked. 'And even if I was, I'd have my own babies.'

'*Our* own babies.' He smiled. 'That's fine by me.'

'No!' It wasn't what she'd meant. He knew it.

He was still smiling and her heart was twisting…

'Doctor…' It was Mike and he sounded panicky. 'She's pushing.'

The medical imperative.

'We'll resume this conversation later,' Ben said, striding back to Kathy. 'Do you want to take Dusty out of earshot? Kathy sounds like she's going to use her lungs to push.'

'Dusty's an obstetrician's kid. He's spent a whole lot of his life in waiting rooms outside birthing suites when I've just needed to pop in and check. He knows there's screaming and screaming.'

'He's a great kid.'

'Go and welcome another great kid into the world,' she said, a trifle unsteadily. 'And we're not discussing anything more about us personally. Nothing at all.'

It wasn't as easy as they'd hoped. Kathy moved into second stage and nothing happened.

The fear and loneliness of the last few months had taken its toll, Jess thought, as had the fact that Kathy had worked to the end. She was too thin. She was tired. She simply didn't have the energy to push.

In Jessie's big London teaching hospital Kathy might find herself whisked off for a Caesarean, especially as there was no equipment other than a stethoscope to monitor the baby. But Ben appeared totally unfussed. He used the stethoscope to check the baby's heartbeat but he seemed to do it almost as an extension of checking Kathy. There was no hint to Kathy that he was worried.

As Kathy grew more panicked he took her hands. He waited for the next contraction to pass, and then he moved deliberately into her line of sight, holding her so she had to look at him. She was wild eyed and frantic.

He simply held.

'Kathy, you can do this,' he said, strongly and firmly. 'But your baby needs you to stop panicking, now.'

'I can't… I can't…'

'You can,' he said, in a voice that brooked no argument. 'I know it hurts like hell. We don't have drugs here to help you so you need to do this on your own. But the pain you're feeling… Imagine there's a pumpkin in there trying to get out. Your body's squeezing and squeezing. There's about a quarter of an inch extra room it needs, it's hurting every time you push, but if you can just manage one or two mighty heaves…'

'I can't!'

'You must because while the pumpkin's still in there, it'll keep on hurting. One mighty push, it's out and the pain's on the other side. Over. That last little bit, Kathy, it's so close you can touch it. Use the time between contractions to gather your strength

nd then when your body pushes you go for it. Push with every-
ning you have, push through the pain and then there'll be no
ain. I promise. I know it's like biting on a broken tooth, but at
ne end you won't have a broken tooth, you'll have a pumpkin.'

'A pump—'

'I mean a baby,' Ben said, hastily, and smiled, and she almost
nanaged to smile back.

She met his eyes. He looked at her calmly and surely, and
nen he slipped her hand back into Mike's.

'Okay,' he said, moving to the far end of the bed, to where
e needed to be to catch a pumpkin. 'You have you two up your
nd of the bed, pushing, and you have Jess and me at this end,
vaiting to catch. Mighty effort, Kath, love. Push!'

She pushed.

She stopped screaming and pushed again.

She pushed once more. Yeah, okay, a scream, but… 'Here's
ne head,' Ben said, jubilant. 'Black hair!'

'A black-haired pumpkin,' Kathy moaned, and pushed once
nore, fiercely, strongly, with everything she had, and one per-
ect little girl slid out to greet the world.

he rest of the day passed in a blur.

It wasn't exactly a restful Christmas afternoon. Animals still
eeded feeding. Babies needed caring for. Half the resort staff
eemed to find an excuse to pop over and see the action.

One baby girl, two dazed, proud parents, four puppies, a re-
ort full of animals.

What a Christmas!

The hotel buggy appeared at dusk with turkey sandwiches,
nango trifle and champagne. They ate like they were starving.
Vhat had happened to their midday meal?

They could have Christmas pudding for breakfast.

As dusk fell they tucked Kathy and her precious bundle—
umpkin until something more dignified occurred—into Sally's
ed. Ben decreed Mike have Dianne's bed; he'd sleep on the
eranda.

Dusty wilted and headed for bed as well.

'But I'm worried about Slash,' he said as Jess tucked him in. 'He's still not eating and he has a bump on his stomach.'

Slash. The snake. A bump.

Infection? Uh-oh.

'I'll take a look,' she promised.

'Get Uncle Ben to take a look.'

'Hey—are you saying Ben's a better doctor than me?'

'Just…different,' he said sleepily. 'Like my skateboard and field glasses are different. I want them both.' He hugged her and snuggled. 'Like I want you and Uncle Ben.'

Right.

She should go to bed too, she thought. It was barely nine. She needed to check on Slash.

She walked out into the starlit night, avoiding the veranda. Chicken.

'I'd rather be a chicken than a dead hen,' she told herself, thinking she wasn't exactly making sense. She'd had one glass of champagne for dinner. One glass too many?

Slash's pen was by the side of the house, one of a series of small enclosures for patients who might, as part of their re cuperation, feel the need to eat other patients. It wasn't such a problem in her normal line of work, Jess acknowledged, smiling a little to herself as she rounded the corner. She flicked on the flashlight she'd brought with her and saw Ben lying full length in front of the wire. Shining his own flashlight through the net ting.

Had Dusty warned him, too?

She almost retreated, but he'd seen her light. He turned and waved his flashlight.

'Hey,' he said. 'Dr McPherson. Just who I need for a second professional opinion.'

'Infection?' she asked, cautious.

'Come take a look,' he said, and wiggled sideways on the grass so she could lie beside him.

Lie beside him? A girl would have to be mad.

A girl didn't have much choice. She lay beside him.

He was back peering into the enclosure, totally focused. 'Dusty told me Slash had a bump,' he said.

'He told me that, too,' she said. 'That's why I'm out here.' It was good to get that clear. Just in case he had the idea she might have come looking for him.

'The bump's moving.'

The bump was what? Had she heard right? 'Sorry?'

'Look for yourself,' he said, and edged a tiny bit further, but not far. She still had to lie hard against him.

She lay hard against him. Not so wise—but he was focused on Slash. A professional opinion. Right.

Her flashlight joined his.

A bump…

Definitely a bump.

And…definitely moving.

The thickening was around the snake's rear third. She'd noticed it…the thickening…when they'd treated the wound, but… 'I—I thought she'd just eaten something,' she stammered, awed. 'I mean…she looked thickish but not…'

'Pregnant? And here I was thinking you were the snake expert.' Reproach at its finest. 'I believe we even discarded the diagnosis… "Pity it's not pregnant."'

'I don't even know where its heart is, much less its uterus,' he admitted. 'You're sure? I mean, it's not just worms or something?'

'Look,' he said, and directed his flashlight further down.

Slash's tail was slightly raised. There was a flap of what looked like, well, snake skin for want of a better description, toward the tip. It was also raised. And as they watched, a tiny, membrane-covered bump emerged from underneath and then retreated. The snake's body rippled. The lump heaved inside her.

'It must be worms,' Jess said, not sure whether to be awed or revolted. 'For heaven's sake, baby snakes?'

'I'm sure of it. I did a dash inside to the internet,' Ben said.

'First puppies. Now snakes. It's a bit late for an ultrasound now but apparently they can have up to forty.'

'Forty!'

'This one's taking a while. Do you think forceps?'

She shook her head in disbelief. This night was crazy. 'Why don't we order an epidural while we're at it?' she muttered. 'I'm sure she's hurting.'

'It'd be an interesting anaesthetic case,' Ben admitted. 'Wow, it's all out.'

It was all out. A membranous bulge, like a shell-less egg, was emerging from under the flap of skin. There was a moment of squirming and then a tiny snake was coiling out onto the ground beside its mother.

'One,' Ben said in satisfaction.' What do you call forty babies? Like quads only quads by ten. Deci-quads. I need to count. One down. Thirty-nine to go. Give or take a snake.'

'You're going to lie and count all night?'

'A good obstetrician never leaves the hospital until the patient's safely delivered,' he said, sounding pious. 'You never know… If the seventeenth is breech…'

'She'll sue if you're not here with forceps?'

'She'll be entitled to. By the way, do you still think Slash is a good name for a girl snake?'

'It'll have to be Sasha,' she said, still feeling winded.

'Okay, how about she's Sasha, also known as Slash. That makes her sound like a biker snake. Excellent. And the first baby out will have to be Noel. Then Merry. We'll do Tinsel and Jingle and Donner and Vixen and… Who are the other guys?'

'You want forty Christmas names?'

'Forty-five,' he said. Puppies and Pumpkin as well. 'As Christmas deliverers, we rock, Dr McPherson. There's no one to touch us. What a team.'

And then suddenly laughter faded. Craziness faded.

He took the flashlight from her suddenly shaky hands.

He gathered her into his arms and he kissed her.

* * *

She was lying on the grass outside a snake enclosure, being kissed.

She was being kissed by Ben Oaklander.

No. She was being kissed by Ben.

Christmas night. The stars were hanging low in the sky. They'd had five, no, six babies so far, counting snakes, and there were more coming. They'd had a truly extraordinary Christmas.

It was ending as it should end, with a kiss.

She'd told herself to be sensible. She'd told herself this was far too short a time frame to decide anything. She'd told herself to force her head to rule her heart, to not let this man near.

All of those were excellent decisions.

But one kiss for Christmas. She let herself have one, wondrous, drawn-out moment, she took as well as gave, she kissed as she wanted to be kissed.

But her head was handling it. Somehow her head was still in excellent decision mode. One kiss and she managed to pull away. But only just.

She didn't look at him. She fumbled for her flashlight and checked the patient.

'She's doing fine,' Ben murmured, running a finger down her cheek. Touching the corner of her mouth. Making her heart twist. 'You want me to fetch a blanket so we can keep on supervising?'

'Stay out here all night? While forty babies are born?'

While the night grew darker and Ben grew nearer. A rug and starlight and Ben.

'No,' she said, and she knew she sounded panicked but she couldn't help it.

'No?'

'No.' Somehow she shoved herself to her feet. He rose as well, and stood, too close. Too Ben.

'You know I won't hurt you, Jess,' he said gently. Surely. Truly. 'It would be my wish and honour to stop anything hurting you ever again. More than anything else in the world, I'd like to try.'

'Ben…'

'I know,' he said. 'It's too fast, too soon, you can't trust m
because I look like Nate, you can't trust me because you don'
know me, you can't love me because it's not sensible. I know al
those things and yet… I do seem to love you, Jess.' Then, as sh
wavered, and she did waver, he put his hands on her shoulders
drew her to him and kissed her on the lips, a gentle, searchin
kiss that was a message all by itself.

'Go to bed, Jess,' he said gently. 'I'm on duty tonight.'

'What, snake watching?'

'Until all my babies are delivered.'

'You're nuts.'

'I didn't think I was nuts until I met you,' he said softly. 'Bu
I am now. Go to bed, and Merry Christmas.'

How was a girl to sleep after that?

She lay in the little bunkroom with Dusty asleep beside her
with Pokey snuffling in her basket under the bed. Some tim
during the afternoon she and Ben had decided night baby dut
would be split into Pumpkin and family for Ben, puppies an
family for Jess. So she supervised Pokey and she thought…sh
thought…

She just thought. A million thoughts were tumbling in he
head.

All centred around Ben.

She lay, wide awake, for an hour. For two.

Go to asleep, she told herself. Be sensible. It's been a weird
wonderful Christmas, time out of frame, a dream.

Dianne and Sally would be back tomorrow. The ferries woul
start running. They could leave.

Dream over.

The rest of the house was in darkness. Kathy and Mike an
Pumpkin were obviously asleep, gloriously happy. Dusty wa
asleep. He was pretty happy as well. Pokey and her pups wer
asleep, and by the sound of Pokey's snores there was content
ment there too.

Which left her.

And Ben.

Ben would be trying to sleep on the settee on the veranda, he thought. The settee would be too short for him. He shouldn't have given his room to Mike.

He had, and it was too late to offer to swap now. He might even be asleep as well.

Or counting snakes.

Surely he wouldn't…

Once thought, she had to know. She slipped out of bed and edged the curtains aside.

Out in the dark, a sliver of light. By the snake pen. Definitely a flashlight.

He was still lying full length where she'd left him?

Welcoming babies.

Waiting for problems?

She should have given him a book on snakes for Christmas, she thought. The perils of snake-birth.

Here was another thought in the jumble. Dusty had given him two of his books. What had she given him?

Nothing.

She stood staring out into the night at the pinprick of light that was Ben's flashlight.

Ben.

And then she thought, what had he ever been given?

A fortune by his father. He'd never touched it.

Blame from Nate. That must have been gut-wrenching. She remembered the scorn she'd heard in Nate's voice the first time she'd met him. 'My sainted brother.'

Ben as an eleven-year-old, being dragged to a strange country in order to punish his father. Ben, with a family that wasn't a family at all. Ben finally finding a way to contact the little brother he loved, only to meet with hatred.

She thought of her own parents, her family, of tragedy but of the love and joy and tears and laughter they'd shared. To not have that…

To not give it…

The thought slammed home with savage certainty, leaving her breathless. To not give it because she was afraid it might be snatched away…

Snatched away from her, or snatched away from Ben?

He had far more courage than she did. He knew, far more than she, how much love hurt, yet here he was, looking at her as if she was all he ever asked in life.

To offer a love like that…

Love came in all forms.

He'd sorted this whole Christmas. He'd seen Kathy's need. He'd arranged for Mike to be here. He'd taken the chance with Pumpkin's birth—there were insurance issues, she knew, small risks, and it would have been simpler to decree Kathy go to the mainland to hospital.

But he'd taken those risks on. He'd cared for Kathy.

He'd given his bed to Mike.

He'd given up his Christmas, his precious isolation, so two elderly ladies could go to the funeral of a friend they loved.

He'd sat up through the night researching puppy birth. And now he was out in the dark, just watching. With all the patience in the world.

How could she ever compare him to Nate? Because they had the same smile?

They didn't. The outward smile was the same, but Ben's had love behind it; not just love for her but love for all he cared for.

Enough to form a family?

He didn't need to form a family himself. It took two. If she could just find the courage.

For she had love to spare. She'd just packed it away. Allocated it to her mother and to Dusty and to no one else.

If she opened her heart…

Pokey snuffled in her sleep and she found herself smiling. 'I guess even you,' she said softly. 'I have no idea how this will work but this love thing…why not take a leap of faith? For all of us?'

* * *

was pretty stupid lying on the rough native grass counting baby snakes.

It was better than the alternative, which was lying on the too-small settee on the veranda, thinking of Jess.

She was leaving tomorrow, packing up, returning to England.

He could follow her.

But even if he did, how could he eradicate the fear in her eyes? Once back on her home turf, wouldn't it just intensify? Back in her nice safe life, with no monetary considerations now, why would she ever think about him? Nate's brother.

Snake baby number twenty-seven slithered into the world. Twenty-seven! This was getting ridiculous.

'Have you needed forceps yet?'

He didn't move. He couldn't. She was right beside him, kneeling on the grass.

She was wearing those gorgeous pink pyjamas. He could feel them brush against his arm. His skin.

Jess.

'No…no,' he managed. 'Textbook delivery so far.'

'I brought out my tweezers, just in case.'

'So you're here in a professional capacity?' It was hard to get his voice to work. She was so close.

She lay down beside him. Why hadn't he got a rug? To lie down on the grass in those gorgeous pyjamas…

She was so close.

'Nope,' she said softly. 'I'm here because I just checked the time. It's a quarter to midnight. It's still Christmas. I'm here in Santa capacity.'

'Santa…'

'I've been thinking…' she said. 'About everything you've said.'

'About what in particular?' All he wanted to do was turn and take her in his arms. Somehow he managed to keep himself still. Focus.

Baby snake twenty-eight was hardly noticed.

'About loving me and what a gift of faith that is. And how

amazing it is that you've offered it. And how a girl would have
to be a coward not to accept that gift. There's that saying…rather
be a chicken than a dead hen. I was thinking dead hen was the
only alternative. But a girl would be nuts to think that's what
would happen. For to love you… I just can't see it.'

'You can't see you as a dead hen?' he said, cautious now.
Twenty-eight was starting to wriggle. He was running out of
names. Cupid, he thought suddenly. Wasn't that a Christmassy
name? It felt Christmassy to him.

It felt perfect.

'Ben…'

He let himself turn then, so he was face to face with her.
Their noses were inches apart. He so wanted…

No. Be still. This was her step.

'Mmm?'

'I've decided that boys' own adventure books do not a
Christmas make,' she whispered. 'You gave me a gift that'll
change my life for ever. Nate's money. And then you offered
me another. Your love. In return you get two lousy books…'

'They seem,' he said cautiously, 'to be excellent books. I've
read the first story. Pirates and buried treasure and a mad and
bad sea captain.'

'Ben?'

'Yes?'

'Would you like another gift?'

'I don't need…'

'Try it on for size,' she said, and she tugged his hand and
pulled it up to her.

She was holding a plain gold ring. Before he could react, she
slipped it onto the little finger of his left hand.

It slipped on as if it was meant to be there.

'It's my father's wedding ring,' she said. 'I had it cut down.
I've worn my mother's engagement ring and my father's wedding ring since they died. I loved my mum and dad very much
and their love was big enough to share. So tonight I thought I
should share. I thought I could just ask if you'd wear my father's

wedding ring until…until I can give you your own to take its place.'

There was enough in that statement to take a man's breath away.

'You're saying…' he said, not actually knowing what *he* was saying. 'You're saying…'

'Is it proper to ask a guy to marry you?' she said. 'I'm not sure what the etiquette is anymore. But if it's not proper, you could simply regard this ring as a gift and…and a hint.'

'A hint that you might consider marrying me?' He had to ask. It was important for a man to get his facts right.

'If you'll have me. And Dusty,' she added hurriedly. 'You'd have to have Dusty as well. And maybe even Pokey.'

'This is getting big.'

'Huge,' she admitted. 'Enormous. I don't know how I have the temerity to ask.'

Twenty-nine. Twenty-nine would have to make up its own name, Ben thought. He was concentrating on other things.

'So if it's not proper for a woman to ask a man…' he ventured.

'Then of course I rescind.'

He hardly had any breath left to speak. They were lying face to face, under the starlit sky, and she'd just given him her father's wedding ring.

It behoved a man to act fast.

'Will you marry me?' he asked before the moment had a chance to slip away.

'Yes,' she said, with no hesitation at all.

'And live happily ever after?'

'Yes.'

'And trust me with your heart?'

'Yes and yes and yes.'

And suddenly there was no more to say. There was no more to ask.

There was only a man and a woman under the stars, a man taking his woman into his arms, into his heart, into his life.

He held her and held her. Christmas Day came to an end, and snake babies twenty-nine, thirty and thirty-one had to manage their births with no obstetric attention at all.

Sally and Dianne returned the next day, sad, grey, grieving for their friend.

They were met by babies.

Alicia Jessie, one day old, was voicing displeasure at her first bath when the two elderly ladies arrived. Grief turned to intrigue and the beginnings of the way forward.

A baby, in their house...and staying? They were delighted.

'Of course you must stay,' Dianne told the new parents when she realised what had happened. 'Sally and I can use the sleep-out.'

'And could we make Marge's room the baby's room?' Sally asked, shyly. 'That seems...right. Please, stay as long as you can. For what little time we have left here, we need to make thing happy. And...can I have a cuddle?'

She cuddled Alicia Jessie, she wept a little, the resort buggy arrived with high tea of macaroons, sponge cake and strawberries, and over the third macaroon Sally let out her heart.

The news had kept getting worse.

'Marge said she was leaving her money to the sanctuary,' she said, trying hard not to cry. 'We all intended that. This was our dream. Only it seems Marge never got round to changing her will. So there's not enough left to keep the sanctuary going. The university will take it over as a research site but we'll have to leave. And...and Marge's daughter doesn't even want Pokey.'

She finished on a wail and Kathy took Alicia Jess back and hugged her and Alicia Jessie wailed in sympathy.

They were all on the veranda. Ben and Jess were sitting on the top step. Holding hands. Soppy, but no one was noticing. Soon they'd share their news, Jess thought, but for now it was all theirs, a secret joy, building and building.

Tempered now with sadness.

'Do you own this place?' Ben asked, looking around. A ram

ling old house. A research shed out the back. Pens, pens and more pens.

'We have a ninety-nine-year lease,' Sally said.

'In Marge's name?'

'No, dear, we were sensible about that at least,' Sally said. 'It's designated as Cassowary Island Habitat, a separate entity. We paid up front. It's only the running costs we can't cover now. Bringing the vet over. Medical supplies. We can't keep doing it. We won't compromise on quality.'

'Could you extend the house, if you wanted?' Ben said, curiously. He was still holding Jessie's hand.

Dianne noticed. She glanced at the linked hands, glanced at Ben, glanced at Jess. She managed a tiny smile, then retreated back to sadness.

'I guess,' Sally said. 'If we wanted. If we had the money. But...why?'

'Could you build a couple more bungalows?'

'We're free to do what we want within this compound. We bought the lease years ago, before they started to protect this island. While we were still working and this was our dream. Actually,' she admitted, 'it's only about an eighty-year lease now.'

'I think that'll be long enough,' Ben said, and smiled.

'Long enough for what?'

Ben's pressure on Jessie's hand increased. She knew he was smiling inside. He'd run this idea past her some time last night, or was it some time this morning? Her happiness just kept growing.

'You might not have enough money to keep caring for this place,' he told Sally and Dianne now, simply, bluntly. 'But I do. If you agreed to my terms I could set this place up so you could care for your animals for ever.' He hesitated. Corrected himself. 'Okay, not for ever. For the terms of the lease. For eighty years.'

'H-how?' Sally stammered, bewildered.

'I have family money,' he said simply. 'A lot of family money. I've been waiting...until I had a family to spend it with.'

'But…'

'If you agree,' Ben said, 'we would very much like to help Jess and I would be honoured to be a part of what you're doing here.'

Jess and I…

The words hung.

Dianne's eyes went back to their linked hands. 'Oh, my,' she breathed. 'You're not…'

Ben held up his hand. On his little finger, a band of gold 'Engagement ring,' he said simply. 'I said yes.'

'You're…'

'What…?' There was a confused muddle. Clarification Congratulations. Laughter.

Dusty had been sitting beside Ben. He'd been checking out the surrounds with his field glasses. He'd been listening.

He finished looking at what he was looking at—and then he looked at his mother.

'Engaged,' he said.

'Ben asked me to marry him,' she told her son.

'I believe it was the other way round,' Ben said, smiling at Dusty. 'She's very pushy, your mother.'

'She's bossy,' Dusty said. 'Why do you want to marry her?'

'So I can be a proper uncle to you?'

'You're a proper uncle anyway.'

'I guess I am.'

'If you were married to Mum…' he said, thinking it through 'You'd be…almost a dad.'

'I guess I would,' Ben said diffidently. 'How would you feel about that?'

'Ace,' Dusty said, deeply satisfied. 'Could we live here?'

'No.'

'No?'

'Your mother and I talked about that last night,' Ben said apologetically. 'We'd love to, but our job is delivering babies And though we seem to have delivered a whole lot in two days…

'A whole lot?' Sally breathed. 'Pokey?'

'You don't know the half of it,' Ben said. 'But can I tell you ur plan?'

'*Our* plan,' Jess repeated, and grinned and grinned. All was ooking very neat in her world. Neat as in Dusty's use of the ord. Neat as in cool. Neat as in ace.

'The thing is, the resort manager told me a couple of days ack that there was local concern about this sanctuary's long-rm viability,' Ben said, sounding a little apologetic. 'With just e three of you running it he said there were problems. So I ad a bit of warning. I've had time to think. And I think…if my amily money was used to bring this place to what it could be, reckon we'd even get the cassowaries back.'

'We have sixteen already,' Dianne said, sounding defensive.

'Which is a great start and with more money for research we an truly make this place Cassowary Island again. We can have full-time vet. We can work with threatened species. We can ork with the university.'

'It'd cost a fortune,' Dianne breathed, her eyes shining.

'Just lucky I have one,' Ben said. 'Just lucky my father and y brother didn't waste their money doing what they should ave done.'

'But you…' Sally said.

'That's a problem,' he admitted. 'Jess and I deliver babies. usty needs to go to school. But we thought…if Jess is prepared o move from London, I'd be prepared to move north. I can do y research through the university here. We can work on the ainland, Dusty can go to school, but whenever we have time ff we could come and help.'

'I could keep coming here?' Dusty breathed.

'We'd need a bungalow,' Ben said. 'And we'd need vet quar-rs. And room for more staff.' He hesitated then, and Jess looked t Kathy and smiled and smiled. She knew what was coming. his was her part of the plan. How neat was this?

'We also think,' Ben said diffidently, 'seeing neither of you adies drive… We think you need someone here permanently ho can do some hard physical work. Kathy says you, Mike,

aren't enjoying the mines. Kathy, you tell us you love this i
land. If there was a decent house here, and decent wages…'

'Oh, my,' Kathy breathed.

'Hey,' Mike said, startled, and took Alicia Jess back fro
her. 'You'll drop our baby.'

'I could help here?' Kathy breathed.

'Don't go near the snakes,' Dusty said. 'Not till you've learne
how. I'm going to learn how.'

'Me, too,' Kathy said.

'Could we do this?' Sally breathed, as awed as Kathy. '
mean…could we really do this?'

'We can do anything we like,' Ben said. 'Forty-five babies i
one night. Give or take one or two. I believe I stopped countin
There's nothing Dr McPherson and Dr Oaklander can't achieve

'Forty-five…' Sally said, confused.

'We're quite a team,' Ben said, and rose and tugged Jess up t
stand beside him. He put his arm around her waist and hugge
her close. 'My wife and I. A unit. A family. Did I tell you th;
we're getting married? Should I repeat it?'

'When?' Dusty demanded.

'How soon would you like?'

'Now,' Dusty said. 'Make him sign something, Mum, so h
can't change his mind.'

'He can change his mind if he wants,' she said serenely, fee
ing the strength of his arms holding her, feeling the strength (
his love. 'No one's making him do anything.'

'Yes, you are,' Ben said, and despite his audience he drev
her round to face him. 'Yes, you definitely are. You, my lovel
Jess, are the reason for all of this. You've pulled me out of m
boys' own world and you've made me family. I love you wit
all my heart, for ever and ever, and if it's not possible to marr
you legally today, know that I'm marrying you at this momer
in my heart. I love you, my Jess. From this day forward.'

'You can have babies together,' Dusty breathed.

'Thousands,' Ben said.

Whoa…

'Professionally speaking, of course,' Ben added hastily. 'Personally...one or two?'

'Can we talk about this later?' Jess said, feeling desperate.

He smiled. He tugged her forward and he kissed her.

'Why, yes, my love, I believe we can,' he said. 'For I believe we have all the time in the world.'

'Only eighty years,' Dianne warned.

'That's just the start,' Ben said, kissing his Jess again. 'Watch this space.'

* * * * *

A sneaky peek at next month...

Medical Romance

CAPTIVATING MEDICAL DRAMA—WITH HEART

My wish list for next month's titles...

In stores from 2nd December 2011:

☐ New Doc in Town & Orphan Under the Christmas Tree
– Meredith Webber

☐ The Night Before Christmas – Alison Roberts

& Once a Good Girl... – Wendy S. Marcus

☐ Surgeon in a Wedding Dress – Sue MacKay

☐ The Boy Who Made Them Love Again – Scarlet Wilson

Available at WHSmith, Tesco, Asda, Eason, Amazon and Apple

Just can't wait?

Visit us Online

You can buy our books online a month before
they hit the shops! **www.millsandboon.co.uk**

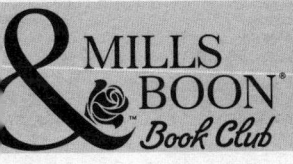

MILLS & BOON®
Book Club
2 Free Books!

Get your free books now at
www.millsandboon.co.uk/freebookoffer

***

r fill in the form below and post it back to us

E MILLS & BOON® BOOK CLUB™—HERE'S HOW IT WORKS: Accepting your
e books places you under no obligation to buy anything. You may keep the books
d return the despatch note marked 'Cancel'. If we do not hear from you, about a
onth later we'll send you 5 brand-new stories from the Medical™ series, including
o 2-in-1 books priced at £5.30 each and a single book priced at £3.30*. There is
extra charge for post and packaging. You may cancel at any time, otherwise we
l send you 5 stories a month which you may purchase or return to us—the choice
yours. *Terms and prices subject to change without notice. Offer valid in UK only.
plicants must be 18 or over. Offer expires 28th February 2012. **For full terms and
nditions, please go to www.millsandboon.co.uk/termsandconditions**

s/Miss/Ms/Mr (please circle)
_____

st Name
_____

urname
_____

ddress
_____

_____
                                      Postcode

mail
_____

**end this completed page to: Mills & Boon Book Club, Free Book
ffer, FREEPOST NAT 10298, Richmond, Surrey, TW9 1BR**

Find out more at
www.millsandboon.co.uk/freebookoffer

*Visit us
Online*

0611/M1ZEE

Have Your Say

You've just finished your book.
So what did you think?

We'd love to hear your thoughts on our
'Have your say' online panel
www.millsandboon.co.uk/haveyoursay

- 🌹 Easy to use
- 🌹 Short questionnaire
- 🌹 Chance to win Mills & Boon® goodies

POINT BLANK SEAL

BY

CAROL ERICSON

MILLS & BOON

First Published in Great Britain 2017
By Mills & Boon, an imprint of HarperCollins*Publishers*
1 London Bridge Street, London, SE1 9GF

ISBN: 978-0-263-92923-2

46-1017

Our policy is to use papers that are natural, renewable and recyclable products and made from wood grown in sustainable forests. The logging and manufacturing processes conform to the legal environmental regulations of the country of origin.

Printed and bound in Spain
by CPI, Barcelona

Carol Ericson is a bestselling, award-winning author of more than forty books. She has an eerie fascination for true-crime stories, a love of film noir and a weakness for reality TV, all of which fuel her imagination to create her own tales of murder, mayhem and mystery. To find out more about Carol and her current projects, please visit her website at www.carolericson.com, "where romance flirts with danger."

For my two Wildcats

Prologue

A light glimmered among the rocks to his right, and Miguel Estrada shifted his MK 15 in response, his heart thudding against his chest. He whispered into the mic clipped to his flak jacket. "Twenty degrees to your right, up another thirty yards."

Miguel couldn't tell if the SEALs on the ground were following his directions or not. They'd moved out of his view behind some rocks, and they couldn't answer him and risk giving away their position. He just had to trust they'd heard him and reacted accordingly, especially since this wasn't his regular team and they were missing that natural rapport.

His world became the area in his scope, and his eyeball tracked back and forth to scan that world, looking for any movement or more light.

These caves tucked into the rugged interior of Afghanistan were a maze, deep and complex. The intelligence they'd received on the whereabouts of Vlad had led a team of SEALs, including him on sniper duty, to this godforsaken part of the world.

The intel suggested Vlad would be lightly guarded and relaxed, not suspecting the hell about to be unleashed upon him. Miguel just hoped Vlad didn't have any children with him. That made everything more complicated—like the two boys the team had run into on their trek up here.

Thank God, it hadn't been Miguel's call to make on how to deal with the boys. Elias had decided to release them, and it looked like that had been a good call since they hadn't seen them—or anyone else—since those boys had scampered across the rocks.

A light flickered again in the same area, and Miguel held his breath, waiting for an opportunity. If he could take out Vlad or anyone with Vlad from this vantage point, he'd do it and save the SEALs clambering over those boulders a few bullets.

The night scope on his sniper rifle cast a green glow on the rugged terrain, with every rock and every edge standing out in stark relief. If only he could see a person, other than the SEALs, he could help verify this location for them.

The brush behind him rustled and he tensed his muscles. He could probably handle one of those little gerbils or moles, but if that was a bat flapping his wings behind him he just might lose it.

Miguel tapped his fingernail against the trigger. Snipers generally had all the patience in the world, but those SEALs down there should've emerged from that cluster of boulders by now. Maybe they'd discovered something out of his sight. Miguel's own team would've found a way to signal that news.

He licked the grit from his lips and shifted his rifle again, zeroing in on the area where the SEALs had disappeared earlier. If they'd gotten his message, they should've popped up twenty degrees to the right of the jagged outcropping that looked like a mouthful of bad teeth.

He mumbled under his breath, "C'mon, guys."

A shift and a scrape behind his location had the hair on the back of his neck quivering. Before he had time to analyze this latest noise behind him, movement on the rocks below had him tightening his finger on the trigger. A light flashed behind the rocks and a pop echoed in the distance.

What the hell just happened? Miguel hissed into his mic, "What was that? Send me a signal."

The only signal he received was another flash and bang. Had the SEALs come upon Vlad's hideout? Were they taking him out now?

The crack of a twig behind him didn't sound like a nighttime rodent or even a bat, but his mission right now was to protect those men down there. Breathing heavily, Miguel swept the rocky hillside, looking for anything that hadn't been there before.

He hadn't liked the look of those particular rocks from the get-go, but the team had to traverse them to get to Vlad's cave—if that *was* Vlad's cave.

A head rose above the highest boulder and Miguel's gut lurched. A man, a keffiyeh wrapped about his head, waved his arms in the air, a weapon clutched in one hand.

Miguel swallowed hard as he recognized the weapon. Then he swore when he realized the man was gesturing—toward him...or someone behind him.

In a split second, he took the shot and dropped the man while he was still waving. Then he rolled to his side, hauling his rifle with him, but it was too late. As he tried to reposition his weapon to the target behind him, he heard the click of a gun.

A heavy boot crushed his arm holding the rifle and Miguel gritted his teeth. Someone else kicked him in the head, and the tinny taste of blood flooded his mouth.

A man growled in English, "Drop your weapon and get on your knees. Your team members are all dead."

Instead of releasing his rifle, Miguel swung it behind him, making contact with someone's leg. The target grunted and one of his cohorts kicked Miguel in the midsection.

The cold metal of a gun pressed against Miguel's temple.

"I'm going to tell you one more time. Release your weapon and get on your knees."

They seemed to have given up on the idea of Miguel releasing anything because someone began to pry his fingers off the rifle, bending them back and breaking a few in the process. They weren't about to wait for him to get on his knees either, as he was yanked up by his jacket.

Miguel raised his eyes for the first look at his captors. Three men—one pointing a gun at his head, one rubbing his shin and the third assessing him through narrowed eyes.

Miguel cleared his throat and spit some blood out of the side of his mouth. "Was this a trap?"

His question earned him another kick to the gut, and he doubled over.

There was no way anyone could've known their position, even if those two boys from earlier in the day had ratted them out, which they probably had. This had been a setup from the start, and in the off chance that he got out of this alive, he'd make it his life's mission to root out the mole that had been responsible for the deaths of those SEALs down there.

"We ask the questions, pig. How much do you know about the man you call Vlad?"

Since Miguel had no intention of answering any of their questions—now or ever—it looked like he wouldn't get that chance to track down the mole.

He spit blood again, this time at his interrogator's foot. "Go to hell."

As the butt of his own rifle came at his head, Miguel had one thought before the darkness engulfed him.

Jennifer.

Chapter One

Two years later

Jennifer herded her fifth-grade students into the park and yelled at two boys straggling behind. "Chase and Noah, you are not in middle school yet. I can still keep you from walking at promotion this week."

The two boys laughed and shoved at each other, but they caught up with the class.

Jennifer pressed the smile from her lips. She couldn't help it if she had a soft spot for rambunctious boys. Her own son kept her on her toes and he was only eighteen months old.

When her class got to the picnic area with the other fifth-grade classes already there, she set them free and she joined the other teachers by the barbecue area, sipping sodas and drinking from water bottles.

Jennifer pointed to the parents grilling the burgers and hot dogs and setting out bags of chips. "Are we helping or what?"

Olivia Gutierrez, who had the classroom next to hers, shook her head and raised her can of soda. "Our wonderful parent volunteers are taking care of everything and told us to relax."

"We have the best parents." Jennifer stooped next to

a cooler and pulled a bottle of water from the ice. She cracked open the lid and then tipped it toward a man at the edge of the parking lot next to the park. "Is that one of ours?"

Susan Burke, the other fifth-grade teacher at their school, shrugged. "I don't recognize him, but it's not like I've seen every parent in the fifth grade. Could be a parent from Stowe."

The man's attention seemed to float from the kids to the teachers, and a whisper of fear brushed the back of Jennifer's neck. She called to Mrs. Garrett, one of the teachers from Stowe. "Mrs. Garrett? Is that man in the blue shirt by the parking lot one of yours?"

Mrs. Garrett adjusted her glasses and squinted. "I've never seen him before, and I don't like the way he's looking at the kids."

Olivia smirked and elbowed Jennifer in the ribs.

"I'll find out right now." Mrs. Garrett, her gray, permed hair waving at the top of her head, marched toward the parking lot like an angry bird.

One of the other Stowe teachers laughed. "Once Pilar gets done with him, he's gonna wish he never set foot in this park."

Jennifer smiled, but her muscles tensed as she watched Mrs. Garrett confront the stranger.

Mrs. Garrett gestured toward the kids, waved her arms and pointed toward the barbecue area. When she was done with him, the man hightailed it back to his car.

Jennifer murmured, "Guess he wasn't a parent."

"What?" Olivia had turned around from her conversation with a parent.

Everyone else had lost interest in the confrontation. Nobody had watched Mrs. Garrett talk to the man… except Jennifer. She'd been very interested.

"The man at the edge of the parking lot. He left."

Olivia snorted. "Even if he'd been a parent, Mrs. Garrett had probably scared him off. She scares me."

Jennifer wiped her clammy palms on the thighs of her slacks and intercepted Mrs. Garrett when she returned to the barbecue area, her low heels clicking on the cement.

"Who was he?"

"Just an office worker from the area on his lunch break. He didn't realize the schools were having our end-of-the-school-year picnic today, but I set him straight."

Jennifer's gaze shifted to the squat office buildings scattered across the street from the park. If he worked in one of those, why had he driven a car and come through the parking lot? He should've crossed at the crosswalk and come in the way the kids had entered.

"Ms. Lynch, Ms. Lynch!" One of the girls from her class was waving her arms. "Do you want to do the Hula-Hoop with us?"

"Duty calls." She put her bottle of water on a picnic table and promptly forgot about the man in the parking lot as soon as she slipped that pink plastic circle around her waist.

After a few more games, a cheeseburger, a hot dog and enough candy to put her in a sugar coma, Jennifer clasped a clipboard to her chest and raised two fingers. "Anyone in my class leaving with a parent, check in with me before you take off."

Olivia bumped her shoulder. "With any luck, all of them will leave with a parent and we can stagger back to the school on our own."

"I doubt that's going to happen." Jennifer smiled at one of her free spirits, Chase, approaching with his mother. "Thanks for your help today, Mrs. Cannon."

"Thank you for a great school year and all your understanding for our son. We're hoping Chase matures a little in middle school."

Jennifer's smile broadened. She hoped Mom wasn't counting too much on maturity in middle school, or she'd be heartily disappointed. "I'm sure Chase will do just fine in middle school. He won't have any problems with math. Right, Chase?"

"It's my favorite subject."

"I know it is."

For the next fifteen minutes, Jennifer continued to check out her students. Then she and the other fifth-grade teachers from Richmond gathered their classes, took a head count and started the trek back to the school.

When they reached the corner, Olivia shouted, "As soon as the light changes, cross the street, no dillydallying."

The kids, giggling at her word choice, surged into the street. Jennifer brought up the rear to make sure all the students made it into the crosswalk. As she glanced back toward the park, her heart stuttered when she spotted the so-called office worker Mrs. Garrett had set straight earlier.

Leaning against a car in the parking lot, he watched the students crossing the street. Or was he?

Jennifer couldn't tell the precise focus of his gaze from this distance, but he seemed to be looking at the back of the line…at her.

A horn beeped and she jumped. Everyone had made it across the street before the light changed, except her. She jogged to the curb as the kids laughed and called out, "C'mon, Ms. Lynch."

"Just showing what you're *not* supposed to do."

One of the girls, her face serious, grabbed Jennifer's hand. "You need to be careful, Ms. Lynch."

The girl's words caused a little trickle of fear to drip down her spine as her gaze darted to the park's now empty lot across the street.

"You're right, Maddy. I do."

LATER THAT EVENING, Jennifer cuddled her son, Mikey, against her chest, her feet kicked up on the coffee table. She pressed her face against his springy, dark hair and inhaled the scent of…toddler, very different from the scent of baby.

His lashes fluttered against his cheek, and she held her breath. She'd just gotten him to sleep after a wild play session that had involved cars, stuffed animals and crackers. She slid her feet from the coffee table and held Mikey close as she threaded her way through the toys on the floor to his bedroom. She liked that Mikey had his own room, even if they shared a bathroom. Two bedroom, one bath places in the nice areas of Austin weren't all that easy to find, but now she had to move.

She hadn't felt safe here ever since the break-in.

Kneeling next to Mikey's new toddler bed, shaped like a car, she pulled back the covers and tucked him in. She kissed his forehead and whispered, "Mommy loves you."

On the way out of the room, she flicked on his nightlight. For being a fearless daredevil, Mikey didn't like the dark. She needed a night-light as much as he did these days.

After that day when she'd come home from picking up Mikey to find that someone had broken into her house, tossed it and had stolen some small electronics, she had a hard time falling asleep at night. Every little noise had her bolting upright in bed, and then lying awake the rest of the night with eyes wide-open.

She shuffled into the kitchen and uncorked a bottle of red. She splashed some into a glass and swirled it around before taking a sip. She took another sip and closed her eyes, allowing the warmth of the alcohol to seep into her tight muscles.

Having a drink shouldn't feel so good. She shouldn't let it feel so good—not with her mother's alcoholism running through her genes. Mom beat her drinking problem, but Jennifer would never let it get to that point. She sucked in another mouthful of wine and returned to the sofa, dragging a pillow into her lap.

Having Mikey had probably saved her from traveling down the same road as Mom. She couldn't be impaired and take care of her son. She'd never do that to him.

But, oh, those nights when Mikey stayed with Mom and Dad? The booze was the only thing that allowed Jennifer to forget.

A tear seeped from the corner of her eye. Who was she kidding? She'd never forget. Would never forget the day that crisp naval officer stood on her porch and delivered the news that would shatter her world.

She stabbed the power button on the remote and clicked through the channels, settling on a comedy she'd seen before. She couldn't laugh, not even with a half a glass of wine swirling in her veins.

As she switched the channel, the dog next door started barking. Max never barked unless something— or someone—wandered into his yard.

Jennifer set down the wineglass. On her way to the sliding door to the patio, she picked up a bat that she'd propped up in the corner of the room after the break-in. Staring outside, she flicked on the light, which illuminated the table, chairs and small barbecue that clustered on one side of the cement slab that passed for a patio. The potted plants and flowers on the other side remained in darkness. She turned the light on and off again and then sucked in her lower lip.

The bulb on the left side of the door must've burned out. When had that happened? After the robbery, she'd checked all her locks and lights.

A dark shape moved in the shadows beyond the patio, and her knees almost buckled. Was that an animal? She cupped her hand at the glass and peered into the night.

She needed a dog. She needed a gun. She *had* a bat.

Hoisting the bat in one hand, she clicked the lock down and slid open the door. She advanced toward the dark side of the patio, raising the bat like Babe Ruth.

"Jennifer?"

She spun around and faced a man standing on her patio, bathed in an otherworldly light.

Her mouth dropped open and she grabbed on to a trellis rising from one of the pots.

"Jen, it's me. Miguel."

Miguel? It couldn't be. How much wine had she drunk in there? She cleared her throat and said the only thing that made sense. "You're dead."

Chapter Two

Miguel eyed the bat still clutched in Jennifer's hand. He didn't come this far to have it all end on her patio with a crushed skull, although he wouldn't blame her for taking a swing at him.

He spread his arms, palms up, and stated the obvious, "I'm not dead."

She dropped the bat. It bounced once before toppling over. Then she breathed his name. "Miguel."

In those two syllables, she expressed all the hope, longing and love that had kept him alive for a year and half in captivity.

She reached out her arms and seemed to sway toward him, her feet apparently rooted to the cement beneath them.

He closed the space between them and swept her into his arms, holding her body so close he couldn't tell where his ended and hers began. He pressed his lips against her soft hair, the blond strands almost glowing in the dark as if they had collected all of the moonlight.

She wrapped her arms around his waist, tilting her head back, her cheeks wet. "My every prayer has been answered, but how…? Why did they tell me you were dead?"

The navy and the CIA had their reasons, but he didn't need to tell her those reasons—right now.

"The navy thought I was dead. Everyone on that mission died."

She jerked in his arms. "Where have you been all this time?"

"I've been… I've been a prisoner of war." Was that a nice enough way to put it?

Gasping, she took his face in her hands. "Are you all right?"

"I am now." He kissed her lips and felt as if he were living a familiar dream, one that had kept him alive… and sane.

She returned his kiss like a woman starving. He broke away first as the passion rose, and she grabbed his hands.

"Come inside. You have to see Mikey. Miguel, we have a son."

He cupped her face with one hand, and smoothed the pad of his thumb across her cheek. "I know and I can't wait to see him, but I have to tread carefully."

"What are you talking about?" She tilted her head farther into his hand.

He touched his lips to her soft earlobe. "You had a break-in recently, didn't you?"

She drew back from him, her eyes wide. "How do you know that? How long have you been here, in Austin?"

"I'll tell you everything later, Jen." He jerked his thumb toward the small house where his son was sleeping. "There's something I need to do in the house first."

"What? Is Mikey in danger?"

"No." The lie felt right on his lips—for now. "Before we talk inside, I need to sweep the place for bugs."

If he discovered a hidden camera, that would be a different matter completely. He'd have to leave immediately.

"Why would someone want to bug my house?" She grabbed handfuls of his shirt and tugged.

"To get to me."

"I don't understand any of this, Miguel. I don't even know if you're really here."

"Oh, I'm here all right." He pressed another kiss against her lips to prove it.

"D-do I need to wait outside?"

"No, but when we're inside don't talk to me. Pretend you're alone."

"I can do that. I'm good at that."

He pinched her chin. "I'm sorry."

"Okay, let's do this. I'm getting cold." She rubbed her arms.

He stopped to pick up the bat and held it up. "Glad you still have my Louisville Slugger for protection."

"You almost got a hit upside the head for sneaking around out here." Pressing her fingers to her lips, she led him into the house and slid the door closed behind her.

Miguel's eye twitched as he watched Jennifer pluck up the wineglass from the coffee table and carry it into the kitchen. She'd vowed never to drink like her mother, but he guessed a dead fiancé and raising a child on your own could change plans.

He pulled the electronic bug detector from the front pocket of his jeans and began scanning the living room. He'd gotten lucky with the size of this house.

It shouldn't take him long to get through the house… and into the bedroom to see his son.

Jennifer rinsed her glass in the sink and turned toward him.

He put his finger to his lips and flicked the switch on his bug detector. He had it set to the display option. If there were any listening devices planted in Jennifer's house, he wouldn't want the sound of his bug sweeper to transmit to the people on the other end of the device.

Facing the wall, he waved the tracker from corner to corner, sweeping across the bookshelf. The listening device would most likely be in this area, across from the TV.

Miguel's pulse jumped along with the squiggly red line on his tracker. He followed its lead and was rewarded with the gleam of a tiny mic wedged between two books.

He became aware of Jen hovering over his shoulder, and he jerked back. He pointed at the TV and then cupped his ear.

She dipped next to the coffee table and picked up the remote control. Aiming at the TV, she clicked, and the sound of a commercial jingle filled the small room.

Perfect. He plucked the listening device from its hiding place, and pinched it between his thumb and forefinger.

They'd hear a bunch of static on the other end and not much more. With the mic still squeezed between his two fingers, he mimed drinking a glass of water.

He didn't remember Jennifer being very good at charades but she was catching on quickly to this game.

She scurried in the kitchen and filled a glass with water from the tap. When she put it down on the kitchen table, he dropped the device in the water.

Her blue eyes widened as she stared at the black spec settling at the bottom of the water glass. She parted her lips, but he shook his head and placed two fingers against them.

This might not be the only bug in the place. He continued his search by sweeping the kitchen, but beyond a few false reads from the microwave, he found nothing there.

Swallowing hard, he moved toward the hallway. He turned into the first room on the right and turned on the bathroom light. He gestured toward the sink, and Jennifer cranked on the water.

His throat tightened when he saw the yellow rubber duck on the edge of the tub and the cartoon fish on the shower curtain. He'd missed so damn much.

A familiar sharp pain lanced the back of his head and he dragged in a long breath. He had to stay focused if he didn't want to miss even more of his son's life.

With the bathroom clear, Miguel turned back into the hallway, holding his breath. He stepped into his son's room, a gentle glow from a night-light illuminating a path to his bed.

Miguel followed the light and crouched next to his son's bed. Pride and joy overwhelmed his senses, and he reached out and traced Mikey's chubby cheek with the tip of his finger. He wanted to gather the boy in his arms and never let go, but he had unfinished business.

Jen had come up behind him and squeezed his shoulder.

He covered her hand with his own and squeezed back, hoping to convey all his regret and sorrow at not being here with her during her pregnancy and the first year and a half of Mikey's life.

His nose stung, but he knew there would be no tears. He'd lost the ability to cry, but crouching here next to his son, inhaling the smell of his hair and skin, he knew he hadn't lost the ability to feel.

That thought had been the one thing that terrified him during his months of captivity.

Miguel pushed to his feet and scanned this room with even more vigor than the others. The guys who'd planted that bug obviously hadn't wanted to listen to the crying and fussing of a toddler.

Miguel shook his head at Jennifer and she straightened Mikey's covers before leading him out of the room.

When he walked into Jen's bedroom, the scent of her signature perfume hit him like a wave. Some nights he'd wake up in his cell smelling that fragrance. He knew it was a dream or hallucination at the time, but he'd wallowed in it anyway.

His gaze tripped over the king-size bed, and he momentarily squeezed his eyes shut. Had she shared that bed with anyone else since his…disappearance? He couldn't hold that against her if she did. She had every right to move on with her life.

But the way she'd kissed him and clung to him outside gave him a selfish hope that she hadn't.

He swept the room and got a hit. The blood boiled in his veins as he removed the device from a picture frame above her bed. He dropped that bug in the same glass of water and then finished his search of the rest of the house.

He tossed the bug detector on the kitchen counter and enfolded Jen in his arms again. "I'm just glad they didn't plant a camera, or all of that would've been for nothing."

She squirmed from his grasp and pressed her palms against his chest. "You're going to tell me what's going on, where you've been and why someone is bugging my house." Her fingers curled into the material of his shirt. "Not that I'm not thrilled you're back and safe, even if I am still pinching myself."

He took both of her hands and kissed one wrist and then the other. "Let's sit down."

"Do you want something to drink? To eat?" She skimmed her hands down his sides. "You've lost weight."

"I'll just get some water." He pushed aside the glass with the two bugs. "*Not* this glass."

She filled a glass with water from a dispenser in the fridge and handed it to him. "Let's talk."

As he followed her to the sofa in the living room, his mind whirled with images from the past two years of his life. What could he tell her? What would she want to hear?

The truth? Nobody could bear that. He'd barely survived it.

Jennifer sat on the sofa, curling one leg beneath her. "Can you start at the beginning?"

He settled beside her and draped an arm around her shoulders. "God, it's amazing to see you. Unbelievable."

"How do you think I feel? At least you knew I was alive. You even knew about Mikey…somehow." She threaded her fingers through his. "I thought— They told me you were dead."

"I'm sorry." He kissed the side of her head. "If I could take it all back, all those months, everything."

"The beginning, Miguel." She pursed her lips together in that schoolteacher way she had.

"We received some intel on Vlad. You remember I told you about him, right?"

"He was the sniper for the other side you guys kept coming up against until he disappeared from the field."

"He seemed to have dropped off the face of the Earth. We thought he might be dead, but we heard chatter and then received specific intelligence that he was regrouping in the caves of Afghanistan, which seemed totally likely."

"The last I heard from you was that you were going off on some assignment as a lone sniper, apart from your team."

"That assignment was tracking Vlad to his hideaway. I was pulled off a mission with my own team to help this one." He might be revealing classified information to Jen, but he didn't give a damn. The navy, his brothers, had never turned their backs on him, but he couldn't say the same for the shadowy intelligence agencies that called the shots.

"And it all went horribly wrong. The navy wouldn't tell me much, but I knew others had died with you." She bumped her knee against his. "Are they alive, too?"

"No. They're all dead."

She covered her eyes with one hand and sniffed. "So I'm the only one who gets the homecoming."

Miguel closed his eyes and clearly saw the ambush of the other SEALs at the cave, the pop of the guns, the flash of the gunpowder.

"What happened to you, Miguel?"

His lips twisted. "Do you have a few days?"

She snuggled closer to him and rested her head on his chest. "I have all the time you need, *mi amor*."

Smiling, he ruffled her soft hair. He'd been teaching her Spanish and she'd picked it up quickly, despite her atrocious accent.

"The mission went to hell. Someone set a trap. The SEAL team on the ground was ambushed and killed, and I was captured."

Her back rose and fell with quick, panting breaths. "H-how long? How long were you a prisoner?"

"Just over eighteen months."

She must've been doing the calculation in her head because her shoulders stiffened. She mumbled into his shirt. "Where have you been the past four to five months? Why didn't you contact me?"

"Various hospitals, starting with the one in Germany, debriefing sessions, intelligence meetings." He didn't mention the psychiatric units. He didn't want her pity.

She finally raised her head from his chest and met his gaze. "I'm sure you needed…treatment. I'm sure the navy and the CIA wanted to pick your brain. But those places didn't have telephones?"

"No. Literally, no. None for me anyway."

"They wouldn't allow you to use the phone?"

"No."

"And they wouldn't notify me? Your father? Your brother? Miguel, your father…"

"I know he's dead." His nostrils flared. "They wanted you to go on believing I was dead, too. They still want you believing that."

Her eyes narrowed. "Those bugs you found—is that the navy, the FBI, some intelligence agency I don't need to know about?"

"It's not the navy. At least the navy is not calling the shots on this one."

"But you have reason to believe forces in the intelligence community broke into my home and planted listening devices?"

"Yes…maybe." He didn't know who was behind the sinister vibe he'd picked up at the debriefing center.

"Miguel, why? They should be treating you like the hero you are. They should be throwing you a ticker tape parade."

"Part of it is the sensitive nature of the assignment. They never went public with it."

"Part of it." She smoothed a hand across the shirt she'd wrinkled earlier. "What's the other part? Why wouldn't they allow you to contact me?"

Running a hand through his hair, longer than he usually wore it, he said, "I don't know."

"They don't know you're here."

"They don't know where I am, but I'm sure they can make an educated guess that I'm coming here."

"You spent eighteen months as a prisoner of war and now your own government wants to imprison you again?" Her cheeks flew red flags, indignation making her voice squeak.

"I don't know what they want, but I wasn't going to stick around anymore to find out." Guilt stabbed at his gut. The FBI had warned him that he could be putting Jennifer in danger by showing up on her doorstep, but he was afraid she already was in danger and he knew he was the only one who could protect her.

She trailed her fingertips along his tense jaw beneath his new beard. "What did your captors do to you, Miguel?"

"Tried to get information out of me." He rubbed a spot on his hip, still sore from the wounds he received from his captors.

"How?"

He thought he'd imagined the whispered question, spoken so softly, but the question lingered in Jen's blue eyes.

If he told her everything would it be worse than she imagined? He gazed into those baby blues and a knot tightened in his gut. Never.

"It was rough, Jen, but I'm here. I survived it." He brushed his lips across hers. "The thought of you gave me strength, pulled me through the most brutal moments of my captivity."

"How did you know I'd be waiting for you? You must've figured the navy would tell me you died. You didn't even know I was pregnant before you left. I didn't know I was pregnant."

"I tried not to think about it. Tried not to think of you moving on with someone else." He scooped her hair away from her face, his fingers tightening involuntarily. "Have you?"

"Of course not." Her lashes fluttering, she leaned in for the kiss he had waiting for her, and then she jerked back. "How did you know where I lived? How did you know about Mikey?"

"After the hospital in Germany, I went to a debriefing center near DC. I kept asking about you, kept asking for a phone. All they'd tell me was that you were okay and I needed to concentrate on getting better." He ground his back teeth. "As if seeing you wouldn't make me feel better immediately."

She grabbed his hands. "Did you escape this center? Leave without their permission?"

"Yeah, but not before breaking into an office and looking at my file." He pulled away from her and smacked a fist into his palm. "They didn't even tell me I had a son."

"A-are you AWOL or something?" Her gaze dropped to his clenched fist and then back to his face.

He shrugged, rolling his shoulders and flexing his fingers. "They debriefed me. It's not like I'm going to confess anything to you about my captivity or about Vlad that I didn't already spill to them."

"But you're not supposed to be here."

He ran a hand across his mouth. "This is the only place I'm supposed to be."

"I thought I was dreaming. I didn't think I'd ever see you again—except in those dreams."

He curled a hand around her neck and pulled her close, but before he could plant another kiss on her mouth, a crash resounded from the room next to them.

Then he smelled the smoke…and heard the screams of his son.

Chapter Three

Miguel bolted from the sofa and Jennifer lunged after him, tripping over the coffee table and banging her shin. The acrid smell of fire invaded her nostrils and terror ripped through her body like the jagged edge of a knife when she saw black smoke pouring out of Mikey's bedroom.

"It's Mikey's room."

Miguel charged into the smoke-filled room as Jennifer hung back coughing, her eyes watering. The heat from the flames licking at the drapes spiked her adrenaline, and she stumbled into the room after Miguel.

"Stay back, Jen. I've got him."

Miguel emerged from the dark gray cloud, Mikey clutched against his chest. He slammed the door behind him.

"Get out. Get out of the house now—back door."

She grabbed her phone on her way to the sliding glass door and gulped in the fresh air when she hit the patio. The smoke and fire from the front of the house hadn't made it back here yet, hadn't escaped from Mikey's room.

She got on the phone with 9-1-1 while stroking the back of Mikey's head as he sobbed against Miguel's shoulder. After giving emergency services the details, she held out her arms and Miguel transferred Mikey to her.

Even amid the terror, she couldn't help noticing how Mikey, in his fear, had clung to Miguel. She whispered in Mikey's ear, "It's okay. You're okay now. Mommy's here."

She rested her chin on top of Mikey's head and met Miguel's gaze as he pulled her away from the house. "What was that?"

"As far as I can tell from the smell, it was a Molotov cocktail."

"Meant for you? The FBI would go to those measures to get you back? Risk harming a child?"

Miguel cocked his head at the sound of sirens in the distance. "No, but who said I was being debriefed by the FBI?"

"You're scaring me even more, if that's possible." She squeezed Mikey so tightly, he squirmed in her grasp. At least the FBI had some accountability, rules to follow, public exposure. But these shadowy black ops organizations? Who held them accountable?

The sirens wailed louder, and Jennifer pointed to the side of the house. "Should we meet them?"

Her neighbor Stephen called over the back fence, "Is that you, Jennifer? What's going on?"

She yelled, "Fire in the front bedroom. Everyone's okay. I think the fire department just got here."

"Oh, my God. Mikey's room?"

"Yes, but he's fine. We're going out front now."

She led Miguel to the front of the house on the other side of where the fire was blazing.

Mikey lifted his head when they got to the street, now bathed in red light. Neighbors clustered on their porches in their pajamas. The firefighters started working before the trucks even came to a full stop.

Jennifer waved at a police officer getting out of his car, and he approached them.

"Is this your house, sir?"

Miguel pointed to her.

"I rent it. I live here with my son."

"Is the boy okay?"

"Scared but not injured." She shifted Mikey to her other hip.

"What happened?"

She felt Miguel stiffen beside her. They hadn't discussed what to tell the authorities. The truth?

"I—I'm not sure. We were talking in the living room, heard a crash from the front bedroom window and smelled smoke. I heard my son cry out, and my... friend went into the room and grabbed him. We all ran outside to the back of the house then, and I called 9-1-1."

"A crash, like a broken window?"

Miguel cleared his throat. "Like somebody threw something through the window."

The cop narrowed his eyes. "You know anyone who would do something like that, ma'am?"

"Of course not."

Taking out a notebook, the officer asked for their names.

Jennifer didn't blink an eye when she heard Miguel identify himself as Mike Esteban.

As they continued talking to the police officer, the firefighters seemed to be making short work of the fire that had engulfed Mikey's bedroom, where flames were shooting up to the roof through the broken window.

Mikey squirmed in her arms, kicking his legs against her hip.

"We need to stay here, Mikey."

"Do you want me to take him to watch? He seems interested, not scared."

Miguel hadn't even formally met Mikey yet. This was his first real contact with his son, and it couldn't be more disastrous.

With her throat tight, she spilled an all-too-willing Mikey into Miguel's outstretched arms and murmured, "He likes action. He's his father's son."

Miguel wandered to the other side of the house where Mikey could get a good look at the firefighters at work.

"Ms. Lynch, is that the boy's father?"

"N-no."

"Where's the boy's father?"

Was the officer trying to imply some former husband had a motive for firebombing her house? A case of jealousy while she enjoyed the company of another man?

"His father's dead."

"I'm sorry." He scratched his chin. "If what you heard is accurate, this sounds like a deliberate act. The arson investigators will do a full analysis, but I'm just trying to get as much information as I can from you to assist them."

"I understand. I'm a fifth-grade teacher at Richmond Elementary. I don't have any enemies that I know of and no irate parents that would go to these lengths."

"You never know what lengths people will go to—until they do."

Jennifer crossed her arms and shivered. "I suppose I'd better call the rental management company and let them know what happened."

The cop looked up from writing in his notebook, peering over her head at the house. "You won't be staying here tonight."

About an hour later, the fire chief on the scene allowed her to go into the house to collect some of her things.

Miguel joined her inside the house, a sleeping Mikey nestled against his shoulder.

She touched Mikey's cheek. "Thanks for sitting in the car with him while I talked to the police and firefighters and called the rental agency. You even got him to sleep."

"After the excitement of watching the firefighters at work, he conked out." With one finger, Miguel pushed a lock of dark hair from Mikey's forehead. "He's incredible."

"You can put him on my bed while I pack up some of my stuff. The fire didn't get much farther than Mikey's room, but I'm going to have to replace his clothes. What the fire didn't destroy, the water did."

"It's just stuff." Miguel walked past her into the bedroom and put Mikey's head on the pillow.

A firefighter called into the house from the front door. "Folks, you're going to have to hurry it up."

"Just a few more minutes." She wheeled a suitcase from her closet and shoveled clothes into it. She dumped Mikey's dirty clothes from the laundry basket into a plastic bag and shoved that into the suitcase.

When she came out of the bathroom with a bag of toiletries, Miguel was on his knees by the side of the bed studying Mikey's face, stroking his hand with one finger.

Her nose tingled. Miguel's introduction to his son might not have been ideal, but Mikey had his father back and that's all that mattered.

"I'm ready. Did you come in a car?"

"It's a few blocks away." He slipped his arms beneath Mikey. "You can give me a ride to my rental and then follow me to my motel."

"I didn't even ask where you were staying."

"I think we had other things to talk about. The motel is here in Austin." Miguel put a finger to his lips, as they walked into the living room where the firefighter still hovered at the front door.

"Everything okay, folks?"

"Not perfect, but we're all safe." Jennifer grabbed her phone and laptop from the kitchen counter, and then shoved the computer into her school bag.

She still had to show up for class tomorrow and get through two more days of school.

With one arm still holding Mikey, Miguel took her bag from her and slung it over his shoulder.

When they got to her car, Miguel placed Mikey in his car seat and she buckled him in. "This takes some practice."

"I want to learn everything. I want to do everything, everything I missed."

She slammed the back door of the car and kissed Miguel. "Thanks for getting Mikey out of that room."

"We got lucky. That was a small Molotov cocktail, never really exploded and didn't project far into the bedroom."

"We'll be in touch, ma'am."

She jerked her head to the side to acknowledge the firefighter. Had he heard Miguel? Did it matter? One of the firefighters had already mentioned something about a Molotov cocktail.

They weren't the suspects here.

She drove Miguel to his car a few blocks away and then followed him to his motel near the university.

He waved her into a parking spot in front of the two-story building while he swung into a space in a lot at the end of the building.

She waited in the car until he walked up to it. Then she released the trunk and he hauled out her suitcase and school bag.

She followed him to his room on the first level, carrying Mikey in her arms. She eyed the king-size bed and put Mikey in the middle of it.

The motel room had a little kitchenette and Jennifer

wedged her back against the counter, folding her arms. "Now that we have some privacy, what do you think happened back there? Who's responsible?"

Miguel collapsed in a chair, his legs stretched out in front of him. She'd noticed the weight loss before, but his gaunt face and lanky appearance really hit her. Miguel had played baseball in college and had kept himself in peak condition throughout his navy SEAL training and beyond. The months in captivity had taken their toll on his body. What about his mind? How did anyone go through that without requiring psychological help to recover? Was that why the people in DC hadn't wanted him to leave?

He ran his knuckles along his jaw, which now sported a scruffy beard. "I don't think that was the government."

"You don't *think*? Would a government agency toss a Molotov cocktail into a child's bedroom?" She pressed her folded arms against her belly and the knots forming there.

"The FBI? No."

"But you weren't being debriefed by the FBI, were you? Or the CIA?"

"No."

"Would this…other agency do something like that?"

"That room in the front of the house could've been any room. Maybe Mikey wasn't the target."

She pushed off the counter and did a quick circle around the dumpy room. "That excuses them? They knew there was a child in the house. You said that's how you found out about Mikey—from their files."

He held up his hands. "I'm not excusing the inexcusable, but it would be easier to believe this other agency tossed that Molotov cocktail into a house without targeting a child, but…"

"But what?"

"What would be their motive? They want me to come back, for sure, but they don't want to kill me."

"Then who?" Jennifer hunched her shoulders. "Who *would* want to kill you…or us?"

Miguel jumped from the chair and perched on the edge of the bed. He placed a hand on Mikey's back. "I'd never let anything happen to you or Mikey. You know that, don't you?"

"You didn't answer my question, Miguel. Who?"

"There's only one person I know who wants me dead."

Jennifer licked her lips. "You don't mean Vlad?"

Mikey stirred and flinched in his sleep, and Miguel rubbed a circle on his back.

How did he instinctively know what Mikey needed? As far as she knew, he hadn't been around small kids much. He'd been a younger brother, and while his older brother, Roberto, was married and had children, Miguel hadn't seen much of his niece and nephews.

"Vlad."

"That doesn't make sense either. Vlad had you, didn't he? You said you were captured and the rest of the team was killed while on a mission to find Vlad. It must've been his people who had you imprisoned."

"At that time, I was more valuable to Vlad alive. He probably thought he could lure the rest of my sniper team out and pick them off one by one."

"That didn't happen."

"My team thought I was dead. It almost worked once when Austin heard some chatter about Vlad's whereabouts."

"Austin Foley?"

"Yeah. He still thought I was dead, but Vlad's people were responsible for an IED that killed Austin's brother.

He was all-in to track down Vlad, but the navy nixed the mission."

"Now that you're not useful to Vlad anymore, you think he's out to kill you? In Texas?"

"He has operatives working Stateside now. You know the incident at the JFK Library a few months ago?"

"That was Vlad?" She plopped down in the chair that Miguel had vacated. "He's built himself a terrorist network, hasn't he?"

"It wasn't just the attempt at the library. We destroyed a training camp he was running in Somalia, and he had entered into a deal with a Colombian drug cartel to exchange drugs for weapons and passage into the US."

"Oh, my God, Miguel. This is bad. And this is the man who's after you? After us?"

"I can't be certain because…" Miguel absently smoothed the pad of his thumb across a lock of Mikey's hair, over and over.

"Because what?"

"Something seemed off at the debriefing center."

"What do you mean by that?" The faraway look in Miguel's eyes had her digging her fingers into her upper arms. How much psychological counseling had he received after his imprisonment? Miguel had nerves of steel, but conditions like he'd experienced, even though he wouldn't tell her about them, would be enough to break anyone.

"What seemed off, Miguel?" She glided slowly across the room until she hovered above him, still seated on the edge of the bed.

"I felt like I was being held captive again."

"That's understandable." She dropped her hand to his shoulder and squeezed.

"I escaped the compound in Maryland just as surely

as I escaped from my cell in Afghanistan." He threaded his fingers through hers and she felt the slight tremble of his hand. "Something wasn't right at that compound, Jennifer—something or someone."

"You're scaring me, Miguel." Was he imagining things? Paranoid? She untangled her fingers from his and stepped back, shooting a quick glance at Mikey.

A stab of guilt lanced her belly. Miguel wouldn't hurt his son. He'd been nothing but tender with him ever since he rescued him from that burning room— and that fire hadn't been the figment of his imagination.

His dark eyes flickered, and he pushed to his feet. "I don't want to scare you, Jen. Maybe I never should've come back into your life. I probably led the bad guys— whoever they are—right to your doorstep."

"That's not true." She pressed a hand to her hot cheek. "They'd already found me. They broke into my house. Th-they've been watching me."

His head jerked around. "How do you know that?"

"I just felt it, even before the break-in."

He curled a hand around her neck. "You need a safe place, you and Mikey."

A safe place? Away from him? "I have to finish out the school year. There are two more days of class this week and the fifth-grade promotion the day after to-morrow. I'm not going anywhere."

"I'll get you through the rest of the school year." He pulled her close and kissed her forehead. "Now you need to get to sleep. You and Mikey take the bed and I'll bunk here on the couch."

She drew her eyebrows over her nose. He wasn't going to sleep with her his first night back? She'd dreamed of lying in his arms so many times over the past two years and now that she had him within her reach, he was slipping away.

Was it because he saw the doubt in her eyes?

He pressed his index finger between her eyes as if to flatten out her frown. "I'm not going to sleep. I'm going to keep watch over you and Mikey."

"You look tired, Miguel. You need to sleep, too."

"I've gone without a good, full night's sleep for so long now, I don't even know what I'm missing anymore." He pointed to the bathroom. "You first. Go brush your teeth and all that."

Ten minutes later when she came out of the bathroom, Miguel, sitting on the edge of the sofa, glanced up from his cell phone, his face drawn, his eyes hollow.

Jennifer forced a smile to her face and swallowed. "All yours."

He turned his phone facedown on the table beside the sofa and jumped to his feet. "Crawl into the bed next to Mikey. I'll be done in two minutes and then I'll keep watch over both of you."

As soon as the bathroom door closed behind him, she rushed to the phone, grabbing it before it could go to sleep. She tapped the display and the most recent text message came to life.

As she read the words from Josh Elliott, one of Miguel's sniper teammates, her heart did somersaults in her chest.

She was still clutching the phone when Miguel emerged from the bathroom, and she held it up to him, reciting the words she'd memorized.

"'Mole. Don't know how deep. Gunning for you—and Jen.'"

Chapter Four

A muscle in Miguel's jaw jumped. "You read my text?"

"That's all you have to say?" She waved the phone at him. "When were you going to tell me?"

"About the mole?" He ran a hand through his hair. "I just found out."

"I repeat. When were you going to tell me about it? Ever?" She tossed the phone against the back cushion of the sofa, and it bounced and landed on the floor. "You're not back twenty-four hours and you're already keeping things from me."

Heat burned in his chest, along with the guilt. "Jen, this is different."

"Really? Aren't you going to tell me that I'm better off not knowing for my own safety? Why don't you let me decide what's best for my own safety? Were you planning to leave me again *for my own safety*?"

Clasping the back of his neck, he bit the inside of his cheek. The thought had crossed his mind that with him out of the picture, Jen would be safe, but Josh's text indicated the mole was after Jennifer, too.

As she studied his face, her eyes grew round. "You were. You were going to leave us—me and Mikey."

In two steps, he ate up the distance between them and pulled her stiff body into his arms. "I'm never going to leave you again. Yeah, I did think maybe you'd be better off without me back in your life, but I learned to be selfish in captivity. I'm not gonna let you go—not now, not ever."

She struggled against him for a few seconds until he cupped her face in his hands and planted a desperate kiss against her lips. Then she seemed to go boneless in his arms, melting against his chest.

She pulled away from his kiss and whispered hoarsely in his ear, "Don't ever leave me again, Miguel. I almost died when they told me you were dead."

He massaged a circle on her back and rested his chin on top of her head, the honey-blond strands of her hair clinging to his beard.

She hooked one arm around his waist and slid the other hand up the front of his shirt, splaying her fingers across his bare chest. "Make it real. Let me know you're back."

Throwing a quick glance at his son's sleeping form, Miguel stepped back from Jennifer's searching hands. If he needed an excuse for not being intimate with his fiancée, that excuse lay in a flushed tumble on the bed. "Is this a good idea?"

Tugging at his shirt, she replied, "He's not even two. He's not going to know what's going on over here even if he does wake up. And he won't."

All his muscles tensed, but Miguel tried to put a smile on his face. "If you say so."

"I say so." She bunched his shirt in her hands and yanked it up. "Help me out here."

Holding his breath, Miguel pulled his shirt over his head.

Jennifer gasped.

Miguel crumpled his T-shirt in one fist. "Yeah,

maybe this isn't such a good idea after all. I probably should've warned you."

Her fingertips traced the scars crisscrossing his chest. Then she nudged him with her hands to turn around.

"Not much better back there."

She smoothed her hands across the various wounds on his back, exploring them as if committing them to memory. "H-how did you ever survive this?"

"By thinking of this." He turned to face her and wrapped his hands around her waist. He slanted his mouth across hers, slipping his tongue into her mouth, where it did a familiar tango with hers.

He could do this if he just maintained a certain level of control. He wouldn't allow himself to let go.

Jennifer wedged her fingers in the waistband of his jeans and yanked at his zipper.

"Mama." A wail quickly followed the single word.

Miguel jerked back from Jennifer. What had he been thinking? He could never maintain control with Jen.

She kissed Miguel's chest. "Let me settle him. I'll be right back."

She sat on the edge of the bed and a few minutes later Miguel joined her, kneeling on the floor.

Mikey rubbed his eyes and let out another wail. Jennifer pulled him into her lap. "It's okay, Mikey. We're in a hotel, but you're with Mama…and your daddy."

A knot twisted in Miguel's gut. He'd wanted to be a dad for so long, but the conditions couldn't be worse. "Do you think he's ready for that, Jen? Ready for me?"

"The sooner the better. Might as well get him used to the idea."

"Doesn't look as if he much likes the idea of a daddy."

Mikey's face had crumpled, and fresh tears rolled down his cheeks as he stared at his newfound father.

"He's probably having a delayed reaction to that explosion in his room and the fire. He hardly had time to react before you swooped in there to save him. Now he's waking up in a strange place." She shrugged.

"With a strange man."

"Not for long, Miguel. He'll adapt quickly. Kids do."

"We're not giving him much to adapt to—a motel room instead of his home, most of his clothes and toys ruined." He touched Mikey's little fist, curled around a lock of Jennifer's hair. "Has he had many men in his life?"

She sucked in a quick breath of air. "Dad and Mom have been to visit a few times, but Alicia's husband, Troy, has probably been the most prominent male in Mikey's life, since I see Alicia and Troy a few times a month."

Her words left a sour taste in his mouth. He didn't even like Troy, the husband of Jen's best friend, and that guy had a more important role in Mikey's life than he did.

Miguel met Mikey's watery gaze and winked. He supposed he should be feeling grateful that Troy was there for Mikey…and Jen.

Jennifer kissed the top of Mikey's head. "I'm going to change his diaper and try to get him to go back to sleep."

"Can I watch? If I'm gonna be a dad, I'd better start learning the basics."

"Of course. Nothing to it." She scooted off the bed with Mikey clutched to her chest. Pointing to the corner where he'd stashed her bags, she said, "Bring me that green diaper bag. We'll do it here on the floor."

He strode to the corner and swept up the bag. He crouched beside her at the foot of the bed. "What do we need?"

"Changing pad in the side pocket, fresh diaper, wipes, a little tube of cream in the zipper pouch inside and a plastic grocery bag."

He pulled out all the items she'd requested and lined them up on the floor, holding the diaper in his hand. "This looks like a complicated operation."

"Only when he's squiggly." She grabbed Mikey's kicking feet and pressed a kiss on each sole. "I'm going to start potty training him in about six months. Alicia said boys are slower than girls, but Bella was potty trained at twenty-six months."

"If Bella can do it, Mikey can do it. Right, big guy?" Miguel poked Mikey's belly with his finger, and his son rewarded him with a giggle.

Jennifer made short work of the task, and let him secure the fresh diaper into place.

He wrapped up the soiled diaper in the plastic bag and put it in the bathroom trash. Then he washed his hands and put everything back in its place in the diaper bag.

Jennifer had returned to the bed with Mikey and curled up beside him. "He's still a little restless, so I'm going to cuddle with him until he falls asleep. Then we can get back to what we were doing. You got me all hot changing that diaper. Nothing sexier than a man changing a diaper."

He shook his head. "That's weird. Is the TV going to bother you?"

"Just keep it low."

Miguel pulled his T-shirt back on and settled on the couch, clicking on the TV. He scanned through the channels until he found a news program and then glanced at Jennifer, her eyes closed.

Bending forward, he retrieved his phone from the floor and texted Josh, asking if he had any more details about the mole.

Josh responded quickly and Miguel read the text with growing dread. Josh had had some contact with Vlad's people on Josh's recent Stateside assignment, protecting the daughter of the drug kingpin Hector De Santos. Vlad's guys had implied they had someone on the inside, and Josh had no reason to doubt that, at least he hadn't wanted to bet against it.

Miguel clenched his jaw as he thought about Vlad, their nemesis. They'd been on Vlad's trail when Miguel had been captured. He'd had a long time to think about a mole then.

Where had the SEAL team gotten the intel about Vlad's location in those caves in Afghanistan? Through the Vlad task force? Was it just bad information, or was it very, very good information planted for the SEAL team, and him as the sniper, to walk right into an ambush?

Almost eighteen months later and after his escape from his captors, the CIA didn't seem all that interested in finding out. Could this mole have infiltrated the top echelons? The task force itself?

Josh ended their text exchange with a curt directive. Watch your back.

Miguel tossed his phone on the cushion next to him, his gaze shifting to Jennifer, her body curved around Mikey's, both of them sound asleep.

Miguel pulled his gun from beneath the cushion of the couch and hunched forward, watching the blue light from the TV flicker over Jennifer and Mikey. Instead of weakening him, his captivity had made him strong, hard—maybe too hard to be a family man.

But not too hard to protect them with every inch of his life.

A LITTLE HAND grabbed her nose, and Jennifer opened one eye while puffing a strand of hair from her face. "What are you doing, rascal?"

"Wake up, Mommy."

"I'm awake." She rolled to her back and raised her head. "Tell me you got some sleep on that couch."

Miguel, showered and fully dressed down to a pair of scuffed cowboy boots, pushed up from the couch where he'd been perched. "I slept some."

"How long has this one been awake?" She jerked her thumb at Mikey.

"Not long. Woke up, stared at me for a few minutes and proceeded to tweak your nose." He stretched. "If I'd known it was that easy to wake you up, I would've used that method years ago."

She ran her tongue along her teeth. "I remember how you used to wake me up…and I distinctly prefer your method."

He gave her a tight smile. "What time do you have to get to school?"

She swallowed. Except for their desperate kisses last night, Miguel didn't seem all that interested in picking up where they'd left off. "I have to be there at eight, but I need to drop off Mikey at his day care about fifteen minutes before that."

"It's close, the day care?"

"It's a few blocks from the school." She lifted Mikey and swung him over her head. "Can you watch him while I take a shower?"

Miguel's eyes widened as his gaze darted around the hotel room. "This room isn't babyproofed. Is it safe?"

Hooking Mikey on one hip and placing her hand on the other, she surveyed the room. "Don't let him rip up the brochures on the credenza, keep the remote out of his picky little paws and, by all means, keep him away from the electrical outlets and the minibar. Otherwise, I think you're good. I'll change his diaper before I hit the shower."

"Let me do that." He took a step forward, holding out his arms. "I need the practice."

She cocked her head to one side. "You sure would've come in handy these past eighteen months."

A shade dropped over Miguel's dark eyes and she bit her bottom lip. Miguel's captivity had made him even more intense, but she couldn't contain her own elation. Since his return yesterday, despite the challenges they faced, the heavy, dark cloud that had been following her around for two years had dissipated into fairy dust.

"I'm sorry, Jen."

She went to him and placed Mikey against his chest, wrapping her arms around both of them. "Dear God, you have nothing to be sorry about, Miguel."

"I should've never volunteered for that assignment."

"I thought you didn't have a choice. Besides, you did what you thought was right. You always do." She brushed her lips across Mikey's soft hair and then pressed them against the stubble on Miguel's jaw. "Diaper duty for you."

She spun around, blindly lurching for the bathroom, tears blurring her vision. When she slammed the door behind her, she hunched over the vanity and peered at her reflection. The woman who gazed back at her had dropped ten years since yesterday.

She knew she couldn't expect Miguel to be the same person he was when he left her two years ago, but had his feelings for her changed? No. He'd told her she'd been the one keeping him strong, keeping him alive.

Did he really think she cared about the scars on his body? She snorted as she cranked on the water for the shower. Even though he'd lost a little muscle as a prisoner, he still had the hottest body she'd ever had the pleasure of exploring—scars or no scars. And she planned to do more exploration, damn it.

Maybe having Mikey in the same room had scared him off. She tipped her head back and let the warm spray course through her hair. He sure seemed eager to make up for lost time and learn everything he could about toddler care. Alicia's husband, Troy, had probably changed a grand total of ten diapers in the past two years of Bella's life.

The bathroom door burst open and Miguel's voice rose above the water. "I think I need some help out here."

Grabbing the edge of the shower curtain, Jennifer peeked into the bathroom at Miguel looming in the doorway with a squiggling Mikey tucked under one arm. "What happened?"

"First, he wouldn't let me put his clothes on after I changed his diaper. Then he started jumping on the bed. When I tried to grab him, he crawled off the edge and fell on the floor." Miguel took a deep breath. "I think he's okay."

"Well, these are the terrible toddler years." She pointed to her soapy head. "I'll be done in a few minutes." She grinned at Miguel's panicked expression. "Welcome to fatherhood. You'll think of something."

She whipped the shower curtain back in place and

stuck her head under the water to rinse. When she finished her shower, she dropped the towel on the floor and slipped into some clean underwear.

She opened the bathroom door a crack and put her eye to the space. Two lumps, one large and one small, moved beneath the covers of the bed.

She swung open the door. "Everything okay?"

Miguel lifted one edge of the blanket. "We're under the ocean waves here, swimming."

Mikey's muffled voice echoed Miguel's. "Swimming."

"In your diaper?"

Mikey wriggled from beneath the covers. "Swimming."

"I see that, but now you have to get dressed so Mommy can drop you off at Ms. Lori's room."

"Does he need breakfast?"

"They feed him there."

"What about you?"

"If I get moving and leave a little early, I can pick up something on the way."

"We." Miguel shrugged off the blanket and held Mikey's arm as he clambered off the bed. "I'm taking you to school, and I'm picking you both up."

She nodded, a pinprick of fear needling the back of her neck. "What are you going to do all day or at least until noon? We get out early today since the kids just have graduation practice."

"I'm going to do some research."

"On?"

"Moles."

AFTER THEY DROPPED off Mikey and picked up some breakfast burritos, Miguel parked around the corner from the school.

Jennifer peeled back the yellow paper from her burrito and pointed to the bag. "Any hot sauce in there?"

"Thought I saw some." Miguel plunged his hand into the bag and pulled out two packets of hot sauce. He ripped one open with his teeth and handed it to her.

"Who do you think broke into my house and fire-bombed it? Same group for both actions?" She squeezed the red sauce onto the end of her burrito and took a bite.

"Not sure." He raised his hand and ticked off the recent events on his fingers. "You think someone's been following you. Someone broke into your place and planted those bugs. Someone threw a Molotov cocktail into your house, but it wasn't a big one."

"Yeah, I feel so much better that someone threw a fiery rag in a glass bottle into my son's bedroom, but it was just a little, bitty one."

Miguel dabbed at a spot of hot sauce on his chin. "What I meant was that act could've been more of an attempt to warn and not kill."

"It could've killed." The hot sauce burned in her belly. "It could've killed Mikey."

"I know." He grabbed her hand. "I'm just trying to figure out motivation here. Is it the CIA trying to scare me back to Maryland or is it some terrorist cell trying to kill me?"

"And us."

Miguel's jaw tightened. "Maybe I never should've come back to you."

"We've been through this already. Before you even got to Austin, someone was following me and bugging my house."

"Probably just because they knew I'd return here. If I'd never come back, they probably would've lost interest in you and continued their search for me."

She dropped her burrito and dug her fingers into the denim covering his thigh. "Do you think you could've kept your return from me? I'm sure I would've found out somehow, and then nothing would've kept me from your side."

Drawing her toward him, he kissed her with his spicy lips. "I love you, Jen, more than anything, but that means keeping you safe."

"Yeah, yeah. I've heard that line before." She cupped his jaw flicking her fingers through his longish hair. "This is no military cut, sailor."

"They weren't offering and I wasn't asking. Had more important issues on my mind."

She glanced at her cell phone. "I have one more question before I head off to class. How could one mole in the intel community get to you?"

He jerked his thumb at the laptop stashed in the backseat. "That's what I'm going to try to find out."

"Can Josh Elliott help you?" She crumpled up the waxy paper around the rest of her burrito and tossed it into the bag at Miguel's feet.

"No. He's headed out for another deployment. He had a little time off after his last assignment. Guess he met a woman."

"Josh?" Miguel's sniper teammate was more intense than Miguel. "I hope she's tough as nails."

"She's…" Miguel shrugged. "I hope so, too. I'm going to be waiting right here for you at noon, and then we'll pick up Mikey."

"And then?"

"We should find another house. Mikey can't stay in a motel forever."

"Tomorrow is the last day of school. Let's deal with it then."

A bell rang in the distance, and Miguel raised his eyebrows. "Are you late, teacher?"

"That's the first bell. I'm not late until the second bell." She kissed him again just because she could and he was inches away from her. "Noon."

Before she turned the corner, she glanced back at the car and waved. She still felt like she was moving through some crazy dream. Miguel alive, back home— and their lives in danger. When would they catch a break?

She had no time to pop into the teachers' lounge like she usually did, so she headed straight for her classroom.

The first bell had called the kids to class, and they jostled and nudged each other as they lined up in the hallway outside the door.

"You're almost in middle school. Behave yourselves." She jingled her key chain at them and then opened the door.

"What're we doing today, Ms. Lynch?"

"I must've told you a hundred times, Chase." She dropped her bag on the floor and nudged it under her desk with her toe. "Cleaning up the room. You guys are going to take all your stuff home, projects, papers, supplies, and then we're going to walk to the high school to run through the promotion ceremony."

The morning passed quickly, and at ten thirty Jennifer got her class ready for the walk to the high school. As she gathered the kids in the hallway, Olivia sidled up next to her.

"What happened at your house last night? I heard there was a fire."

"That news spread quickly." Jennifer snapped her

fingers. "Girls, stop talking. There are classes in session across the hall."

"Are you and Mikey okay?"

"We're fine. M-my friend discovered it quickly, got us out of the house and called 9-1-1."

"Thank goodness. When you didn't make it to the teachers' lounge this morning, I got worried. Do you have a place to stay?"

"Motel for now. I'll start looking for a new place soon. I was done with that place anyway."

"It's a good thing it's the end of the school year." Olivia took Jennifer's arm. "One more day until freedom."

Freedom? Jennifer had been feeling a noose tightening around her neck ever since Miguel appeared—no, that wasn't fair. She'd been feeling that noose even before. She just hadn't understood its significance.

Just like they had the day before, the fifth-grade teachers herded their students through the park and across the street to the high school. The school had reserved its auditorium for their practice.

Once inside, the students were assigned a place in line alphabetically. The teachers gathered in the back while the principal and vice principal ran the kids through their paces.

Olivia took a sip from her coffee cup. "Are you and Mikey still going to visit your sister in San Francisco this summer?"

"Maybe." Olivia knew all about her dead navy SEAL fiancé. When would she be able to tell everyone the good news about Miguel? She was pretty tired of being the poor, young fiancée, left to raise a child by herself.

She wanted to shout the news from the rooftops. She

wanted to tell Troy that Mikey no longer needed a father figure—he had his own father.

Jennifer sighed. "You still going out to visit the in-laws?"

"God, yes, for two long weeks."

A buzzing sound had Olivia patting her pockets. "It's not mine."

Jennifer reached for her purse hanging over the back of a chair in the last row of the auditorium and scrambled for her cell phone in the side pocket.

Her heart did a little flip when she saw the number for Mikey's day care. She held up one finger to Olivia. "Excuse me a minute. I have to take this."

"Hello?"

"Oh, Jennifer. I—I…" Franny, the owner of the day care, dragged in a ragged breath. "First of all, let me assure you that Mikey is safe."

The blood rushed to Jennifer's head all at once, and she grabbed the edge of the seat. "What does that mean? What happened?"

"Mikey's fine and we already called the police."

"The police? Franny, tell me what happened."

"A man broke into the center, into Ms. Lori's room. Jen, he tried to take Mikey."

Chapter Five

Jennifer gulped and pressed two fingers to her throbbing temple. "Where is Mikey now?"

"He's in my office with me. We're waiting for the police right now."

Shifting the phone away from her mouth, Jennifer tapped Olivia's arm and said, "I have to leave. Mikey's okay, but something happened at his day care. Tell Sandra I'll be gone the rest of the day."

Olivia's eyes grew round. "Go, go. I'll get your class back to the school and dismiss them."

As Jennifer hustled from the auditorium, she continued with Franny. "What happened? What do you mean someone tried to take him? Was it someone who tried to sign him out and pretend I sent him?"

Had Miguel tried to pick up his son, not realizing the security measures in place at the day care?

"I mean take, Jen, as in forcibly try to remove him from the center." Franny released a little sob.

A blast of adrenaline shot through Jennifer's body and she quickened her pace back to the school. "Are you sure Mikey's okay?"

"He's fine, sitting here having a snack. I don't know what we would've done if that other man hadn't charged into the play area and challenged the man who had Mikey."

"What? Another man?"

"As the man ran into the playground with Mikey under his arm, another guy leaped over the fence and knocked the kidnapper down. He got Mikey away from the man and handed him over to us. The kidnapper ran and the last I saw of Mikey's protector, he was going after him."

Mikey's protector? It had to be Miguel. He'd saved his son's life twice in two days.

Jennifer's heart was still beating erratically by the time she jogged the two blocks to Mikey's day care. When she got there, a police cruiser was stationed out front.

She bolted through the front gate and ran to the play yard, where two cops were talking to Franny and Lori. Panic stabbed the back of her skull when she didn't see Mikey with them.

"Where's Mikey?"

Franny hugged her. "He's back in Ms. Lori's room. Ms. Tina is watching the class. We thought it best not to isolate him from the other kids to get things back to normal for him. Is that okay?"

Jennifer clung to Franny for a few seconds before nodding. "Yes."

One of the officers stepped forward. "Ms. Lynch, I'm Officer Grady. The teachers were telling us that there are no custody disputes or family issues, is that correct?"

"That's right."

"And the father is...?"

"Deceased."

"His family?"

Jennifer blinked. This cop would have a field day with Miguel's family, but she already knew who was behind this attempted abduction, and it wasn't Miguel's brother, Roberto, or any of Roberto's enemies. "Mikey's paternal relatives are not involved in his life."

"Do they wanna be?" The officer chewed on the end of his pen. "Kidnappings like this usually end up being family members."

"Not in this case."

"What about the man who stopped the abduction." The other officer turned to Franny. "Was he a parent?"

"No, never saw him before." Franny shook her head so that her long, gray braid flicked back and forth.

Jennifer sucked in her bottom lip. Would Miguel want to be outed to these police officers? Probably not. He didn't seem to know whom to trust, outside of his sniper team. She wouldn't put him at risk now.

Jennifer pressed a hand against the knots in her belly. "Maybe he was just a passerby who saw what was going on. I'm going to see my son."

She broke away from the group and entered the building. She had to tiptoe through the infant area to get to the toddler classroom. After all the excitement, most of the babies had conked out and were nestled in their bassinets.

Jennifer poked her head around the doorway into the toddler room and waved at Mikey, who was sitting at a table playing with blocks of different shapes and colors.

He waved a red square at her, a big grin on his face, punctuated by a few cookie crumbs.

Rolling her shoulders, she took a deep breath and plastered a smile on her face. "Hello, big boy."

"Hi, Mama."

She swooped in and lifted him from the plastic chair.

She hugged him so tightly, he squirmed in her arms. "Are you having fun?"

"Yes." He put the corner of the block in his mouth. "Red square."

"That's right. Good job. Are you ready to go home?"

Mikey's little face crumpled and he showed her his elbow. "Boo-boo. I fell."

Tears stung the backs of her eyes while she kissed her son's scraped elbow. "I heard. Are you okay?"

Mikey put up his fists. "Boom, boom. The mans were fighting."

She clasped her hands over Mikey's fists and pressed her lips against his knuckles. Had he recognized Miguel? Had the teachers and the police asked him anything about the other man?

"I heard about the fight. You can tell me all about it when we get home, okay?"

"Policemans?"

"Yes, we can see the police officer again before we leave." She didn't know exactly how they'd leave, since Miguel had her car. She didn't want to call him to pick them up in case the day-care teachers recognized him.

She collected Mikey's things from Tina and walked back out to the play yard, squinting in the midday sun.

The police officer who'd been questioning the teachers had put away his notebook and the other seemed to be scouring the rubber surface of the playground for clues.

Officer Grady asked, "Ah, Ms. Lynch. How's your son?"

"He's fine, thanks." She approached the group, holding Mikey against her side. "He wanted to say goodbye to you."

"Bye-bye, Mikey." The officer waved. "Let us know

if you think of anyone who would do this, Ms. Lynch. I've already asked the teachers to call if the man who interrupted the…ah…incident comes back. We'd sure like to talk to him."

The officer searching the ground popped up, holding a white napkin in his hand. He held it up, the bright letters of the fast-food place where she and Miguel had eaten that morning blazing yellow and orange against the white backdrop. "Does this belong here?"

Franny sniffed. "We don't allow fast food at our day care."

"That place isn't far from here. It could've come from anyone's pocket." Jennifer lifted and dropped her shoulders quickly. "It might even be mine since I ate there this morning."

The eyes of the officer holding the napkin narrowed. "Is that right?"

As the heat crept into her cheeks, Jennifer rested her face against Mikey's head. "Maybe it fell out of my purse. It's not much, is it?"

"Maybe, maybe not, but it's something." He whipped out a plastic bag and placed the napkin inside. "I'm sure you're happy we found something."

"Of course, and I'm going to talk to Mikey tonight to see if he'll tell me anything." She patted Mikey's head against her shoulder. "D-did he tell you anything?"

Officer Grady answered, "I asked him a few questions, but he's pretty young. We didn't expect much from him."

"Maybe I can find out something tonight."

"If so, let us know." The suspicious officer with the napkin pressed his card into her hand, even though Officer Grady had already given her his card earlier. "Don't go anywhere, Ms. Lynch."

"For how long?" She glanced at the card before pocketing it. "I'm a teacher and tomorrow is the last day of school. We have vacation plans."

"Just keep us posted, so we know where to reach you—in case something comes up."

"I'll do that." She hugged Franny again. "Thanks for everything."

"I'm afraid we didn't do much. If we ever locate that Good Samaritan, you can thank him yourself."

She would, personally.

Readjusting her bag over one shoulder and Mikey's bag over the other, she walked through the gate and landed in the parking lot, looking both ways. As she started making her way back to the school, she pulled out her cell phone and called Miguel.

He picked up after a half a ring. "Thank God. Is Mikey okay? Are you okay?"

"We're both fine. It was you, wasn't it? The man who saved Mikey?"

"Make a right at the first block. I'm parked across the street from the park. Did you tell the police anything about me, about your hunch?"

"Of course not. I know you're trying to keep a low profile." She cranked her head around to make sure the police were still at the day care and then veered to the right.

Before she could utter another word, her car rolled backward on the street and idled next to her, Miguel at the wheel. She opened the back door and secured Mikey in his car seat. Then she slid into the passenger seat next to Miguel and slammed the door.

"Why are they after Mikey?"

"Because they're after me."

"But you don't even know who it is, do you?" She

gripped her knees with both hands, tension lacing her shoulders. "Are you trying to tell me the CIA is going to kidnap a child, an American child from a day care center, to bring a navy SEAL into line?"

"I told you, Jen—" he wheeled around the corner and pulled up to a signal "—someone has infiltrated the Vlad task force. That person may be calling the shots or maybe has gone rogue. And then again…the people who just tried to take Mikey may not be with US intelligence at all."

Her nails dug into the fabric of her slacks. "I don't know which prospect is worse—a rogue CIA agent or a terrorist group."

Mikey shouted from the backseat, "Boom, boom. Mans fighting."

Miguel's brows shot up and he reached into the backseat to squeeze the toe of Mikey's light-up sneakers. "That's right, big guy. Your daddy had to take care of some business."

Mikey rewarded him with a big grin and started kicking the back of Jennifer's seat.

"Great. He's getting all aggressive." She turned and cinched Mikey's ankle above his sock. "Stop kicking, Mikey."

He gave the backseat one more shot from his toe, and then started singing.

"I'm sorry he had to be a part of that fight, but there's no other way I would've been able to get him out of that man's grasp—unless I pulled a gun, and I wasn't about to do just that."

"I'm sorry, Miguel." She brought her hand to the base of her throat. "I know you did what you had to do. If you hadn't wrestled Mikey from that man…"

"I wish I hadn't lost him, but he got away when I grabbed Mikey."

"Tell me what happened. Why were you at the day care?"

"After I dropped you off, I started thinking about the day care and how easy it would be for someone to walk right in there."

"You already figured Mikey was in danger?"

"If someone didn't care about firebombing your house with a child inside, I knew we were dealing with some hard-core people."

Her jaw tightened and she felt as if she might break into a thousand brittle pieces. "You went back to the day care?"

"I parked around the corner and took up watch across the street."

"Across the street? There are houses across the street."

"I saw a husband and wife leaving for work, so I hopped their fence and tucked myself into a corner next to a tree. I knew nobody could see me from the street."

She studied his profile, more angular than she'd remembered. "How long did you sit there?"

"Dropped you off at eight, slipped into that yard around eight thirty and the guy showed up at the day care around eleven—about two and a half hours."

"In the same position for two and a half hours?"

He quirked one brow at her. "You forget what I do, Jen?"

"Yeah, I suppose that's nothing for you." She grabbed his forearm. "I'm so glad you were there. I knew it was you as soon as Franny told me a man had jumped in to rescue Mikey. When did you notice what was happening?"

"As soon as the guy walked up to the day care, my

sensors went on high alert. He just had a look. Didn't look like a dad."

"Really?" She glanced in the backseat at a drowsy Mikey and turned down the radio. They didn't need to drown out their words now. "Dads come in all shapes and sizes."

"I know. I guess I'm stereotyping, but this guy looked tense, alert."

"Takes one to know one."

Miguel grimaced. "When I saw him, I jumped onto the sidewalk. It didn't take him long to come barreling out of that building with Mikey under one arm and a gaggle of teachers on his tail."

"Maybe this will prompt the day care to put some barrier between the open front door and the kids."

"I'm not sure any barrier would've stopped this man. Nothing but a bullet would've stopped him...or a well-placed fist."

"That's what you did? Knocked him out?"

"Like I said. I was afraid to come in with a gun blazing. I tackled him, and he held onto Mikey as he fell. I was able to apply enough pressure that he had to release Mikey. I rolled over to shield Mikey, and that's when the man got up and started running. I think he saw the gun in my waistband, and that made his decision for him."

"You went after him?" Her knees had started bouncing in some sort of delayed reaction.

"Once I secured Mikey with his teacher, I chased him. I saw him go around the corner, but he must've had a car waiting because he just disappeared when I rounded that corner."

"H-how was Mikey when it happened?"

He took her hand. "He was scared, crying. I don't think he recognized me or realized it was me. His teachers did a good job of calming him down. I don't know that he even realized what was going on, but the violence had to have frightened him." He slammed a fist against the steering wheel. "It's just that type of violence I want to protect him from."

"I think you had a good excuse, Miguel." She traced a finger over his knuckles. "Don't be so hard on yourself. My God, you saved his life."

"Jen, we're going to have to leave here."

"Here?"

"Austin. We have to leave Austin."

She pulled on her earlobe. "I figured we would."

"At first I thought it would be good enough if I left." He held up his hand as she opened her mouth. "Not forever. I would've been back once I resolved this… problem. But now they're onto you and Mikey. It's not going to matter if I stay with you or not. If I don't stay with you, I have no way of protecting you—and you need protection."

He'd hit the freeway and took the exit back to the motel.

"I'm glad you see it that way because I'm not letting you out of my sight, Miguel Estrada."

He squealed into the parking slot in front of the motel room. "Pack your stuff, and we'll return to the house so you can pick up a few more things."

"Everything is still pretty much packed from our escape from the house. I'll go through our things tomorrow after school to see what else I can salvage."

He cut the engine and stared straight ahead, gripping the steering wheel. "You don't get it. We need to leave right now."

She jerked her head toward him. "Now? I can't leave now. I have one more day of school."

"You said it's graduation or promotion or whatever tomorrow."

"It is, but I still need to be there."

"Are your grades done?"

"Yes."

"End-of-the-year party, picnics, conferences all over."

"Yes."

"Then you can leave—and you have to."

"I suppose I can call in sick." She eyed the cell phone in her lap. "I hate to miss the ceremony."

"I'm sure you do, but Mikey's safety is more important, isn't it?"

"Of course, if you think…"

"Jen, someone found out where he attended day care, knew when he'd be there, knew there was light security and attempted to snatch him from beneath the teachers' noses. I think we need to leave—now."

"All right." She released a deep breath. "Where are we going to go?"

"I think I have a plan. Can you just get your stuff ready right now? I need to turn in my rental car. We'll get back to your house to get your things, and maybe you can call a packing and moving service to have the rest of the house boxed up and moved to storage. Is that possible?"

"I can do that. In fact, the management company would be thrilled if I took care of that, and then the insurance adjusters could move in and do their assessments of the damage."

He flipped the door handle and stopped, glancing at her frozen in the passenger seat. "Are you okay? I know this is all a huge shock and disruption to your life."

"I guess I'm just being a princess." She folded her arms. "Remember when you used to tease me that I came from a perfect world with a white picket fence and 2.5 kids?"

"I was a cocky idiot because that's exactly the world I want with you right now, except maybe we could have three kids instead of two and a half."

She gurgled and punched his arm. "I knew what you meant though. I'd never faced any adversity growing up. Mom had even been clean and sober for a few years before she had me and my sister. For a few seconds there I was just wishing that your homecoming could've been different."

"There's nothing wrong with that. I wish it could've been different, but I'll take what I can get."

"So will I—I'll take what I can get if it means having you." She flung open the door. "So let's get going."

As she ducked into the backseat to retrieve a sleeping Mikey, Miguel stood guard over them as if he thought a car might come screeching up at this very minute—and maybe he was right.

He hustled them into the room, bolted the door and took out his weapon. "I'll pack up what little I have. We can buy anything Mikey needs on the road."

She settled Mikey in the middle of the bed and went into the bathroom to collect her toiletries. She called over her shoulder. "You said you had a plan? What is it? Where are we going?"

Miguel loomed in the doorway of the bathroom. "Desperate times call for desperate measures. I thought we could go to Roberto's."

Jennifer dropped her bottle of shampoo in the tub. "You thought we'd be safe with a criminal?"

Chapter Six

Miguel gripped the doorjamb, his knuckles white. "I think it's our only option right now."

"You're kidding." Jennifer bent forward and swept up the shampoo bottle. She waved it at him. "You avoided Roberto like the plague. You even had the bright idea to break up with me to protect me from your family. Now we're running straight into the lion's den?"

"It's different now. Roberto's different."

"Oh, right. He gave up committing petty crimes with your father to be some kind of fixer. I'm sure he's completely legitimate." She snorted and fired the bottle of shampoo into her bag.

"It's because he lives on the edge that I thought he could help you—us. Think about it. Security is so tight at his compound, I doubt the mail carrier even gets through."

"It feels like we'd be swapping one dangerous situation for another."

"It's not my first choice." He ran a hand through his hair. "But I'm not sure where else Mikey and you would be safe from these people. There's a mole, Jen. I don't know who to trust. I'm not even sure I can trust Ariel."

"Who's Ariel?" She tipped her head to the side. "I thought all your sniper buddies were male."

"I honestly don't know if Ariel is a male or female, but she—or he—has been running the show in regards to Vlad. She coordinated three different missions Stateside, and Austin, Slade and Josh all worked with her. Josh told me to contact her."

"But you think she could be the mole?"

"I don't know." He stepped aside to let her out of the bathroom with her toiletries hastily tossed in a bag. "Maybe it's not her, but it could be someone close to her. I don't trust anyone. That's the problem. The CIA or the FBI might offer you protection at this point, but how do I know it's not some trap?"

Dropping her toiletry bag on top of her suitcase, Jennifer sighed. "If you can't trust the FBI, who can you trust?"

"Roberto."

"The criminal."

"The fixer."

"Can he fix this?" She spread her arms out to her sides to encompass the dumpy motel room.

"He can keep you and Mikey safe. I know that."

"Will he want to?"

Miguel's eye twitched. "My big brother has been wanting to get back in my good graces for some time. I cut him out of my life when he chose to go down the wrong path with Dad. I'd always looked up to him. Since he was ten years older than I was, he always did play the protector. He always took the brunt of Dad's anger to shield me. I even think that's why Roberto joined our father in his criminal pursuits—to keep the pressure off me."

She crossed the small room in two steps to stand in front of him and brushed her hands over his face. "I